To Echo and Remain
A Love Story

By

Gregory E. Lang

To my wife, Jill,
who from beginning to end
is my true love story,
forever and ever,
to echo and remain.

INTRODUCTION

Appalachia is a geographic and cultural mountain region in the southeastern United States. It is easy to get disoriented, if not overwhelmed, by her landscape's dense shade, thick and varied vegetation, and the many sounds that echo within her woods. Generations of inhabitants believed good and evil spirits roamed the land. It is a region ripe with colorful depictions of hillbilly life... some accurate, many exaggerated.

Appalachia has long been a source of enduring myths and distortions regarding the temperament and behavior of her mountain people. They are often portrayed as ignorant and prone to impulsive acts of violence, marriages within their bloodline, and engaging in such pastimes as moonshining, snake handling, river baptisms, and clan feuding. While there were a few such characters, most mountain folk were honest and humble people, simply doing their best to get by with what they had. Families hunted and gathered their food, living off bear meat, venison, fish, and what vegetables they could grow and protect from hungry nocturnal critters. Neighbors shared what they could when it was found that anyone was unable to provide for themselves.

Native Americans first arrived in Appalachia more than 16,000 years ago. Enslaved Africans were brought to the region by Spanish expeditions during the 16th century. When English explorers arrived in the late 17th century, the central part of the region was controlled by the Algonquian Indian tribe, and the Cherokee controlled the southern part.

Between 1790 and 1840, a series of treaties with the Cherokee and other Native American tribes opened up lands in north Georgia, north Alabama, the Tennessee Valley, the Cumberland Plateau regions, and the Great Smoky Mountains along what is now the Tennessee-North Carolina border. The last of these treaties, spurred on by the white man's lust for the undisturbed earth of Indian territory during the Gold Rush of North Georgia, culminated in the removal of the bulk of the Cherokee population from the region. This forced displacement of the tribes and their long march to a new reservation settlement in Oklahoma became known as the Trail of Tears. Only a few Cherokee remained behind after a private landowner permitted them to establish a village on his property. Today, that land is the reservation of the Eastern Band of Cherokee Indians in North Carolina.

The Cherokee taught the region's early European pioneers how to plant and cultivate crops such as corn and squash and find edible plants such as ramps and fiddlehead ferns. The Cherokee also passed along their knowledge of the medicinal properties of hundreds of native herbs and roots and how to prepare tonics from those plants. Before the introduction of modern agricultural techniques in the region in the 1940s, many Appalachian farmers followed the Indian traditions of planting or fishing by the phases of the moon or when certain weather conditions occurred. Many a seed was sown simply because a full moon could be seen in the night sky within the imaginary borders of the Capricorn constellation. Many a fish were fried the day after a Bluegill full moon.

After the Civil War, parts of Appalachia experienced an economic boom. As a nationwide demand for lumber skyrocketed, lumber firms turned to the virgin forests of southern Appalachia. The mountains and valleys of Appalachia once contained what seemed to be an inexhaustible supply of timber. However, the general inaccessibility of the region prevented large-scale logging in most of the area throughout much of the 19th century. But by the 1880s, an increasing demand for lumber forced logging firms to turn their eyes back to the virgin forests of Appalachia.

Logging in Appalachia peaked in the early 20th century when lumber companies cut the virgin forests on an alarming scale. This led to the creation of national forests and state offices staffed with foresters to manage the region's timber resources.

Yet, in spite of decades of large-scale deforestation, much of the undulating terrain of Appalachia remains untouched by chainsaws and greed. The woods and wetlands range from a palate of dark, misty red spruce forests and skinny, soaring Appalachian Lily trees to layered oak and poplar forests towering over Bloodroot, Crested Dwarf Irises, and Painted Trillium that thrive in the ground made fertile with leaf decay. Silver maple swamps are along the many streams and rivers, and

Cottongrass ferns and colorful wildflowers grow on the high plateaus. There are hollows and thickly wooded slopes, and cold springs rising unexpectedly out of dark holes and vanishing again farther downhill or beneath a tangle of mountain laurel and rhododendron bushes.

Appalachia is indeed a landscape full of hidden things. In these mountains that are said to kiss the sky, there are lingering remnants of dashed dreams, traces of the grotesque and vulgar sins of the past, whispers of many mysteries and sorrows, and the echo of unfinished love stories. Within the branches of every tree, there are memories — those almost forgotten and those being made.

Love is made out of ecstasy and wonder;
Love is a poignant and accustomed pain.
It is a burst of Heaven-shaking thunder;
It is a linnet's fluting after rain.
Love's voice is through your song, above and under,
And in each note to echo and remain.

In Memory, 1917

Joyce Kilmer

Chapter 1

Friday, September 1, 2000

Quinn Bulloch was the last person Owen Montgomery expected to encounter in the courtroom that morning. Yet, there she sat with her client in the middle row of benches behind the rail that separated the defendant's table from curious onlookers and those waiting to be called before the judge. She was impossible to overlook. He immediately saw that she was as beautiful as she ever was, and he remembered the night she threw her engagement ring to the ground at his feet and walked away, leaving him with a heartache that sometimes still awakened him in the middle of the night. He quickly scanned his surroundings to see if he had entered the wrong courtroom. He had not. He clenched his teeth and, annoyed, grunted. He tried to ignore her as the day wore on, but he simply could not stop looking her way.

"You're goin' to save my tree, ain't you, Mr. Montgomery?" asked the old woman seated beside him. She was tugging on his sleeve and reminding him of why he was there in the first place. She followed the direction of his gaze and saw that he was staring at their opponents. They were leaning into each other, grinning and whispering. "I know what they are thinking," she said. "They're bettin' I am just a simple old woman, and this mess is goin' to be too much for me."

"You will prove them wrong, Emma," Owen said. "I know you will." He sat straight, pressed his back against the cool wooden bench, and squared his shoulders. He fingered the buttons on the cuff of his dark blue suit jacket, chewed on his lower lip, and, try as he might, could not take his eyes off of Quinn. "You will do just fine. You can handle this," he reassured his client.

"Mr. Montgomery?" Emma said, leaning closer to his ear.

5

"Yes," he answered, still looking toward Quinn.

"What about my tree?" she asked.

Owen turned his gaze away from his former fiancé and faced Emma Troutman. "I'm going to save your tree," he said, forcing himself to stay in eye contact with her. He really wanted to take another look at the woman who once shared his bed. They hadn't been together in more than two years, but he remembered her every detail as if he had just awakened by her side.

"You promise?" A short and frail woman, Emma's voice was soft and raspy. Her hair was curly and stark white, and her face, crisscrossed with deep wrinkles, was dark as coffee with a drop of cream stirred in. Her fingers, knotted and twisted with arthritis, were intertwined as best she could get them. Her hands, trembling slightly, rested in her tiny lap. She slowly unlaced her fingers, reached up with one hand, and pushed her thick trifocals higher on her nose.

Owen looked into her tired brown eyes. "It's been a long day of nothing happening, hasn't it?" he asked.

"We've been here since ten o'clock," Emma huffed. "And this hard bench is cruel to my old bones."

"We will be out of here soon," he replied. "And, yes, I promise to save your tree and those belonging to your neighbors." Whitaker might show me the door if I don't, he thought nervously. After watching another associate lawyer recently being shown the door, he knew that the senior partners of Morehead, Sterling, and Whitaker didn't give anybody second chances.

He turned to look at Quinn again. She had nagged him for months about taking his career more seriously, and now here she was, the very one who would try to keep him from creating a potentially lucrative opportunity for himself. He was determined to be at the forefront of the emerging field of Internet security, and all that stood between him and that goal was Emma's tree.

"You keep lookin' at that girl," Emma said.

"I'm sorry; I don't mean to ignore you," Owen said.

"Do you know her?" Emma asked.

"Yes I do, from a few years ago," he said.

"I hope she don't distract you too much 'cause we don't want to be spendin' all our money on a lawyer that can't keep his mind straight," Emma said.

"You won't spend any of your money," he reassured her. "You know this is a pro bono case. There will not be a bill, Emma. I promise you that, too."

"I'm still havin' a hard time believing a lawyer ain't gonna send us a bill," she chuckled.

"Don't worry. I'm sure we'll get a permanent injunction," he said. "The law is clearly on our side."

"I planted it myself and watered it every day until its roots took hold. It's my tree," Emma insisted.

"And I'm going to see that it stays that way," Owen answered.

"They painted a big red X on it. I can see it from my front porch!" she exclaimed.

"All rise," the courtroom bailiff suddenly barked as the door of the judge's chambers pushed open. The Honorable Judge Hardwick's recess, more likely the judicial relic's well-guarded naptime, Owen thought, was finally over.

Owen stood and, not thinking, gave Emma his left hand to help her rise to her feet. When she grabbed it and pulled herself up, a sharp pain stabbed his chest beneath his neatly folded pocket square. He winced and braced to ensure his arm didn't give way under her weight. Once on her feet, Emma stood beside her lawyer, the top of her head barely reaching the height of his shoulders.

Owen reached under his jacket and rubbed his chest. The pain subsided slowly.

Emma saw him wince. "Are you okay?" she asked.

"It's nothing," he answered.

Edward Hardwick, Circuit Court Judge, took his place behind the bench. "Be seated," he said, looking across the room at the restless lawyers, plaintiffs, defendants, witnesses, and bystanders who were likely as eager as he was to go home. He jerked his hand to his mouth, but not in time to hide the sudden erupting yawn. He wore wire-rimmed glasses, and under the bright lights, his scalp shined through a comb-over of thinning grey hair.

Owen peered at the clock on the wall above Hardwick's head. It was three-thirty-five, about the time for Atlanta's infamous afternoon traffic jams to begin. Congestion would soon clog the downtown streets. He knew his girlfriend, Nicole, was probably already antsy and waiting for him at his house. They were to drive to the mountains of North Carolina for the weekend.

"Liberty Park Homeowners Association versus Capital City Developers," the bailiff called out.

"That's us," Owen said, still holding his client's hand, moist and slick from her nervous last-minute application of hand lotion. Emma pushed down on her hip to force her back straight and then stepped forward with a little hop to get herself moving. Arthritis wreaked havoc throughout her body but age had been helpless to slow her mind. Although she was eighty-three years old, she was the good sense of her neighborhood, the one everyone confided in or turned to when advice was needed. All understood at the outset of their lawsuit that she would be the one to sit with their lawyer at the plaintiff's table. When they elected her President of the homeowners association, she proudly said it was the first time she had ever won anything.

Owen guided Emma toward a chair while watching Quinn lead her client to their table. She moved in a distinctive gait he remembered well. Strutting in perfect posture, she commanded attention as she went. Hers was the well-heeled walk of old money and high expectations.

It was a walk his father admired.

"That girl is going places," Dr. Lewis Montgomery once remarked, watching his son's fiancé saunter across the room at the Paces Ferry Club one Saturday afternoon, gliding toward a select cluster of Atlanta's elite citizens. "She's going to be a hard dog to keep on the porch, son," he said with a grin, lightly punching Owen on the shoulder.

"She'll run over anyone she thinks might get in her way," Owen muttered, "and won't think twice about it."

"You can't fault ambition, Owen," his father said.

"That depends on whose ambition we're talking about," Owen frowned, "and who's getting run over."

"You can't blame her; she comes from a long line of over-achievers. She wants what's best for both of you, Owen," Dr. Montgomery said.

They watched Quinn work the crowd. She was intentional about the order in which she greeted people and how much time she allotted each person.

"It's funny how you can act like you're going to kiss someone but never let your lips touch their skin," Owen quipped.

"Have a drink, Owen," his father said sharply. "Your spring is wound a little too tight." Then, summoned by Mrs. Montgomery, he walked away. Owen watched as his father disappeared into the crowd and then turned toward the bar. He nearly ran headfirst into Quinn.

"You should be working the room with me," she said tartly.

"Quinn, every social occasion isn't an opportunity to find an advantage," he answered.

"You still don't get it, do you?" she scolded. "To get ahead, to win, you've got to have an advantage. Advantage is everything. Wake up, Owen." Annoyed, she shook her head, turned on her heels, and walked away from him.

The judge coughed, and Owen's attention snapped back to the present.

Quinn paused at her chair at the defendant's table and waited. Her client sat down, but seeing her still standing, he quickly jumped up and pulled out the chair for her.

She sat down without thanking him or giving an appreciative nod.

Owen watched the judge scratch his head vigorously, leaving a few tufts of hair standing upright on the crown of his head as he glanced over the papers on his bench. Whitaker, who had thrust this case upon him at the last moment, warned Owen that while old man Hardwick looked and sometimes acted like a fool, he wasn't. Instead, he was brilliant but quick-tempered and impatient; he liked to get to the bottom of things quickly. He hated for his calendar to become backlogged. Worse, he hated unsure lawyers who moved slowly. "If you don't have the balls to be in court, you shouldn't be a lawyer, lady lawyers excluded, of course," he supposedly once said after a few too many glasses of single malt scotch.

Owen placed his briefcase on the table, nodded to the judge, and then pulled out the chair for Emma. She shuffled toward it, and he rubbed his hands together to rid himself of her hand lotion that had rubbed off on him. A vaguely familiar scent reached his nostrils.

Before sitting down, Emma looked to the back of the courtroom at the small gathering of her neighbors who had come to watch the hearing. The men were dressed in their best. That was an old suit with a carnation pinned to the lapel for a few, but most were in shirtsleeves and ties that had seen a lot of Sundays. One or two propped their hands on the handles of walking canes. The women all wore dresses, and a few sported netted Sunday hats. Most of her neighbors were nearly as old as she was, although some were as young as thirty.

"They have been my neighbors for so many years. It sometimes seems like we were raised under the same roof," Emma said. "They want to keep their trees, too." She pointed a bent finger toward her friends. "We're all countin' on you, Owen."

Owen looked over his shoulder at his other clients. He'd met most of them a week ago but couldn't recall their names, except for the most unusual ones. There was Frog, the retired brick mason and chain smoker since the age of nine; Ruby, the woman who wore a thick coat of deep red lipstick and checked it often in case it needed a touchup; and Mr. and Mrs. Roundtree, the happily married forever couple who lived in the little blue house next door to Emma.

Their first homeowners association meeting was held at the neighborhood church. Everyone brought food and dessert and hugged one another as if it were a family reunion rather than a business meeting. Before Owen could get everyone focused on the matter at hand, they had insisted he eat while they spent time getting to know him. And he got to know something about them while he gulped sweet tea to wash down vinegary and ham hock seasoned collard greens, black-eyed peas with raw white onion, and greasy but irresistible fried hoe cakes. His clients were more than mere neighbors; they were lifelong friends and family who had established time-honored traditions and a strong sense of community pride within the boundaries of their old and crumbling neighborhood.

"We're going to save all the trees, Emma," Owen said as he sat down. He opened his briefcase, pulled out a folder thick with stapled and highlighted documents, and glanced cautiously again at Quinn.

She watched him now, her blue eyes vibrant beneath her perfectly plucked brows, and she smiled a little as if she wanted to say something but had talked herself out of it. She was sitting askew in her chair, her legs crossed at the knees, a tanned and sculpted calf and ankle pointing toward him, the sharp toe of her designer shoe bobbing in a lazy rhythm in the aisle.

"I don't intend to disappoint anyone," Owen added quickly. Turning back to his folder, he randomly began thumbing through its contents. A paperclip came loose from a stack of documents and shot across the table.

"Hello, Owen. So nice to see you," Quinn said, leaning into the aisle.

"And you as well," Owen said flatly.

"I see you still have a soft spot for the underdog," she wisecracked as she righted herself in her chair. Her thick, soft hair was draped behind her shoulders, ensuring it didn't hide an inch of her flawless face.

Owen snapped his head around and looked eye to eye with her. "Don't insult my client," he said tersely.

"It's been a while, hasn't it?" she nearly cooed. "I'm eager to see how well you perform today." She tucked her legs under the table and turned to her client to whisper in his ear.

Owen glared at her, shook his head, and turned his attention back to Emma.

"Why'd she call me an underdog?" she asked, offended.

"It's best to ignore her," he answered, meaning it as much for himself as for Emma.

"Can't hardly ignore a woman like that," she said. "We don't see much of the likes of her in Liberty Park."

Until now, the residents of Liberty Park were a quiet and passive group who managed their neighborhood simply by being good neighbors to one another. They observed an unwritten code of conduct. It required them to keep their front yards clean, watch each other's grandchildren, and never start a lawn mower on Sundays until after church let out. In Liberty Park, no one walked the walk of old money and high expectations.

"Shoot, you the first lawyer I ever spoke to," Emma added.

"I've read your pretrial motion, Counsel," Hardwick fanned a handful of papers in the air, addressing Owen, "but humor me a moment. The Board of Education has the right to sell its land, and the developer has the right to remove those trees in keeping with the architectural plan that was approved when the property was rezoned. So tell me, why should I give you a permanent injunction against Capital City Developers?"

Owen stood, cleared his throat, and quickly scanned his notes again. His tie suddenly felt too tight around his throat, so he grabbed the double Windsor knot and tugged on it.

The extra cup of strong black coffee and throbbing music of REM that had pumped him up earlier that morning now failed him. He had a detailed knowledge of the law, but his courtroom experience was limited. After finishing law school, he had chosen to work for a legal aid organization, believing it was a good move to prepare himself for a state prosecutor role. He provided legal services to the poor, but those cases seldom went to court. Most were handled with a few phone calls and some paperwork.

The Liberty Park case had been handed to him less than three weeks ago when Whitaker agreed to take it after a golfing buddy, supposedly distantly related to one of the homeowners, called in a favor. Whitaker had no interest in the case; it didn't have a payoff other than returning a favor. After securing a temporary emergency injunction against removing the trees, he punted it to Owen. "I want to see how well you work under pressure," he said when he tossed the file onto Owen's desk.

"Sir, with respect," Owen responded at the time, "I am one of the most productive associates in the firm. I billed nearly 2,100 hours last year, almost 200 more than the quota."

"It takes a lot more than a few extra billable hours to climb the ladder here, Mr. Montgomery," Whitaker retorted. "Prove you can handle a curve ball, get that debt off my back, and maybe we'll sit down to talk about that new law specialty you are so interested in."

"Your Honor," Owen began, "the residents of Liberty Park are here asking you to save a small grove of yellow poplar trees that stand on the subject property. Many of these residents planted the trees as small seedlings around the old elementary school during an Arbor Day ceremony decades ago. After the school burned down, the students who never moved from the neighborhood spent their time and money maintaining the area, cutting the grass, pruning the shrubs, and planting flowers each spring and fall. They turned the old schoolyard into their neighborhood park."

"So your clients' are trespassers," Hardwick remarked.

"Your Honor," Owen started.

"I said humor me," Hardwick interrupted, "not bore me. Skip the monologue and get to your point."

Quinn thumped her pen impatiently on her notepad.

Owen glanced up at the clock again. Nearly twenty minutes had passed. Nicole had to be chomping at the bit by now, he thought.

"Your Honor, we certainly don't want to cause any ill will with the defendant," he continued, "but we intend to see that these trees are preserved in compliance with the Tree Protection Ordinance. To assure that, we'll resort to the recourses made available by the Ordinance, no matter how aggressive. It is our position the permit to remove the trees was issued in error." He turned toward the well-dressed developer sitting beside Quinn and addressed him directly. "If we see that any of those trees have been damaged, if you so much as spray paint another X on even one of those trees...."

"An X?" Hardwick interrupted again.

"To mark 'em for cuttin' down!" Emma blurted out, leaning forward in her chair and pounding the table with her little gnarled fist.

"That's right, Your Honor," Owen said, grinning and raising his hand to calm his client. "A red X has been painted on the trees they plan to remove; eight were marked before the homeowners intervened. We are here to preserve the trees, Your Honor. We'll do whatever it takes to make sure they remain standing."

"Counsel, the gentleman sounds serious about those trees," Hardwick turned to Quinn and pointed to Owen with his glasses. "How do you respond?"

"Your Honor," she began as she walked toward the bench and posed in the middle of the floor. Her suit was hand-tailored to look appropriately conservative yet hint at the shapely body it clung to. Hardwick couldn't help but take notice.

"This is a clear and simple case," Quinn asserted. "My client properly applied for the rezoning permit and lawfully obtained the necessary approval. As directed in the rezoning decision, he will replace the trees to be removed with new plantings elsewhere on the property. Furthermore, he intends to add other landscaping elements that will leave the neighborhood even more beautiful than it has ever been. My client fully intends to minimize disruption to the plot and leave Liberty Park a better place to live for the current residents and those who will eventually purchase his new condominiums."

Owen stood, pressing his fingertips together, and felt a twitch starting under his left eye. He wasn't sure the Honorable Hardwick had heard a word Quinn had said, the way his eyes were surveying her from top to bottom. He turned to face Quinn. "If your client is so well intended, you might think he would have accepted at least one of our invitations to meet with the homeowners."

Emma nodded in agreement, and her neighbors' chorus of approval rose in the background.

Hardwick rapped his gavel, and Emma jumped in her chair.

"Your Honor," Owen continued, stepping forward, "the former school site is the only public green space in the neighborhood. The trees are integral to what makes Liberty Park beautiful, and it is beautiful right now, just as it is," he said, darting a glance at the developer. "The trees represent the childhood history of these taxpayers; they play with their grandchildren and great-grandchildren in the shade of these trees. Furthermore, this park is only a short walk from the birthplace of Dr. Martin Luther King, Jr. The proposed condominiums and possibly other future development threaten the unique character of a historic neighborhood. Your Honor, we believe the zoning variance was awarded in error. This case is a glaring example of how the city arborist arbitrarily enforces the code. We see a clear pattern of far more decisions favoring this developer than any other company requesting to remove trees. The variance clearly violates the language of the Tree Ordinance, plain and simple. We respectfully request that you give a permanent order today that enforces the letter and intent of the Ordinance."

"Today, you say? That's rather ambitious, isn't it, Mr. Montgomery?" Hardwick looked at Quinn again and smiled. "I'll review both the Ordinance and the rezoning decision in question, and I'll hear your arguments," he paused to look at his watch and then his calendar, "next Tuesday morning, ten o'clock. In the meantime, the temporary injunction stands. No action is to be taken with respect to altering the land and trees in question. And that includes painting any additional red Xs." He hit his gavel on the bench again and motioned for the bailiff to clear the courtroom.

Owen interrupted the movement toward the exit door. "Your Honor," he began, "the Ordinance expressly states...."

"I said Tuesday, Counsel. Now, don't agitate me."

"If I may, sir...."

"Mr. Montgomery, you may not. Earlier today, right here in my courtroom, a man saw himself on camera helping himself to the contents of a cash register that was not his to pilfer. You might say it embarrassed him because he pleaded guilty on the first day of what was going to be a three-day trial. I have a rare opening on my calendar, and you, sir, will help me fill it. Tuesday morning," Hardwick said gruffly, bringing his gavel down again, even harder this time. It echoed like a gunshot, and even Owen jumped. He wisely chose not to press the issue further. He looked over at Quinn, who grinned and gave him a little nod. "Let's go, Emma," he finally said as he reached to pull his client's chair away from the table. "I'm afraid we're finished here for now."

"Does he mean we get to keep our trees?" she asked.

"For a few more days, at least," he answered.

"A few days? That's all?" she asked, bewildered.

"We'll know more on Tuesday," he said.

"You can talk him into longer, can't you?" Emma nearly begged.

"I intend to persuade the judge to see the situation just like we do," Owen said. "We will win this, Emma."

"Well, that was fun," Quinn said, closing in on Owen with her client tagging along close by her side. "This is so much better than your days working with legal aid, don't you think," she said in a condescending but honey-dipped tone.

"There's no cause for celebration, Quinn," Owen said. "The Tree Ordinance was written to prevent circumstances such as this. The old man," he nodded toward the judge's bench, "just wants to see you strut in here again." He turned to the developer. "You thought you were paying for legal representation, but instead, you're going to get a bill just so he," now pointing to the empty bench, "can get his eyes on her again."

"I like how you promised to be aggressive," Quinn retorted, unaffected.

"What are you doing here anyway?" Owen asked sharply. "I was expecting Richmond."

"It was a last-minute change, that's all," she said. "Don't let it upset you. Besides, I'd hoped you'd be glad to see me."

"I don't mind that you are sitting in for Richmond, but that is hardly the same thing as being glad to see you again," he said. He reached for his briefcase and then looked back at Quinn. "I'll see you Tuesday, and come prepared."

Quinn nodded and walked away, followed by her client, who kept looking over his shoulder at Owen.

"Tell me, how do you know her?" Emma asked.

"We were engaged once, but that is ancient history now," Owen said. Before she could ask any more questions, he quickly guided Emma into the hall, where her neighbors stood waiting patiently for them. He answered their questions, explained the proceedings, and reminded them that the tree ordinance was a relatively new law; it had not yet been tested in court.

After the group broke up, Owen and Emma stood in the nearly empty halls of the courthouse. He looked into Emma's brown eyes again. They were more tired than before and maybe a little disappointed, too.

"Don't worry about Quinn, Emma," he said. He unbuttoned his collar and loosened his tie even more. "Our history is not going to be a problem. I will win this case for you."

She patted his arm and smiled. "You're a good lawyer, I know, 'cause we prayed for one, and then the Lord sent you to us. Now, if you don't mind, I'd appreciate you showin' me to the bus stop."

"I brought you here, Emma, and I'll take you home," he said.

"I don't want to be no trouble for you," she said.

"You're no trouble, Emma, none at all," he said, offering his arm and leading her down the hall toward an exit.

"You did not let me down today, Mr. Montgomery. You did just fine," Emma said. "I especially liked how you told the judge how rude that man was, ignorin' us like he did."

Owen tried to grin but managed only to flare his nostrils and think back to when he tripped and fell while chasing after Quinn.

They say life is a highway
And its milestones are the years.
And now and then there's a toll-gate
Where you buy your way with tears.

Roofs, 1917

Joyce Kilmer

CHAPTER 2

LIBERTY PARK

Owen pushed open the heavy bronze exit door of the courthouse, allowed Emma to exit first, and followed her outside into the humid, sunny Georgia afternoon. Even in September, the unforgiving southern sun baked everything to a crisp and still shined bright enough into the late afternoon to nearly blind you. Emma squinted and shielded her eyes the best she could with her better hand as Owen, wearing his Ray-Bans, led her across the street to his car. He opened the door for her, stood back, and waited as she slowly sat down, her bottom in first and then swinging her feet in last with some labor. Struggling still, she couldn't reach over her shoulder for the seatbelt. He leaned in and buckled her up.

Owen slid behind the wheel and into the driver's seat, turned the key, and then reached to adjust his sunglasses. The air conditioner stirred the hot air inside the car, and he noticed the scent of Emma's lotion once more. Familiar, yes, but he still couldn't place it. He wondered what he and his client would talk about during their brief ride to her home. They didn't have much in common, and there wasn't anything about the pretrial hearing that he hadn't already explained to her. He cringed at the thought she might ask him more questions about Quinn. He looked over and, relieved, saw that she had immediately fallen asleep, her body limp in the soft grip of the leather bucket seat. He listened to her shallow breaths, in through the nose and then out the mouth, each released with a little puff at the end. He grinned and slowly pulled into the flow of traffic.

Within a few minutes, they were driving through Liberty Park, passing the well-worn houses that once characterized the neighborhood, many of them now pushing three-quarters of a century old. Most were single-story structures with clapboard siding thinly coated in blistered and faded paint facing yards hidden behind hedges in need of pruning or rusty chain link fences. Painted concrete front porches were decorated with rocking chairs and one-gallon cans pretending to be flower pots. The rockers waited patiently for neighbors to sit, admire the flowers, and pass the time away with stories about how things used to be before the folks with money started moving in and taking over the neighborhood.

Young professionals of all descriptions were moving into the community. Some bought and refurbished the better-kept original homes, replacing windows, rotted wood, and leaky roofs, and adding new rooms to make space for a home theater or office. Still, most tore down the tired old dwellings and built large contemporary two-story houses on the lot.

Although these owners claimed their new homes were designed to blend in with the original ones, they did not. It was made clear by the near-constant muttering of the newcomers that the neglected original homes compromised the resale prices of the new ones. The fresh coats of paint on angular cement facades, clean brick driveways adorned with shiny new cars, level front porches, and lush green sod growing from border to border, not to mention the low hum of new central air conditioning systems, set their homes apart from the rest. The new home construction was a far better complement to the downtown office and condominium towers seen just across the interstate, the ten-lane-wide asphalt river locally known as the Connector, that separated the established in-town well-to-do from the young up-and-coming and the poor Liberty Park elders who were slowly fading away.

On the next block, Owen drove past the church where Emma and her neighbors attended services each Sunday morning and Wednesday night, where their first homeowners association meeting had been held. It was a clapboard building painted white and sitting firmly on a cinder block foundation painted red. Its simple steeple was the highest point in the neighborhood, a few feet taller than the rooftop outdoor kitchen of a new home built just next door. Standing on one of four corners of the intersection, the church marked the center of Liberty Park. The newcomers were prone to complain about the extended Sunday services, which meant most of the curbside parking was occupied for nearly half of the day.

On two other corners stood the old stores that had catered to the residents for many years. One was a family-owned grocery store with a tattered canvas awning across the front window. Hand-lettered signs advertising produce were taped to the glass doors and windows. Yellow squash and eggplant were on sale, food stamps were accepted, and lottery tickets were available.

The other store sold household products, cigarettes, and beer but did not sell groceries. Years ago, the storeowners had agreed not to compete with one another. "You sell them supper, and I'll cater to their sins," one owner said to the other as they shook hands. At the rear of this store was a small apartment, its porch the daily meeting place for the elderly men of the neighborhood. The store owner lived in the apartment and invited his friends over to play cards, share a joke, or worry about the changes happening in their little haven. He never took long to sell a few cold beers and cigarettes to help move the discussion along.

Those already on the porch nodded politely or waved in the air as Owen and a sleeping Emma rolled to a stop at the intersection.

Owen leaned over the steering wheel and looked ahead. On the fourth corner was the rectangular park where the school once stood. The trees planted over seventy years ago now stood tall and shaded the grass and sidewalk below. A small stone retaining wall wrapped around two sides separating the park from the sidewalk, and the backyards of a few homes bordered the third and fourth sides of the green space. From this corner, Owen could see the tall downtown buildings, which signaled the encroaching high-priced lifestyle threatening to change Liberty Park forever.

He drove on, creeping past a few more houses and then rolling to a gentle stop in front of Emma's house on Irwin Street, a stone's throw from the park. Like so many others they had just driven past, her home didn't sit square on its foundation and needed a new coat of paint and a window screen or two.

He sat and looked at Emma momentarily, hoping she would notice they had stopped and then wake up. He studied the lines in her face and the enlarged knuckles of her hands and fingers and wondered how long she'd been a widow. He remembered the one yellowed photograph he had seen on her mantelpiece, a wedding portrait. She had worn a simple floral summer dress on that special day, a netted pillbox hat, and elbow-length white gloves. The groom was probably a foot taller than she and stood tall and proud in a suit that was too short for his long legs. He looked down on his new bride with a broad smile that conveyed pure matrimonial joy.

"Emma," he finally said as he reached over and nudged her shoulder. After a second nudge, she woke up.

She reached to arrange her hair and then pushed herself upright in the seat. Still sleepy, it took a moment to orient herself. "I'm sorry," she said slowly. "It was rude of me to fall asleep on you. This is the nicest car I ever rode in, and this seat is just like one of those recliners I always wished I had."

"Think nothing of it," Owen said. "I like to take a nap now and then, too."

"It was the cost of skipping my usual after-lunch nap while we were waiting, I guess," Emma said. "Won't you come inside for some iced tea? Or some lemonade? I made it myself."

"Thanks, but not today," Owen answered. He looked at his watch. "I need to get home." He was more than a little late and remembered that Nicole liked to leave precisely on the dot of any and all scheduled departures. "I'd rather be an hour early than a minute late" was practically her motto. He looked at himself in the mirror and, for a moment, forgot he wasn't alone in the car. "You're in so much trouble," he mumbled.

"I'm in trouble?" Emma asked, surprised.

"No, not you; I meant me. I didn't mean to speak out loud; I'm sorry," Owen said.

"What trouble?" Emma asked.

He turned in his seat to look out the rear window and back at the trees. "It's going to be a complicated weekend, that's all." He reached for his door handle. "Let me open your door for you."

Before he could get out, Emma reached over and grabbed his arm. "Complicated? How come?" she asked.

"It's a personal matter," he responded. "Just something I promised my girlfriend I'd do this weekend. Nothing for you to worry about."

With what little strength she had, Emma tightened her grip on his arm. "Are you a promise-keeper or a promise-breaker, Mr. Montgomery?"

"I'd like to think I am a promise-keeper," he said as he shifted in his seat and started to pull away from her grasp but stopped, not wanting to offend her. "But sometimes I try to handle too many things at the same time," he said. "That's all. I'm not unique in that way," suddenly feeling the urge to defend himself.

"Yes, we all do that now and then," Emma said, letting go of his arm. "You need to figure out what is important and what is not. You can't do everything all at once all of the time."

"Sometimes it seems that everything is equally important and happening at the same time," Owen said.

"But it seldom is," Emma mused. "It seldom is."

Owen stared at the dashboard, fiddled with the parking brake paddle beside his seat, and nodded in half-hearted agreement. He got out to open her door, but she had already opened it and was trying to push herself up from the seat when he got to her side of the car. He took her hand and gently pulled her upward, this time using his stronger right arm. She paused when she was upright, gained her balance, and then shuffled to the curb, where she lifted her good leg up first and then hopped onto the sidewalk. Owen reached into the car to grab her purse and slipped it onto her shoulder. She held firmly to his arm as he walked with her to the steps of her porch.

Reaching for the handrail, Emma climbed up, her orthopedic shoes squeaking as she went. Owen stayed close in case she tripped and together, they reached the top step and crossed the porch. She opened the screen door, and he held it while she fished inside her purse. Finding a large brass key, she grabbed the doorknob and pushed it into the old lock, shaking it a bit before the knob would turn. The hinges screeched as the door was pushed open. The smell of mothballs spilled out onto the porch.

Before going inside, Emma turned a parental eye to Owen. "I know I've asked you before, but I want to hear you say it again. You goin' to save my tree, ain't you, Mr. Montgomery?"

"Please, Emma, call me Owen. I would like it very much if you would call me Owen. And yes, I will do everything possible to save the trees."

"You promise, Owen?"

He nodded. "Yes, I promise."

"Good, 'cause those trees are important. Very important to all of us." She waved her hand through the air, her bent fingers pointing out all the homes she could see from her porch. "I'm sure your lady friend will understand. Just tell her you're doin' a good thing for a poor little old woman who can't fix it herself." And then, without another word, she nodded goodbye and disappeared into the house, letting the screen door smack shut but leaving the front door open wide.

Inside, she put her purse on a small table beneath the front porch light switch and a picture of Jesus and shuffled toward the main front window. She leaned over her worn couch, steadied herself with one hand on the window frame, and pushed a dusty lace curtain aside to look out into her front yard. He's a nice man, she thought as she watched Owen step into the street. Maybe too nice, she worried.

Owen opened the car door to get in but then paused to look around the old neighborhood and again at the trees down the street. The grass beneath them had recently been cut, and there was not a speck of litter in sight. Purple irises grew along the boundary of the park and the adjacent backyards. Hostas and daylilies encircled the bases of the trees. The majestic poplars were nearly sixty feet tall with canopies of four-lobed green leaves that spread some forty feet across. Their branches laced together in agreement, casting a tangled shade pattern on much of the ground below.

"The park is the only part of the original neighborhood that has not yet worn out," he muttered out loud.

As he slid back into the car and pulled away from the curb, his thoughts turned to Nicole. They had agreed weeks ago to spend this long weekend with her grandmother, a woman he had never met but had heard much about.

Lo, comfort blooms on pain,
And peace on strife,
And gain on loss.

Pennies, 1914

Joyce Kilmer

CHAPTER 3

OWEN

I grabbed my mobile phone and called Vanessa Dupree, the legal assistant I share with two other lawyers.

"Hello," she answered, "Vanessa speaking."

"Vanessa, I need you to put together a reference list of tree ordinance cases anywhere in the Southeast that developers lost, if there are such things," I said. "Big city zoning boards are nearly always pro-development and leap at opportunities to gentrify old neighborhoods and increase the tax base," I explained, almost as if I were being my opening argument already.

"Well, hello, Owen. How are you?" Vanessa asked with more than a hint of annoyance about my greeting faux pas.

"I'm sorry, Vanessa," I backed up. "I'm fine, thank you. And how are you?"

"And by when do you need this?" she asked hesitantly.

"As soon as you can get it for me, I'm working over the weekend and will be there looking for it first thing in the morning," I answered.

"Owen, it's past five and a holiday Friday," she protested.

"I'll make it up to you, Vanessa," I said.

"You always say that," she snorted.

"I always do, though, make it up to you, don't I?" I answered.

"Mr. Whitaker was asking if I'd heard from you," she said.

"Is he still there?" I asked, somewhat alarmed by the prospect. "He must be worried about today's outcome. That man does not wait around for an Associate," I said nervously.

"He's already left," Vanessa groaned. "Like I said, it's past five. And Nicole called looking for you, too."

"What'd she say?" I asked hesitantly.

"She just wanted to know if I'd heard from you. I told her you were still at the hearing. She said you were supposed to be going to the mountains for the weekend."

"I was supposed to, but now there's this." I rubbed my thumb hard into my temple. I could feel a full-blown headache coming on.

"She sounded eager to leave. I'm glad you're telling her you're working this weekend, and not me," Vanessa said.

My stomach cramped. "Yeah, it won't be the kind of news she wants to hear. She's been looking forward to me going with her to meet her grandmother."

"Owen, why don't you still go with her and just use the Internet like everybody else?" Vanessa asked, almost scolding me.

"The old place where we're staying only has network ports in the lobby, and the Wi-Fi is slow, says Nicole. Besides, you know I prefer the library; it's just my way," I said. "I'm old-fashioned, I guess."

"You guess? Owen, you still write paper checks and use a Rolodex," Vanessa blurted out. "You know that Y2K thing was a hoax, don't you? It's been nine months! ATMs still work, and jet planes are still flying all over the world! Personally, I think it was just a global conspiracy to sell more batteries, rice, and dried beans. And I don't know why somebody so interested in the Internet as a legal practice would also be so afraid to use it!"

I laughed. I enjoy it when she makes fun of me. It reminds me of my beloved older brother who thrived on taunting and teasing me to toughen me up, he'd remind me over and over again just before punching me in the arm or bending me over in a tight headlock. He never hurt me, though. He knew exactly when to pull back just before the pain arrived. He always ended every assault on my body and character with a belly laugh while saying, "You know how much I love you, right, little brother?" Yes, I knew how much he loved me, and I certainly loved him too. Everyone did. He was the gravity in our family; he held us all together. God, I miss him.

"Yes, the hysteria about the digital demise of modern civilization did come to a laughable end," I admitted to Vanessa. "And yes, I am reluctant to put down the time-honored tools of jurisprudence. I like old things. I still use a gold-plated pen given to me as a gift a decade ago and a knife for a letter opener that I won in my Boy Scout days. Vanessa, what I know about how vulnerable the web is keeps me from trusting it."

Vanessa sighed and relented to my request. She said she would email me the notes she could put together on such short notice. "I'm not staying here late," she said. "I have somewhere to be; I have a life outside of the office, and you should get one, too," she said without skipping a beat.

I dropped my phone in the passenger seat and then fingered the logo in the center of the leather steering wheel of my new car, a dark blue 1999 BMW 528i. I had only recently let go of my 1990 Acura Legend, finally finding it a little too worn after 128,000 miles to trust it on the backroads, my preferred route to nearly anywhere. I had waited for the 2000 model-year cars to come out to buy the '99, saving myself a few thousand dollars with my patience. I looked down at the monogrammed cuff of my starched shirt that only partially covered my Rolex watch and then at my conservative but expensive striped Hugo Boss tie draped into my lap. I couldn't deny that corporate law was far more lucrative than working in legal aid. I'm hopeful that breaking ground in the new field of Internet technology law will give me the opportunity I currently lack as a general practice Associate. That was what Quinn had wanted, a reason to be proud of me.

"It makes no sense to me why you don't want to fulfill your potential," she once admonished me before pressing me to explain my apparent lack of ambition.

"I didn't know my potential was best measured in dollars," I shot back.

"Everything is measured in dollars in one way or another, Owen. Like it or not, that's the way it is. I love how idealistic you are, but sometimes it's also the very thing I dislike so much about you." She began to cry.

"I see that I also didn't know that romantic idealism and old-fashioned values were things to be despised," I snapped. She had never come right out and said it to me, but she had planted enough hints that I knew she was beginning to think I was not good enough for her — or at least that I would not be rich enough for her, which I'm sure was the same thing in her analysis.

"I need an equal, Owen," Quinn's voice quivered when she confessed what she had been trying not to say. "I need someone with the same ambition, goals, and potential as I have."

And there it was. It was as if my thinking about it had drawn the words straight out of her mouth.

I forced my thoughts back to the Liberty Park case. I propped my elbow on the door, rested my chin in my hand, and started talking aloud, testing different opening remarks, anything to get my mind off of Quinn.

"Your Honor, we cannot let Atlanta become an asphalt island."

"Your Honor, builders' greed is chasing off those who have given Atlanta its identity since the early days of the Civil Rights Movement."

"Your Honor, if we look closely enough, I am confident we will find irregularities in the conduct of the city arborist."

I sniffed my hand and finally recognized the smell left on me after holding Emma's hand. Lavender.

Suddenly, a vision of Florence Darden, the law school librarian and my friend, oh what a welcome change of subject she was, popped into my mind. One evening, I helped her pull a heavy book cart into a cramped elevator, and we struck up a conversation as we rode to the next floor. It was then, confined in those close quarters, when I first noticed her subtle, floral scent. After that chance meeting, we spoke when we saw one another and eventually learned enough about one another to become friends. Florence encouraged me, tracked down the occasional misplaced law book for me, and shared her wise advice about life and ethics with me every now and then. She was just the kind of woman you might think a librarian would be – intelligent, charming, thoughtful, and unassuming.

"I made these for you," she said one night, placing a paper bag of homemade chocolate chip and pecan cookies on the library table between my stacks of books.

I grabbed one and took a bite. "They are delicious," I said. "They overpower the bitter taste of that cheap vending machine coffee I'm practically living on."

Florence sat down, grabbed a cookie, and bit into it. As she ate, she told me I needed to take a break. I obediently sat back and listened to her talk about ballet, French food, and, finally, flower gardening. That was when I asked her about her fragrance.

"Lavender, my favorite flower," she said. "I wear it because it reminds me of springtime all year long."

I was one of the few law students to attend Florence's funeral. After the service, I spoke to her family and told them of the night when she had brought me cookies. "Her kind and right-thinking example, her desire to serve others, will not be lost on me," I promised them. "She was like a second mother to me, and I am reminded of her every time I open the cover of a heavy law book," I told them while tears rolled down my cheeks.

Florence's kindness was one of two significant influences that shaped who I would later become. The other influence is my mother. In stark contrast to Florence, Blanche Montgomery is a hard woman. She is the kind of woman who answered the request for water from the sweaty black man working in our backyard with a Mason jar instead of a glass from her perfectly arranged kitchen cupboard. Heir to an impressive fortune, faithful tithing member of the First Presbyterian Church, volunteer fundraiser for the medically fragile children's home, and president of the Garden Club, she was the prototype of a steel magnolia. After she's had one too many Belvedere martinis, I've heard my mother speak of the "less fortunate" with more than a hint of superiority when she thought she was in like-minded company. I love her, but sometimes I struggle to like her as much as a son should like his mother.

I drove out of Liberty Park and made my way toward home, a small bungalow I own in Virginia Highland, a nearby neighborhood in the midst of its own resurgence. I crossed the busy intersection at Ponce de Leon Avenue and passed the historical marker mounted on one of the brick columns at the entrance of the neighborhood.

Virginia Highland was as old as Liberty Park, but its homes were much larger and, by comparison, much more elegant. Built of brick or clad in stucco, most had slate or terra cotta tile roofs, carriage houses, and brick paths leading from the sidewalks to the ornate front doors that hung on silent hinges.

In the center of the neighborhood a collection of restaurants, coffee shops, and wine bars added a contrasting dose of urban excitement to the historical surroundings. Nicole and I frequently dined at those restaurants, sitting at small white tablecloth-covered and candlelit tables, enjoying eclectic food, expensive wine, and hushed conversations.

I slowed down as I drove past my favorite restaurant, a quaint spot on a corner fashioned from an old gas station. There, I joined Nicole on our brief first date five months ago.

We met at a networking social hosted by my law firm, where business consultants and legal specialists gathered to mingle with the new associate attorneys. At the time, I was working in corporate law. I was introduced to the principal of a human resources consulting firm, who in turn introduced me to twenty-eight-year-old Nicole Fischer. She had been tasked with generating referrals for her employer while he smoked cigars with the law firm's senior partners. She was certifiable corporate arm candy, and I could not take my eyes off her.

When we were finally introduced, I was immediately attracted to her, and not only because she is almost Meg Ryan's doppelganger. It was more because of the way she smiled at me. It wasn't one of those smiles learned in prep school, well-rehearsed but pleasant enough, used over and over again in the course of meeting strangers. It was more authentic than that and sincere. I felt its warmth, and it drew me in like a moth to a porch light.

"I bet you went to the University of Georgia," she said.

"What makes you assume that?" I asked.

"Well, you are wearing a grey striped seersucker suit, a red and black polka dot bowtie, and a red pocket square. The only thing missing is a pair of white and black buck shoes," she chuckled.

"Just call me busted," I said with a grin before raising a glass of bourbon on the rocks to my mouth.

"Do you own an English Bulldog, too?" she asked.

"No. They are not much good for quail hunting," I answered.

"And you read Southern Literature?" she inquired.

"Of course, when I have time," I answered earnestly. "Carson McCullers, Faulkner, Harry Crews, Tennessee Williams, Erskine Caldwell, Eudora Welty, I love them all. Have you ever been to Andalusia?" I asked.

"Where?" she responded, obviously not familiar with the place.

"Lord, I have much to teach you," I said.

"You are so Southern; it's adorable," she said, flattering me even if she was being sarcastic. "I bet you watch the Kentucky Derby, too."

"The first Saturday in May ought to be a national holiday," I chuckled. "I hope you own a proper hat for the occasion."

From that moment forward, I spent the evening trying to stay close without crowding her. I watched her interact with others, taking in every detail of her appearance, attitude, intelligence, and wit, and smiled at her or raised my glass each time she looked my way. When the event was over, I made sure we exchanged business cards, and as we shook hands to say goodnight, I asked her to have dinner with me sometime soon.

"You move fast," she grinned, obviously flattered. "We're not in a bar speed dating, you know."

"I think it best not to wait," I said. "After watching the other men here tonight taking note of you, I'm sure I won't be the only one asking you to dinner."

Nicole met me at the restaurant the following Sunday evening after refusing to give me her address when I said I would pick her up at her front door. "I'm a cautious person," she explained. "We have plenty of time for you to find out where I live."

That night, after we had exchanged the usual it's nice to see you again and how was your day pleasantries, I asked her, "Please tell me why you are so cautious. You ought to know that bulldogs are noble creatures."

"Honestly, I just prefer to be careful," she said, "to proceed cautiously until I get to know someone."

"Have you had a bad experience?" I asked.

She took a sip of her wine. "I've been disappointed a few times, but never really anything bad," she said. "I learned at a very young age to never let my guard down, to never let myself be vulnerable with anyone. So far, it's worked well for me."

"Wow, that's interesting," I said, unsure what to think of her easy admission and wondering what she was trying to tell me. "And who taught you that lesson?"

"My mother," she said plainly. "She wanted to make sure I knew how to avoid letting anyone take advantage of me."

"Well, that in and of itself is a valuable thing to learn, but, and I hope you don't mind me saying this, it sounds like you might be over-achieving in that regard," I said.

"Maybe," she allowed, "but as I said, so far, it has worked for me."

"I have to know," I inquired, "just how do you avoid being taken advantage of?"

"No one gets close enough to have the opportunity to try," she said, as unapologetically as a Southern Baptist preacher telling a devoted sinner that he was going straight to Hell. She picked up her wine glass and tossed what was left in it down her throat.

"And what does your father think of…" I began to ask.

"I have no father," she interrupted. "I mean, I was fathered by someone, of course, but I never knew him. He and my mother were never married; that's why I'm an only child, and he has never shown any interest in me."

"I'm so sorry," I said. "That must have been so hard for you while growing up."

"Not really," she replied. "My mother was enough for me. She wasn't perfect by any measure; in fact, she was quite flawed, but nevertheless, she did everything she could to keep me from thinking that my glass was only half full."

"You're speaking of her in the past tense," I commented carefully.

"Yes," she said. "I lost her almost two years ago. But that is enough about me for our first date, Owen. Now, it's your turn. You must tell me more about you and your family; it's only fair."

"Well," I began, "my father is a physician here in Atlanta, and my mother was once an antique dealer, but now that Dad is so successful, it has become more of a hobby for her. To be honest, she collects more than she sells these days. She has a thing for oyster plates and rare porcelain figurines."

"And you get along well with them?" she asked me.

"With my dad, yes, very well," I replied, then paused.

"And your mother?" she pressed.

"It depends," I answered honestly. "We have our good days and our bad ones."

"Tell me why," she pressed further.

"My mother is an alpha dog. She expects cooperation and unquestioning obedience at every turn." I fingered my glass, feeling guilty that I had just said such a thing about my mother. "Let's just say I don't always defer to her wishes," I confessed.

"Oh, Owen, you're a rebel! Again, just so southern," she said with a laugh. "Simply charming!" She seemed delighted to hear that I am not a scared little pup. "And how many siblings do you have?" she asked.

I paused. I don't know why I didn't expect her to ask me this question; it was a perfectly acceptable getting-to-know-you kind of question. Nevertheless, I balked.

"Owen, are you alright?" she asked, reaching across the table to rest her fingers on my wrist.

I lifted my wine glass and emptied it. "Yes, I'm fine," I said as I brought the glass back down to the table. "It's just that I lost my brother almost two years ago coincidentally, and sometimes it still comes as a shock to me that he is gone."

"I'm so sorry," Nicole offered sincerely. "I had no idea. And I know exactly what you mean."

"Thank you," I said, "but no apology is necessary. You couldn't have known."

"May I ask what happened to him?" she asked.

"Let's save that for later," I answered.

"So you don't like to share all of your personal details, either, do you?" she said.

"I don't mind sharing everything in due time," I said. "But I don't like dumping all the details of my life onto the table on our first date. It's bad form."

"There, Owen, right there!" she said with excitement.

"Right there, what?" I asked, not following her at all.

"Privacy," she answered. "It's what we have in common, an expectation of privacy. I'd say cheers to privacy, but my glass is empty, too." She raised her wine glass for me to see.

I lifted my glass anyway and tapped it to hers. "I'll order us another," I said.

While we waited for the wine to arrive, I wondered if it was best to let her think I was as much a fan of privacy as she seemed to believe or confess to her that I was afraid that if I told her everything about my family on our first date that it might be our last date. You just don't lead with all your drama, I decided. Thankfully, our dinner arrived along with the wine, and we moved on to lighter conversation as we ate. We shared bites from each other's plates, talked about our jobs, and laughed as we whispered made-up stories about what the couples seated at surrounding tables were really thinking of one another.

"I had hoped we might talk a little longer, maybe stroll around the neighborhood and find a place to listen to some music for a bit," I said, disappointed when she suggested we ask for the check almost immediately after we finished our meal.

"I travel a lot. In fact, I'm going to LA tomorrow morning," she said, "and I want to make sure I get enough sleep before having to head to the airport. Besides, there's really not that much more to know about me," she almost muttered, running her finger around the rim of her wine glass.

"That isn't true about either of us. Our stories are certainly composed of many chapters," I said. "It just takes a while to read a good book."

"Well, maybe there's not that much more I'm willing to share, Owen. Not yet, anyway. But I think I have shared enough to keep you interested." She gulped the last swallow of her wine and smiled at me.

"Why, yes, Miss Fischer, indeed you have. And I thank you for it, too. And to be honest," I said, "I think you have shared quite a lot tonight, whether you meant to or not."

"Really, like what? Have I been telling you more than I realize? Have you been using your dirty lawyer tricks on me to get me to confess to things I had no intention of saying?" she laughed.

"There are no dirty lawyer tricks, Nicole; that's a myth," I laughed with her. "But you did tell me you have never met your father, you are an only child, you don't want pets or children, and you tend to stay in relationships for only a few months before you lose interest."

"I don't like commitments," she said, again rather unapologetically.

"Not even to a dog?" I asked.

"Dogs are too needy. You have to change your whole life to accommodate one," she said.

"Well, I don't mind admitting that I eventually want someone special in my life", I said. "Okay," I put my fork down, "I'll just come out and say it. I'm hoping to find someone who will be as hopelessly attached to me as I will be to her."

"Really?" Nicole asked, choking back a giggle. "That sounds so idealistic. I mean no offense, but really? Is that what you are, Owen, an idealist? A hopeless romantic?"

"I am built to love someone, to share a life and have a history with someone," I said, now myself unapologetic. "Without someone to claim as my own, a woman who would want to claim me in return, well, what's the point of relationships otherwise?"

Nicole sat back in her chair. "Wow, you just put all that right out there, not hesitating at all, even after you said you don't believe in sharing too much about yourself too soon." She paused and watched me looking back at her. My mind raced with thoughts that I had just gone too far for her comfort. "And how do you know this about yourself, Owen? You seem so certain," she said.

"I've been in love before," I answered hesitantly. "Haven't you?"

"Honestly, I don't know." She looked away from my inquiring gaze. "I haven't had much of an example of what love looks like. I'm very close to my grandmother, but she, too, was never married, so there was no help there. And as I've explained, my mom, not so much either. She certainly tried to be everything to me, but she never seemed genuinely attached to me in that unconditional way that moms are supposed to be attached to their children. I grew up feeling somewhat disconnected from the person who is supposed to love me the most."

"I get that," I told her. "My mother runs hot and cold, using affection for rewards or punishments, depending on the circumstances. In my family now, people don't often touch each other or tell each other that they are loved. At least not much since my brother died." I paused. "It seems like ever since we lost Joel, we've forgotten how to be there for each other."

"Owen, I'm so sorry to make you think about your brother. Won't you tell me what happened?" she asked me.

"I thought you said you needed to get out of here," I said quickly. "Not tonight, please. Let's save something to talk about for next time."

"Don't you think you will have to tell me sometime?" Nicole asked.

I stared at her, and I grew angry. "He killed himself," I said plainly, tossing my napkin onto the table. "Are you happy now?" I demanded.

She gasped and quickly brought her hand to her mouth. "I'm so sorry," she said through her fingers. "I'm so sorry I insisted."

"May we say no more about this tonight?" I asked.

"Of course, of course," she said as she leaned toward me. "Owen, I am so sorry. Please forgive me. I won't ask anything else about Joel. You tell me what you want me to know when you're ready to tell me. To privacy," she said as she tipped her glass toward me.

"Thank you," I said, thankful for her retreat. "It is still difficult for me to talk about my brother without being overcome by the realization that I don't have him anymore."

"Promise me this, Owen," she said as she leaned even closer toward me. "Let's not let our respective Greek tragedies be the string that ties us together. I don't want to be the living evidence that misery loves company. If we're going to see each other again, we must have something more than that to share."

"I promise," I said. "Like I said, I want a relationship of real depth, nothing shallow for me."

"Owen," she said, looking intensely into my eyes, "we're only as good as the promises we keep."

"I promise, Nicole. I mean it," I said to her, genuinely meaning it down to the marrow of my bones. "If we see each other again, and I certainly hope that we do, there will become much more to bind us together than our understanding of each other's pain from the past."

I drove onward and tried to believe all would be well between Nicole and me. I wished we were having dinner together again in that restaurant tonight, reliving those first pangs of attraction that had drawn us together. But instead, I'm dreading telling her I cannot make the trip to North Carolina. I remember how excited she was the night she asked me to go with her. "You've lasted longer than anybody," she said when she realized her grandmother's birthday was approaching. "I guess it's time to introduce you to Granna."

"I'm glad to have outlasted your other beaus," I said, "and I'd be very happy to meet your grandmother."

"I've never introduced anyone to her, so it will be a monumental thing for her and a milestone for me, I suppose," Nicole said.

Beyond the restaurants and shops, I drove into the section of the neighborhood where I live. There the homes were smaller than those near Ponce de Leon, but still impressive with manicured lawns and evidence of recent remodeling. I looked in the windows of each house as I passed by and it occurred to me that all my neighbors were strangers. Yes, people occasionally smiled and waved when our eyes met, but no one called out my name or asked me to sit on their porch and visit for a while. No one had come by to welcome me when I first moved in. Unlike Emma, I had no idea who my next-door neighbors were.

Turning onto my street, I saw Nicole's car parked in my driveway, its trunk lid open. I crept to a stop at the curb, looked across the lawn, and saw her through the front window. Pacing back and forth in the living room, she was on the telephone. Smiling and running her fingers through her hair, she looked outside, saw me, and walked over to the window. She quickly waved for me to hurry inside.

I smiled back at her as I stepped out of the car. I grabbed my briefcase and walked across the grass toward the house, bracing myself as each step carried me closer to the front stoop and the moment I would disappoint her. My heart pounded in my chest as I reached for the handle of the front door.

Unbar your heart this evening
And keep no stranger out,
Take from your soul's great portal
The barrier of doubt.

Gates and Doors, 1917

Joyce Kilmer

CHAPTER 4

NICOLE

"He's here!" I sang happily into the telephone while watching Owen walk across the yard. "I can't wait for you to meet him," I told my grandmother. "It's hard to believe I care so much about him."

"It sounds like he is a special fellow," she answered.

"Oh, he is. I care more about him than I had ever imagined that I would," I told her. "Perhaps more than I have let him know."

"And why is that Nicole?" my grandmother asked me.

"You know how I am about expressing my feelings, Granna," I replied. "I'm just not that comfortable with it."

"Honey, you have to use your mouth to let someone know how you think and feel about them," she said. "No one wants to guess about something so important."

"Well, if anyone is going to get to me, it will be Owen," I confessed easily. The truth is he was already getting to me, but I didn't want to admit it to anyone.

"I'm so glad; it's time you found someone," Granna said. "I always worry about you ending up alone. My greatest fear is that you might one day be as lonely as a pine tree in a parking lot."

"Ruth Fischer, you know I'm perfectly happy being alone," I answered confidently. "Besides, look at you. You've always been alone, and it doesn't seem to have damaged you a bit."

"It's not really like that, at least not like you might think," she said. "I've had my share of loneliness."

I should have picked up on this opening she had just given me to inquire deeper into what she was beginning to tell me, but I was so intensely focused on Owen that I hardly heard my grandmother's sadness.

39

He was tall, not too brawny, and handsome in his dark blue suit with his tie pulled loose in his shirt collar. He was a bit of a mess in his housekeeping, and sang Dave Matthews and REM songs when he was in a good mood. His dark brown hair was disheveled from riding with the sunroof open, but I liked that look on him. In fact, it was what I liked most about him. He wasn't perfect, but he was close.

"Are you listening to me?" Granna asked.

"Of course I am," I answered, turning my attention back to our conversation. "We'll be headed your way in less than a half-hour."

"Now, don't hurry; drive safely. There's always a lot of traffic on a Labor Day weekend," she warned.

"I can't wait to see you," I told her.

"It's been too long since your last visit, Nicole," she said. "After your momma died, I was sure I'd see you more often."

"I'm sorry, I've been on the road a lot," I weakly justified my absence.

"You know that's no excuse," she quickly pointed out. "I'm your last surviving family member, Nicole."

"It is just the two of us now, isn't it?" I agreed.

"Yes, it is, and it's high time we start seeing each other as often as a family should," she said righteously.

"I'll do better, Granna, I will. But now I have to go; we'll see you soon." I hung up the phone just as the front door swung open. Owen stepped inside, tossed his briefcase into a nearby armchair, and began to pull off his suit jacket. I rushed over to him and grabbed his lapels, slipped the jacket halfway off his shoulders, and then drew my hands together across his chest, binding his arms against his body and trapping them in their coat sleeves.

"I've got you," I said triumphantly.

"I hope you'll keep me," he answered with a grin.

"Maybe, if you act right," I snickered.

I pulled on his lapels and when he leaned down to kiss me, I pushed him against the door frame and rose up on my toes. I pressed my mouth to his in the open doorway and then parted my lips to greet his tongue, not caring if the neighbors saw us. When my toes began to ache, I dropped down flat-footed, relaxed my grip on his jacket, and threw my arms up around his neck. He stuffed his hands into the back pockets of my jeans and squeezed my ass.

I am a good six inches shorter than he is, and he likes to stand one step below me on the front porch when he comes home so he can look directly into my green eyes before kissing me, he says. But today, I couldn't get off the phone fast enough and this kiss just now reminded me of how short I am.

Eventually, I dropped my head to his shoulder, and he nuzzled his chin in my hair. I hoped for the moment to linger. These easy displays of affection are new to me, but I like them so much. I had finally overcome my impulse to pull away when physical closeness began to scare me.

"I'm crazy about you," he said softly.

"Ditto," I replied quietly and suddenly regretted my impersonal response.

He lifted his head and pulled his hands out of my back pockets. "Just 'ditto'?" he asked.

I took an embarrassed step back. "You know what I mean." I felt a rush of guilt and instinctively changed the subject. I pointed down the hall toward the bedroom. "I started to pack your bag but didn't finish; I wasn't sure what you'd want to bring. How long will it take you to get ready?"

Owen draped his jacket over the back of the chair and inhaled a deep gulp of air. I braced myself, expecting another emotional argument about my all-too-frequent use of the safe word, 'ditto.'

"Nicole," he said, looking at me mournfully, "something has come up. I can't go now."

"Yes, you can. Don't tease me," I said. "Now go change." Was he going to punish me, I wondered.

"I'm being serious," he said, turning his face away from me. "I really can't go."

I backed further away from him. "Why not?" I asked sharply.

"It's that new case, the one about the trees in Liberty Park. Today, the judge only extended the temporary order and then scheduled another hearing on Tuesday. I have to work this weekend," he tried to explain. "I am not prepared for it to have gone down like this so quickly."

"You can't work at the inn?" I crossed my arms tight over my chest and clutched my shirtsleeves in my fingers. I could feel a rage beginning to rise within me.

41

"You've told me yourself the Internet is spotty and slow when all the guests are using the Wi-Fi," he answered. And he was right, but my anger at him accelerated nonetheless. "I have to go to the law library tomorrow," he continued. "I've got to research zoning laws, the Tree Ordinance, and try to track down the city arborist. I'm sorry, but considering everything I now need to do, I just don't see how I can go."

"But you've known about this weekend for almost a month," I shot back.

"I know, but that doesn't change the fact that as of an hour ago, I now have no say in the matter," he said. "I've got to be in court and prepared to represent my client whenever the judge pleases. You know that is how it works, Nicole."

"It's her eighty-fifth birthday, Owen. Couldn't you have asked for a delay or something?"

He looked out the still open front door at my car, sitting in the driveway, the trunk open and waiting for his bag. "I said I'm sorry," he said. "Please try to understand. I'm not happy about this either."

"Did you even ask for more time?" I insisted on knowing. "Did you even try to protect our plans or did you just acquiesce and roll over?"

He cleared his throat and started to rub his chest. "Nicole...."

"Forget it," I interrupted him. "Just forget it. I'll go by myself." I began darting about the room, my hands shaking, my heart racing, and my eyes threatening to rain tears down my hot cheeks. I almost violently grabbed my bag and car keys. "I should have seen this coming," I hissed at him. "You'd think I would know by now."

"Nicole, please," Owen begged as he reached for me, but I stepped out of his reach.

"Please what?" I demanded. "Please overlook yet another example of your work becoming more important than our plans to spend time together?"

"I told you I didn't expect this; I thought it would be weeks before we got to this stage," he said sheepishly. In my heart of hearts, I knew he was telling me the truth. He wasn't the kind of man who would readily lie to cover his tracks. It was his insecurity at work in this moment; I knew that. But that knowledge did little to help me calm down.

"I don't give a damn about the case, Owen," I waved my hands in the air. "I care that you," pointing at him angrily, "apparently care more about your case than spending the weekend with me!"

"This is about more than a case or a weekend getaway, Nicole; it's about my opportunity to establish a name for myself," he said. "You know this; we've talked about it repeatedly. The firm isn't going to let me start a new law practice just because I think it is a good idea. They expect me to earn the chance. If I win the Liberty Park case, I have that chance. Whitaker said so. If I lose, I may never get another one. The firm hates losers."

"I know this is important to you, Owen," I said, managing to soften my attack a bit. "But nevertheless, I'm very disappointed. I need to be able to count on you, to believe that you say what you mean and mean what you say. You know I don't take disappointment very well."

He looked away from me. I saw that sweat had rolled between his shoulder blades, down his back, pooled at his waistband, and soaked into his shirt. "I'm nearly thirty-two years old and still just a damn associate, Nicole," he said over his shoulder. "I've got to do better than this if we...," he paused and looked down at his shoes. "I want to be able to provide a comfortable future one day, that's all," he nearly whispered.

I exhaled deeply, trying to purge the anger from my body, and walked over to him. I placed my hand on his arm. "Must I remind you again that you don't need to be rich to impress me? I'm not Quinn," I said. "Remember?"

As soon as I said her name, I felt his mood change. I had touched a tender spot without meaning too. He turned to face me. "Please don't drag her into this," he said. I saw that his eye was twitching. "This isn't about her," he said firmly.

"Maybe not directly," I said, withdrawing my hand. "But somehow, she always seems to be a factor in whatever is going on with you."

He cleared his throat and swallowed nervously. "I don't think that is true. But, coincidentally," he hesitated a beat and looked down at his shoes again. "I did see her today," he said reluctantly.

"Well, now we're getting to the bottom of it," I said, my anger and sudden suspicion skyrocketing. I nearly sprinted across the room toward the front door. "Don't you see what I mean?" I demanded, but I doubted that he did. "Never mind, I'll be on my way by myself, and you have a great time catching up with Quinn."

43

"It's not like that, Nicole," he insisted. "I saw her in court. She's representing the developer."

I turned on my heels and angrily faced him. "You've never before mentioned that interesting little fact. And why not?"

"I didn't know about it until today," he answered. "Apparently, it was a last-minute change made by her firm, that's all. I haven't hidden anything from you."

"Are you about to tell me that you two need to get together for dinner this weekend and start negotiations?" I asked sarcastically. I was finding it hard to believe that his former fiancé had just coincidentally inserted herself into his day and this case.

He shook his head and looked out the door again, this time at the flower bed we had worked in together last weekend. I remembered how we laughed about getting our hands dirty, and when I said I felt like they were putting down roots as we set the primroses and violas into the soil.

"I can't believe we are treating each other like this right now," he retorted. He looked at me again. "I could not care less about Quinn. I've told you that time and time again; this isn't about her." He reached for my hand, but I wouldn't let him take it.

"I don't want to upset you like this," he said earnestly. "I'll try to work something out. If I work some tonight and all day tomorrow, maybe I can come up on Sunday. How's that? Will that be acceptable?"

"I'm remembering something my mother used to say to me," I growled, shaking my head and maintaining my distance from him. "'Don't believe a single word a man has to say to you'." My pulse drummed in my ears, a new wave of emotion rose up in my throat, and angry words were about to spew out like hot lava. "I'd better go before I say something I might regret," I said, hoping I had not already done so.

"I don't deserve that," he said. I've never lied to you."

I paused long enough to spot that twitch under his eye again, a tic that always signaled when he felt a lot of stress. He hadn't stopped rubbing his chest; I noticed that, too. "That doesn't mean that you've always been honest with me, Owen," I said, my concern for him unable to quell my disappointment. "Hell, sometimes you're not even honest with yourself."

"I'll do everything I can to get there in time for the birthday party," he said, trying desperately to appease me, but I wasn't going to let him.

"Please, don't promise me anything anymore, Owen." I shook my hand in the air, swatting at him to push him back. "Your promises don't keep very well. I'm leaving now; I'd like to get there before she goes to bed."

I marched out of the house, and Owen scurried across the yard to catch up with me. He shut the trunk as I got in the car and started it, and then he walked up to my closed car door window. He leaned down and motioned for me to open it. I did, but before he could say anything, I cut him off. "And all this time, I was hoping that you were different," I blurted out. I felt my face contort, and I began to sob. "And to think I wanted so much to make love with you again this weekend," I said.

Owen, surprised, stammered, trying to say more to explain himself, but I put the window back up before he could choose his words. I shifted the car in reverse, and it lurched backward into the street.

"Wait," he called out, rushing toward the car, but I didn't stop. As I drove away, I watched him in the rearview mirror. He stood at the end of the driveway and watched as I turned the corner in a screech of rubber and disappeared.

There is joy over disappointment
And delight in hopes that were vain.
Each poet is glad there was no cure
To stop his lonely pain.

Apology, 1917

Joyce Kilmer

CHAPTER 5

REFLECTION

Owen kicked at the weeds growing in the crack between the street and driveway and then looked at his hands. His fingers were unfurled, and he could almost see Nicole slipping from his grasp. His chest hurt again, more this time, and his eyes stung, too.

He thought of the earlier events of the day, when he had been in court, and wondered how he could have handled everything differently. He wondered if he would ever be the kind of lawyer he wanted to be and the kind of man Nicole needed him to be. Would it have made any real difference to her if he had been able to leave with her, he wondered, or if the argument was inevitable no matter what he did? Maybe he wasn't cut out for Nicole, he thought. His heart sank, and he struggled to remain confident that the relationship he had waited so patiently for would last.

He stuffed his hands deep into his pockets, hung his head low, and slunk back into the empty house.

*****

Nicole drove along the same route to get out of the neighborhood that Owen had taken to come home. She passed the gas station turned restaurant without so much as glancing sideways at the white cloth-covered tables lined up along the sidewalk, waiting for happy couples to arrive.

Approaching the traffic light at Ponce de Leon Avenue, she saw that the streets were already congested with rush hour traffic. Snarling cars did battle in the intersection and pedestrians did their best to avoid getting run over as they scurried into the crosswalk. Slowing to a stop as the traffic light turned red, Nicole looked in the rearview mirror at a seemingly familiar BMW pulling up behind her. Hoping it was Owen, she readied to jump out and run to him and ask why he had been rubbing his chest so much. She unlocked the car door but realized that it wasn't Owen at the wheel. Disappointed, she locked her door again, leaned forward on the steering wheel, pulled down the sun visor, and looked at her reflection in the vanity mirror.

The sun, a glare just above the horizon and shining harshly into the mirror, was an unflattering light and exaggerated the uninvited creases that were beginning to make their appearance at the corners of her eyes. She tried to smooth her furrowed brow. Signs, she speculated, that anger flowed too freely in her veins while joy stayed tamped down deep inside. Her troubles were aging her, she thought. She tried smiling at herself, but tears began to roll down her cheeks. Her chest heaved, and her throat tightened so much it hurt to suck in a breath. She wondered if Owen had found the glass of wine she had poured for him and left it on the nightstand, next to the new paperback collection of Flannery O'Conner short stories she had bought for him to read during the weekend.

The traffic light turned green, and the driver behind her immediately hammered on his horn. She looked back at him in her mirror, and he threw his hands up in the air. "Go!" he shouted. She quickly wiped her cheeks dry and proceeded through the intersection.

A few blocks later, at the turn that would lead her toward the northbound interstate and North Carolina, she discovered that the intersection was blocked by an accident. She watched as two drivers stood in the street shouting at each other, each calling 911 on their cell phones and pointing to their barely dented fenders. The scene made her wonder how bad she looked in the middle of one of her own characteristic out-of-proportion tantrums. She drove forward a few more blocks, made a turn, and ventured into an unfamiliar section of town. On the horizon ahead was the outline of the tall downtown buildings that she knew stood alongside the interstate. She maneuvered her car in that direction, confident that even though she didn't know the neighborhood, she could navigate her way out of town using the skyline as her guide.

If only I knew how to navigate my way through relationships, she thought. Always expecting something to go wrong, she had her mother to thank for that. She never wandered too deep into the dark waters of romantic relationships, always giving herself plenty of excuses to shun commitments and other entanglements that scared her. She had always found it easier to spend time with someone she didn't care that much about, but the minute she began to feel more attachment than she wanted to, it was time to pack up and go.

She pictured Owen in the seersucker suit he had worn on the night they met. She remembered his warm smile and admiring gaze. His show of interest came across as genuine rather than simply lustful. Something about him had not triggered that familiar impulse to run. Instead, he made her want to be near him.

She turned on the radio to hear Faith Hill singing her hit, "Breathe". She listened for a minute until the lyrics, "I know my heart is waking up, as all the walls come tumbling down," struck a little too close to home. She switched the channel and landed on a talk show. The host was interviewing a technology expert who was singing the praises of a new form of communication called "text messaging." He predicted it was about to explode in popularity and change the way people communicate with one another.

Chancing a turn here and there, keeping herself pointed in the general direction of the downtown skyline, in short order Nicole found herself driving through an old neighborhood. Her eyes were fixed on the landmark buildings ahead. She didn't notice until the last second that the traffic light hanging overhead had changed to red. Her tires squealed as she slammed on the brakes with both feet. The car stopped abruptly, thrusting her forward and then backward into her seat. Embarrassed, she looked around quickly and was relieved to see that no other cars were on the street.

A small group of men sitting around a table on a porch looked up briefly, thumped their cigarettes, and laughed among themselves. They returned to what they had been doing; one of them shuffled a deck of cards.

When the light changed to green, she took her feet off the brake and slowly rolled through the intersection, paying closer attention to her surroundings. Now alongside a small treelined park, a few trees marked with red spray paint, she saw an old woman leaning over and pinching dead blooms from a bed of daylilies that encircled the base of one of the trees.

With a handful of withered blooms, the old woman stood up slowly, ratcheting like rusty gears trying to break free, and looked up into the tree.

After an admiring moment, she reached out and touched it affectionately, letting her fingers trace along the craggy grooves in the bark.

How some people can so easily be affectionate, and others can't bring themselves to cuddle a child is something I will never understand, Nicole thought mournfully. Owen can give affection so easily. He is not afraid of love, even if it might go bad, as it had with Quinn, she thought. Driving with one hand, she propped her elbow on the door and rested her head in her hand. She sighed heavily.

"I'm scared," she remembered telling her mother one night many years ago. "I think something is under my bed."

"Go back to bed, Nicole, it's late," her mother answered coldly.

"Hold me, Momma, please."

"Nicole, I said go back to bed."

Now by what whim of wanton chance
Do radiant eyes know somber days?
And feet that shod in light should dance
Walk weary and laborious ways?

As Winds That Blow Against A Star, 1914

Joyce Kilmer

CHAPTER 6

ELIZABETH

My mother, Elizabeth Fischer, was an only child. She was also a child who had grown up without a father, just as I had. Born to Esther Ruth Fischer, my grandmother of North Carolina, an unwed mother at twenty-one who lived with my widowed great grandfather and her two younger brothers at an inn in the mountain city of Brysonville, North Carolina, the place where I am driving to right now. I have never been sure if my grandmother did not marry by choice, or if being the mother of an illegitimate child in that era made her undesirable as a wife. Either way, she has been single all of her long life. I do not know the full circumstances of my grandmother's pregnancy, nor who was my mother's father. Why has his identity been kept a secret all these years? I don't know that either. The keeping of secrets is a family tradition, I suppose, although it has seldom been beneficial for any of us.

My grandmother remained at the inn after her child was born, helping her father run the business, keeping her brothers out of trouble, and raising her daughter, Elizabeth, my mom, the best that she could as a single parent. Granna, the name I gave her while I was a toddler, never became involved with another man as far as I know. After her oldest brother died in Europe during the Second World War, she became even more devoted to helping her father, Nicholas Fischer, who fell into a deep depression at the time of his son's death.

My mom lived at the inn until she finished high school, at which time she left Brysonville to enter nursing school at the University of North Carolina in Chapel Hill. She was eighteen when she left home to begin her studies, but she returned to the inn every summer and during holidays to relax from her classes and to enjoy talking with the guests of the inn. And to catch up with her mother, of course.

Mom always said she found most of what love and affection she needed from her grandfather and surviving uncle, and they never treated her as less than the delight of their lives. But she was always aware that she did not have in her life the one love that could only be found between a father and daughter. She saw that love exchanged between her mother and her grandfather, but admittedly often with a hint of tension, and she saw it time and time again between the fathers and daughters that stayed at the inn. No matter how much her grandfather loved her, Mom told me once, he could not look at her with the same intensity of pride, unselfish devotion, or unconditional love as what she witnessed in the eyes of the fathers who chased their children across the lawn.

It wasn't that her grandfather didn't have those feelings for my mother because he most certainly did. Rather, my mother was steadfast in her opinion. "It just isn't the same thing," she would say.

According to Mom, she had resigned herself to living without the love of a father until she met Dr. Cecil Williams. He was one of the regular guests, a physician vacationing with his wife, and a man with whom Mom found it easy to talk because of their mutual interest in medicine. Dr. Williams eventually invited her to visit his pediatric practice in Atlanta. He could help her find a job there after she graduated, he told her.

Dr. Williams, or "Doctor C.," as he liked to be called, and his wife Norma were a generous, highly social, and loving couple. They were also without children, Mom said. Dr. C. once admitted to her that he had a strong desire to become a father beginning early in his adult years, long before he had become a doctor. And although he spoke of it only once, Mom remembered his heart was heavy with disappointment when he told her that his beloved wife could not become pregnant. Choosing to specialize in pediatrics was his effort to find a substitute for the role that he so wanted to play, that of a loving father.

He was a successful physician, apparently. Mom said he never lacked enough patients to keep his appointment calendar full. Mom remembered admiringly that he treated generations of children within families, and he kept photos of many of his young patients on a large bulletin board in the hallway of his office. But nothing was a satisfactory substitute for a child of his own who would call him "Dad" instead of "Doctor C."

Mom said Granna noticed the affectionate bond developing between her daughter and the doctor, and she mistook it for something else, something far less innocent than it actually was. She cautiously tried to intervene, but her concern and motherly efforts were not well received.

"It is what I have always wanted," Mom argued. "Why must you think such an unsavory thing? I'd rather have this bond even for a little while than never at all. It is as close as I'll ever get to having a father." Shortly afterward, Mom announced to the family that Dr. Williams had offered her a job and that she had accepted it. She moved to Atlanta that fall after finishing her nursing training.

She worked for Dr. Williams for all of her twenty-two year nursing career, which lasted until he died at the age of seventy. She was forty-two years old by then.

Mom told me once that the first twelve years as a nurse were happy ones for her. She thought she was a good nurse, the patients liked her, and her coworkers respected her. Most of all, Dr. C. loved her as if she were his own child, the child he had always wanted. "And I finally had for myself the closest thing to the loving father I had always wanted," she said to me. I myself miss him to this day. He was the closest thing to a grandfather that I had ever known.

Mom traveled back to the inn often to see our family and to help care for her grandfather when he became sick. She dated men in Atlanta occasionally but never seriously, and she never took a lover, not wanting to be distracted from the time she could spend at the medical practice or with Dr. C. But all that changed, she said, when the young pediatric cardiology resident came to be mentored by Dr. C. for a few months.

Mom told me that he was so handsome she could not take her eyes off of him or ignore the yearning that suddenly came alive and stirred restlessly within her when he was nearby. She was clearly falling hard for him. He befriended her and quickly began to flirt with her, discretely at first and then boldly. She was shy and awkward in responding to him, she recalled, but soon found her confidence and began to return the flirtations. She was thirty-two years old and falling in love for the first time in her life. Looking back, I think that she was so inexperienced in intimate relationships that she could not be realistic about what the relationship might really mean to him. It did not occur to her that he may not have the same feelings for her that she had for him. She dismissed Dr. C's reservations about the budding romance, saying he was just being overprotective of her. Ironic, isn't it, that Dr. C. was doing the very thing a loving father would do for his daughter, and she rejected his advice and ignored his concerns. Instead, Mom pursued her newfound relationship with little caution, enjoying the belated rush of sexual passion that had finally come into her life. When they made love, she believed it meant that they were in love, she said, and that he wanted her as much and in the same way as she wanted him.

She said that she was both excited and frightened when she discovered that she was pregnant with me. She was excited that she was going to bring a life into the world with the man that she loved, and she was frightened that her unexpected condition was not well timed and a wedding might have to be delayed due to his medical school obligations. She was devastated, she told me through bitter tears, when he told her that he was not in love with her and that he did not want to be a father. Mom was alone when I was born, except for Dr. C., who stood outside the delivery room and waited nervously for news about my birth. It still shocks me that Mom hadn't even told Granna by then that I was well on my way into this world.

The resident, who I only know as the "donor", left Mom and me to fend for ourselves. He offered no support of any kind, and Mom refused to pursue legal means to force him to help her in any way. "If I had forced him to be recognized as your father," she said, "he would have had parental rights, and that would have meant I would have to deal with him one way or another until you turned eighteen. I simply could not stand the thought of having to see him again." And that is why I've never met my father, or know where he is. I don't even know his name. I have no idea how much, if anything, he knows about me except that I exist.

Mom raised me as a single mother, sometimes with Mrs. Williams's help and sometimes leaving me with Granna in North Carolina when she needed a respite from the demands of single parenting and full-time employment. Granna was delighted to learn of me when she was finally told, much to Mom's relief.

Dr. C. offered to reduce Mom's schedule without reducing her pay to give her time to look after me, but Mom would have nothing of it. She said she would bear the full consequences of her decisions.

She worked even harder, taking on more responsibility where she could, and spent less time visiting the family at the inn. Granna told me she saw that Mom smiled and laughed less often and could become easily irritated.

Mom said Dr. C. never changed how he treated her, but she believed she had disappointed him and could not bear the thought of that possibility. She spent less time with him away from the practice to save herself from the heartache she feared would come if he were ever to confirm her suspicion.

She tried to be a good mother to me, she really did. She played with me every day after work, she helped me with homework once I entered school, and she did many other things to ensure that I was as happy as I could be. But her heart had been broken, her affections had been shoved down deep and covered up, and her wound never healed. Her experience with love hardened her, and, as a result, she found it difficult to openly express love to anyone, most of all to me. I suppose I was a constant reminder of what had happened to her because of her one and only naïve experience with love. Over time, she did not touch me often enough nor tell me that she loved me as often as I wanted to hear her say those few but powerful words.

"You don't tell me much anymore that you love me," I once said to her, and all she said in reply was, "Don't be silly."

Imagine that. I was so hurt by her cold, vacant words. That day marked the beginning of my own retreat from intimacy and vulnerability.

To her credit, Mom did insist that I be independent, that I care for myself as much as possible, that I expect my voice to be heard, and that I never let a relationship compromise me in any way. My mother had demanded that I consider myself my first priority. She did not allow me to cry, and she did not show any kindness toward my boyfriends, the very few that I had been willing to introduce to her.

I don't like to admit it, but I know the honest truth about me is that I am very much like my mother, whether I want to be or not.

I never go by the empty house
Without stopping and looking back,
Yet it hurts me to look at the
Crumbling roof and shutters fallen apart,
For I can't help thinking the poor old house
Is a house with a broken heart.

The House With Nobody In It, 1914
Joyce Kilmer

Chapter 7

Cool Wind

Nicole glanced in her rearview mirror and saw new creases in the corners of her puffy eyes. Mom wouldn't approve of me acting like this, she thought. She tightened her grip on the steering wheel. Her eyes darted away from her reflection, and she saw the interstate sign ahead. It pointed north.

She accelerated a little to increase the distance between herself and the ugly scene she'd run from and wondered what she could have done or said differently to Owen. She did not like to lose control of her temper, and she felt badly about how she had reacted to the news that he could not go with her for the full three-day weekend. She also recognized that she had behaved in a way that she would not have accepted had another person acted that way toward her. He was right, she thought. If the shoe had been on the other foot, if it had been she who had had to work, she would have expected him to understand and support her decision. That contradiction within herself, that she could sometimes expect more from others than she herself could offer, gnawed at her conscience and sometimes kept her awake late into the night. It was unfair, and she knew it, and she felt powerless to do anything about it.

"You don't even know what love is," she admonished herself out loud as she drove on in the car's otherwise silence.

Even though it felt to her as if only minutes had passed, Atlanta and Friday afternoon traffic congestion were now two hours behind her. She exited onto a state route that traversed the counties of north Georgia. Now, well into the foothills of the Appalachian Mountains, the scenery gave way to hay fields, rows and rows of dried and picked over corn stalks, soybean, carrots, and turnip plants, and trees thickly robed in kudzu vines. Not a single cell tower could be seen for miles.

"Don't put so much of your heart into everything," she remembered her mother warning her. "If you give so much all the time, you won't recognize when someone is taking advantage of you. Before you know it, there'll be nothing left of you."

"What is a heart for, if not to give away?" a young Nicole questioned her mother.

"You'll regret it if you do, so don't," was the answer that was always given.

It was a warning Nicole recalled often until Owen came along. She had never been with a man like him, one who could still say he wanted to be with her even while she frustrated him or, worse, altogether denied him. It seemed she was always torn between consuming him and keeping him at a safe, manageable distance.

But this weekend was supposed to be different. This weekend, she was going to face her fears and let her guard down. And not just a little, but all the way down. She was going to be vulnerable with him, and she was going to make love with him again. She had brought their lovemaking to an abrupt end a month earlier, much to Owen's disappointment. She tried to convince herself at the time that it was her way of making sure he really cared about her, that their relationship was not grounded primarily on the passionate lovemaking that they shared. But she knew the truth about herself and her reason for closing her legs. She found it much easier to have sex with people that she didn't care about because the ones she did care about scared her. And Owen scared her, a lot. And, to her surprise, she realized that even in her fear she missed his body against hers, and she was ready to bring the charade to an end. She wanted Owen, all of Owen, again.

She grabbed her cell phone and dialed his number, but the call didn't go through. The hills and trees refused to let her reach for him at a moment when her thoughts were sweet and her voice ached to be tender. She exhaled in annoyance, tossed the phone onto the passenger seat, and drove onward.

The cool mountain air rushed past the car windows and into the open sunroof, sending a sudden shiver down her spine. It took the warmth from her soul like the night her mother had sent her back to bed without an embrace or comforting word.

She shook her head to rid her mind of bad memories and tried to think about what Owen might be doing. Changing his clothes, grabbing a bite to eat, and sitting at his desk laboring over law books. Thinking about her, she hoped. She looked at her phone again, but still, the hills and trees stood between them. And still, she heard her mother's voice. "You have only yourself to rely on, Nicole."

She could not shake the touch of the cool wind. It reminded her of death.

She was holding her mother's hand when she died. When her loose grip relaxed, Nicole watched as Elizabeth Fischer's thin, pale blue fingers uncurled from around her hand. She had not cried for her mother until then, but at that moment, as she sat alone by her bed in the hospice facility, a flood of tears streamed down her cheeks. "Hold me, Momma," she cried out. "Don't leave me, not yet." But the arms she tried to place around her neck only fell limp onto the bed.

Through miles on weary miles of night
That stretches in my way
My lantern burns serene and white,
An unexhausted cup of day.

Love's Lantern, 1914

Joyce Kilmer

CHAPTER 8

THE ACCIDENT

Owen walked into his bedroom to change. Kicking his shoes off at the foot of the bed, he opened the closet and grabbed a pair of faded jeans and a blue seersucker shirt, a recent gift from Nicole. He had enough red and black in his wardrobe, she had teased as she gave him the gift. He tossed the clothes onto the bed next to his partially packed bag, unzipped his slacks, and then noticed a glass of red wine sitting on his nightstand. He stepped out of his slacks, sat down on the bed, and reached for the wine.

It was sitting next to a photograph, one of Nicole and him that had been taken that spring during a backyard party. He grabbed it, too, and stared at it as he lifted the wine glass to his mouth. The ruby red liquid tasted good, and he thought he recognized that it was his favorite blend, one he had discovered at the restaurant he and Nicole frequented in Virginia Highland. He swallowed and then took another mouthful.

He remembered the party well, the first occasion when Nicole had introduced him to her friends only a few weeks after their first date. Always reserved in public, observing some standard of decorum known only to her, this time she stood pressed against him for the photograph. One arm around his waist and the other across his torso, her hand resting on his chest. His arm was draped across her shoulder, pulling her close. They smiled at each other with the kind of smile that said to everyone watching that they were well on their way to falling in love.

At least that's what he liked to think whenever he looked at the photograph. It reminded him that Nicole did care about him, even when, most of the time, it seemed she didn't care much at all about anyone. He understood her controlled and restrained ways, how she would do something kind instead of simply saying what she thought or felt, like buy him a shirt she might have seen him admire, or rest her hand on his leg when they were sitting on the sofa or driving somewhere. Or surprise him with a bottle of his favorite wine.

He wondered if she was as bothered by their argument as he was. Their mutual awkwardness when trying to be vulnerable with each other never seemed to lessen with time, and he was frustrated about it. He wanted Nicole to ignore her mother's voice when she heard it, and he wanted her to understand what pushed him to work so hard. He wanted her to see that what he was doing was indeed for both of them. He wanted to stop fighting about it. He did not like to argue, but more than that, he did not like to sweep things under the rug. He wanted conflict put to rest. Nicole, on the other hand, avoided what she called "emotionalism" and was happy to wait and see if the conflict would simply go away by itself somehow. Her sudden and intense anger, he reasoned, was her way to thwart an argument, or to get it over with quickly if she thought she had no choice but to deal with the conflict.

He put the photograph back on the nightstand and filled his lungs as if he were about to go underwater. He held it as long as he could and tried to ignore the bursting sensation in his chest, but when he couldn't hold it any longer, he exhaled in a turbulent huff and then admitted it. He understood the consequences he would face if he did not get to the inn on Sunday. How they could be so much alike and yet be so different from one another, he could not understand. He looked at the picture again, and tried to remember the last time she had smiled at him like that.

His bedside telephone rang, and he grabbed it quickly, wine glass in hand. "Nicole?" he answered.

"Owen?" a voice said.

"Dad?" Owen said.

"Are you okay?" his father asked.

"Of course, why?" Owen answered.

"You're not sick, are you?"

"No," Owen insisted.

"Or in any pain?"

"What's this about, Dad?" Owen demanded.

"Quinn called," his father said.

"Jesus Christ," Owen groaned.

"She told us you didn't look well. She said you kept rubbing your chest."

"I'm fine, Dad, really. "She shouldn't have called you."

"She was worried about you, and now so are we," his father explained.

"I'm sure she was quite worried about me," Owen sneered. He gulped a mouthful of wine and tossed his head back to swallow it all. "Don't worry, Dad; I'm fine."

"Don't be mad at her for calling us. She meant well," Dr. Montgomery said.

"Oh, I'm sure she had a reason for calling," Owen said.

"She said she saw you in court today."

"Look, Dad, I said I'm fine. Now I have better things to do than to talk about Quinn. How's Mom?"

"We both talked with her for a while," his father said. "It was nice to hear from her."

"Dad, she was digging for information. I hope you didn't tell her anything."

"Why don't you come by the house and let me check you out?" his father suggested.

"Dad, you're a neurosurgeon."

"I know what a heart should sound like, son."

"I said I'm fine."

"You shouldn't still be so angry with her, Owen. It was an accident."

"What makes you think I'm angry with her?" Owen asked impatiently.

"Son, the very mention of her name nearly sends you into a tantrum."

"You do remember that she dumped me with hardly a moment of hesitation," Owen huffed.

"People change their minds, Owen. Sometimes we don't agree with their reasons or their ways, but you have to respect someone who doesn't go through with what they think is the wrong thing to do."

"So it was wrong for us to be getting married?" Owen snarked.

"I hate to say it," his father paused briefly, "but you weren't ready. Everyone knew it but you."

"I've got work to do, Dad. I need to go. I'll call you later." Owen hung up before his father could say anything else. Now really angry, he took another gulp of wine and held it in his mouth, swirling his tongue through it trying to douse his fire. He shook his head as he swallowed, grunted, and went into the bathroom.

He set the wine glass down next to the toothbrush cup on the shelf beneath the mirror. The cup was finally home to two brushes, Nicole's, and his. For such a long time, she had refused to leave one of hers in the bathroom they initially shared only on weekends. She had said setting up house might lead to expectations she could not fulfill. He wondered now if soon only his toothbrush would call the cup home.

He studied himself in the mirror as he pulled his shirt off and let it fall at his feet on the tile floor.

He leaned into the yellow incandescent glare of the mirror light and looked closer. His shoulders were broad, well-defined, and strong. His neck and biceps hinted at a time when he was more fit. Anyone looking at him naked might guess he had been a gym nut until the long hours of a laboring lawyer kept him from continuing to chisel his body.

Only the asymmetry of his upper left chest suggested there was more to the story than that.

The right pectoral muscles were firm, mounded just enough to show that he had once had impressive upper body strength. The left one was ordinary, flat, and unremarkable against his ribs, except for the ugly, ragged scar just above his nipple.

It had been nearly spring and Colleen Bulloch, Quinn's mother, was having the backyard landscaped in preparation for the upcoming outdoor wedding. The gazebo in the center of the yard was where the groom was to stand and wait for the bride to descend the steps of the back porch and saunter slowly across the pea gravel footpath that led to him. On either side of the unfinished footpath, loose rectangles of Zoysia sod were fit together, making a plush green carpet where the guests' chairs would be arranged. Nearby, flowering azaleas sat in three-gallon plastic buckets waiting to be planted. Tools of the landscaping trade were strewn about, the work to resume and finish the next day. The landscapers had stopped that afternoon after the metal rods were driven into the ground to hold steady the new landscape edging that had been placed at the end of the footpath nearest the gazebo. It had to be widened to make room for the wedding party to stand near the waiting couple during the ceremony.

Their wedding was to be the event of the high society season. The blueblood Montgomerys and Bullochs were to be joined together, a feat that the mothers had daydreamed about for years. They had the makings of an impressive lot - a surgeon, a banker, a socialite and antique dealer, and a lawyer on each side. Both maternal branches of the budding family tree were beneficiaries of obscene amounts of trust fund money flowing in from tobacco and beverage stock. Theirs was a match made in Upper Crust Heaven.

Standing at the far end of the yard in the dark shadows of the night just three days before their wedding, the landscaping lights not yet powered up, the couple fought in such a way that both knew there was no longer a deadline for finishing the backyard. An engagement ring was thrown to the ground and the former bride-to-be ran toward her parents' back door. Owen reached down to scoop up the ring and gave chase in the darkness, not noticing that as Quinn reached out to steady herself in the shifting sod, a carelessly placed gravel rake fell to the ground behind her.

Tripping over the rake and tumbling forward, Owen's only worry at the time of his fall was to not drop the engagement ring. He fell into unconsciousness the moment the rod pierced his chest and lung and ripped into the tissues of the left ventricle of his heart. The end of the rod shattered a rib as it plunged into his flesh and introduced bone fragments and dirt into his chest cavity and collapsed lung, which led to a bad but treatable infection that caused his mother to worry so much that she refused to leave his bedside as he recuperated. She had lost one son, and the possibility of losing Owen, too, left her beyond reassurance or consolation.

The only lingering consequences Owen had to cope with after he recovered from the injury were pain on that side of his chest after physical exertion and the ugly scar. It was the only injury he had ever had, except for the time he accidentally sliced deep into the little finger of his left hand with a box cutter. That injury that left him with a lazy left pinky finger that required him to be more careful when he typed. If he didn't, the first word in a sentence often began with two capital letters.

He brushed his teeth and splashed cold water on his face, slipped into the clothes he had pulled from the closet, shoved his feet into a pair of well-worn loafers, and headed for the kitchen, the empty wine glass in hand.

The bottle of wine Nicole had brought, a cabernet blend he liked but seldom bought for himself, was on the counter. It's little gestures like this that mean so much to me, he thought. Subtle and infrequent, but she does let me know in her own way now and then that she loves me. She didn't know it yet, but he, wanting to encourage her interest in wine, was planning to take her to Napa, California, next summer to visit vineyards and learn about the magic of transforming grapes into liquid happiness. That would make her happy, he thought. Then she would surely know how important she is to me. He paused and then wondered if he was ever going to make her happy or if he was just lying to himself when he thought they had the potential for a future together. He sighed and pushed the wine bottle across the counter and out of easy reach.

He opened one of the drawers of the kitchen counter where they kept menus from the take-out restaurants. After rummaging through the drawer, he chose one from a gourmet sandwich shop that Nicole liked, picked it up, and reached for the phone. He ordered a grilled vegetable sandwich, a cup of tomato bisque, and a cinnamon raisin cookie to go. He looked at the wine bottle again, reached for it, and pulled the cork out. He sniffed the dark cherry and raisin aroma of the wine, then put the bottle to his mouth to take one more swallow before heading to the office. On second thought, he lowered the bottle, carried it to the counter, and corked it again. He pulled the cupboard door open to tuck it away, out of sight, out of mind, he thought, and a calendar that hung inside swung out, swaying back and forth on its hook. He reached to steady it and then saw a big red circle drawn around the first weekend of the month, including Monday, Labor Day weekend. The letters N.C. was written by a woman's hand inside the circle. Then he remembered what Nicole had said as she pulled out of the driveway.

"And to think I wanted to make love with you again this weekend."

And that was about as close as he had gotten to making love with her in just more than a month. It was her idea to stop having sex. The unilateral decision came to her the very evening she invited him to meet her grandmother, her reasons she hadn't thought necessary to explain to him. She wouldn't entertain his questions either but insisted that was the way it was going to be for a while until she was in a better place, whatever that meant. To offer no explanation for pulling away from him hurt. A lot.

He frowned and felt tested nearly to his limits. He closed the cupboard and headed back to the office.

The sun had dipped below the horizon and threw shadows across the front yard. He slid into his car, opened all the windows, and drove toward the sandwich shop to grab his takeout dinner.

He stopped in front of the sandwich shop adjacent to a coffee shop and heard laughter all around and wished he were in a place where he could be laughing, too. Exiting his car, he smelled the strong coffee brewing inside and heard steam from the espresso machine whistling as someone frothed a chilled pitcher of milk. He turned on his heels and went inside to buy a cup to go with his meal. He needed it, he thought, to counteract the effect of the wine. He bought a large cup and then made his way next door to the sandwich shop. His meal was waiting for him at the cash register, tucked inside a brown paper bag with his name written on it in black crayon. He paid for it with cash, left the change on the counter, and walked back to his car. He hurried because the heat of the coffee radiated through the cup and was beginning to burn his hand. Once back in his car and the cup of coffee secure in a cup holder, he started the car and headed toward his office.

The law firm was in one of Atlanta's tallest buildings, overlooking the interstate and Liberty Park. He turned onto Courtland Avenue and then a narrow side street that led to the employee entrance of the parking garage. His hands full carrying his briefcase, food, and hot coffee, he fumbled trying to press the security code into the keypad of the door.

Virgil Ferguson, a night security guard walking his monotonous rounds through the empty building, the keys on his belt jingling with every step, saw Owen and jogged over to open the door for him. "Working late on a Friday night, Mr. Montgomery?" he politely asked.

"I'm afraid so," Owen answered. "It seems there's always more to do."

"You have been here late quite a bit recently. I know because I've seen your car out there after everybody else has gone home. You ever think you work too much?" Virgil asked.

"I'm just trying to get ahead, Virgil," Owen replied. "I have a lot of competition in this building."

Virgil grinned. "Getting ahead ain't all what it's cracked up to be. You know that, don't you?", he asked.

"I've never heard anyone say getting left behind is any better," Owen responded.

"Well, that's a fact for sure," Virgil agreed, "but still, don't stay too late. The ladies don't like us working when we should be home." Virgil pressed the elevator button and when he did, his pleasant mood clouded over. His anguished eyes shifted to Owen's, who had stepped into the elevator and turned to face him.

"Gettin' left behind is never better, Mr. Montgomery. Believe me, I know," Virgil said.

The doors of the elevator closed before either could say anything more.

Owen looked at his reflection in the polished metal doors as the elevator jolted and began to rise. He remembered that Virgil had two kids; he had seen their photograph at the guard's desk. He looked around the elevator as it rose and spotted a travel agency poster. The ad showed a fit young couple in bathing suits running along a beach toward a glowing sunset, hand in hand and grinning at one another with perfect, sparkling teeth and not a hint of cellulite or a hair out of place. "I know, too, Virgil, I know too," he said in a whisper before turning away from the poster.

The elevator reached his floor, and he stepped off and headed toward the office. Inside the dimly lit reception area, he flipped on the lights, made his way into the law library, and set his briefcase and meal on the conference table. In the middle of the table was a folder, his name written on the tab. Inside, he found the notes Vanessa had prepared for him. Counting only three sheets of paper, Owen knew his work was cut out for him.

He opened the blinds on the large windows and looked outside. He could see the silhouette of Stone Mountain on the not-too-distant horizon and the lights of the traffic moving north and south along the wide interstate below.

Hungry, he sat down to eat and took a gulp of coffee, glad to find that it was still warm. He pulled his laptop from his briefcase and, while waiting for it to start up, unwrapped his sandwich and took a bite. The bread was soggy from too much deli oil and red pepper aioli, but he was too hungry to care. He took another bite.

He swallowed, yawned, and took another sip of coffee before pulling the sheets of notes from the folder. Scanning them as he crossed the room, he went to the ceiling-high bookcases that lined the walls. Searching through the Navy Blue, Hunter Green, and Federal Red leather hardbacks, he remembered how many of the weighty books Florence could carry at once. The spine of each book was embossed with gold lettering announcing what content would be found within. He pulled several volumes and took them to the table. With everything spread out before him, he sat down and got to work. Between bites of food and sips of coffee, he thumbed through the books and occasionally stopped to rapidly type some notes on his laptop.

He looked at Vanessa's notes again and realized one page was actually a printout from the online edition of the Atlanta newspaper. His eyes came to rest on a highlighted column heading, "City's Chief Arborist Fired." He scanned it and read that Ludlow Stovall, the very arborist hired to enforce the Tree Protection Ordinance, had recently been fired for "doing my job," or so he claimed. It was alleged by the Executive Director of the nonprofit Trees Atlanta, a tree ordinance watchdog group, that Stovall was unable to resist the temptation of financial gifts being offered by slick developers wanting to circumvent the tree ordinance.

He quickly searched the Internet for more information about Stovall and learned the arborist had generated equal parts controversy and praise for himself in his role in preserving Atlanta's green canopy. He was fired, Stovall asserted, after raising questions about the lack of accountability expected of his fellow arborists, and lack of enforcement in general of the tree ordinance in certain areas of the city. But in the end, it seemed, Stovall had permitted many more tree removals in select areas of high real estate value in his territory than he had secured in tree replacements. According to the Executive Director, citing studies from the University of Georgia and Georgia Tech, trees are an important defense in the battle to maintain air quality. In a city that was home to the world's busiest airport and rush hour gridlock that rivaled that of Los Angeles, Atlanta desperately needed to protect its tree canopy. Stovall, she said, was slowly choking Atlanta to death as he handed out waivers as if they were mere pennies.

Pages of handwritten notes, a neatly typed outline for his opening statement, and numerous trips to the bookshelves later, Owen checked his watch and realized that Nicole had been driving for nearly three hours. He reached for his cell phone and dialed her number.

After a few rings and one gnawed cuticle, he heard her voicemail answer. Suddenly unsure what to say, unsure if he'd waited too long to call, unsure if anyone ever watched the two of them and thought they looked like the happy couple in the travel poster, he hung up without saying a word. One fight was enough for the day, he thought. Maybe it's better to give her time to cool off. Besides, he hated leaving voicemails because so few people ever listened to them, choosing instead just to call back with no idea why they had been contacted in the first place.

Reaching to put his phone away, he saw the corner of a photograph sticking out of a pocket of his open briefcase. He pulled it out and stared at it. It was one he had taken of Nicole during their first weekend trip. She was wearing a sundress and standing barefoot in the powdery white sands of Rosemary Beach in Florida, her hair tossed in a breeze, her eyes full of sparkle, the Gulf of Mexico in the background. She was grinning in laughter. He remembered he had made her laugh with a corny joke.

"What do you call five hundred lawyers sitting on the bottom of the ocean?" he asked.

"I don't know, what?" she said.

"A good start," he said.

In a near whisper, he asked, "Do you really love me, Nicole?" He hesitated, waiting for the photograph to speak to him, and then sighed heavily. "I've laid my heart out for you," he said, gazing into her eyes in the photograph. "Please don't step on it."

Unlatch the door at midnight
And let your lantern's glow
Shine out to guide the travelers
Feet to you across the snow.

Gates and Doors, 1917

Joyce Kilmer

CHAPTER 9

BRYSONVILLE

Driving meandering roads that rose and fell along the contours of the hills, Nicole drove with bleary eyes onward toward Brysonville. Her headlights swept the darkened roadside, briefly lighting up closed fruit and vegetable stands, antique shops, and the occasional hand-lettered "Jesus Saves" sign nailed to a tree or fence post. Although she had eaten nothing since lunch, her stomach remained silent each time she passed a roadside restaurant.

And although she had stopped crying several times, it didn't take much for tears to start up again. Getting angry was her way of hiding her tears from people, but when she was alone, she had nothing to hide from.

Finally tempted by a red neon sign promising hot food, she decided to stop at a place called Thalia's. Maybe just some fries and a soda to go, she thought. Her tires crunched on the gravel as she pulled off the road and parked in the nearly empty lot. It was later than she thought, and she hoped the place was still serving food. She stepped inside to find that only two tables were occupied, both with silent diners, the only noise in the room supplied courtesy of a sitcom on the television over by the cash register. A rotund and big-bosomed woman, probably Thalia, wearing a too-tight tee shirt and an apron with a handful of plastic ink pens clipped to her apron strings, sat leaning forward on a stool laughing at Archie Bunker of All in the Family. "Sit wherever you like," she said automatically when she heard the door open. Her eyes never left the television.

Nicole spied a payphone hanging on the wall in the back. It was partially hidden among mounted Gone With the Wind and Coca-Cola memorabilia that covered the walls. Without giving herself time to change her mind, she walked over, reached for the receiver, dug through her bag, and found a quarter. She dropped it into the phone and dialed Owen's office phone. Shifting nervously from one leg to the other, she waited as it rang.

Thalia looked up during a commercial. "You want anythin' honey?"

Once, twice, three times, the phone rang.

"No ma'am," Nicole answered, her stomach silent again.

On the fourth ring, she hung up. Unlike Owen, she didn't mind leaving voicemail messages, but she hated to admit that she was wrong. She would get to that later, she decided.

Nicole gritted her teeth as her hand hung gripping the receiver, being not too sure who she was most upset with. She finally let go and made a racket when she slid a chair out of her way to open a path to the exit door. "I'm sorry," she said to Thalia, who had switched channels to watch a rerun of The Waltons.

Nicole made her exit and shuffled her feet in the gravel as she walked to her car, certain her vow of abstinence would remain intact for the unforeseeable future. Why would a woman give herself to a man who was probably just one step away from hurting her anyway, she thought? She was unwilling, she admitted, to be at a disadvantage in any relationship. Even one that she wanted.

She slid into her car and drove back onto the road in a sweeping motion as if she were in a hurry to get somewhere or away from something. She glanced at herself in the rearview mirror and quickly turned away from her reflection in a fit of self-loathing.

A few miles beyond Thalia's, the roadside scenery gave way to barbed wire fences clothed in jasmine and honeysuckle, and tall craggy rock faces where the road had been cut through the mountainside. The long stretches of countryside were spoiled only by an occasional satellite dish in the yard of small homes far off the road and perched on a hillside. The darkness hid much of this scenery from view as she drove on toward Brysonville, but having come this way many times before, she knew what lay behind the sights that appeared briefly as her headlights swept past.

She read the street signs that flashed by as she drove onward - Lingering Shade Road, Jot-Em-Down Road, Crooked Creek Road, Gristmill Road. She was definitely in the country now, where residents could tell you who owned the land alongside the road and how long it had been in the family, who was born here or was a transplant. Up here, people's mail was still delivered reliably long after the numbers had fallen off their rusty mailboxes.

Soon, Nicole spotted a roadside sign. Brysonville, twenty-six miles ahead. Hoping to cheer herself up, she forced her thoughts to her childhood memories of the family business located in the little city at the southwestern end of the Great Smoky Mountains Range, nestled alongside the Tuckasegee River.

Brysonville spread out in every direction from the large brick courthouse that stood at its center. A two-story structure with a tall clock tower on one corner, the courthouse rested on a sturdy foundation made from boulders and large stones brought down from the mountains. Its wood trim was painted crisp white, and its shingles were made of slate. In addition to serving its purpose as the legal seat of the county, the courthouse was also the city's welcome center for visitors arriving by train.

An old wood and steel pedestrian bridge spanned the river, connecting the train depot on the mountain-facing side of the river to the city and leading arriving passengers to a gazebo that greeted them at the edge of the courthouse grounds. A drug store, barber shop, hardware store, and others, some old, some new, lined the streets along the square around the courthouse. Park benches were everywhere.

During the long summer afternoons of her childhood, Nicole sat on those benches, eating ice cream cones with her grandmother, counting the cars as the trains left the depot. They would wave and chat with friends and acquaintances as they walked by. Back then she believed her grandmother knew everyone by their first name, and she probably did. Everyone referred to her grandmother as Miss Ruth.

Visitors were attracted to Brysonville year-round for its clean air, cool nights, and spectacular views of the Great Smoky Mountains. Many who traveled to Brysonville came to hike through the nearby Joyce Kilmer Memorial Forest and stay at the Poplar Inn, hoping to meet the old woman responsible for saving the Kilmer forest from the logging company many years ago.

Constructed in 1923 on a small bluff overlooking Brysonville, the Poplar Inn was named for its exterior shingles made from the bark peeled from poplar trees that had been cut and brought down from the mountains. Its interior walls were constructed of American Chestnut that had been harvested before the chestnut blight practically eradicated the tree from the mountains. The inn's long covered side porch was home to more than a dozen rocking chairs where guests in the know sat and waited for Ruth Fisher to make her daily appearance and take her place in her special chair. It was the one on the end nearest the windows of the innkeeper's suite. Anyone who had stayed at the inn at least once before knew not to sit in that rocker and was quick to tell the unknowing that it was off-limits to guests. The porch also offered the best view of the Smoky Mountains, especially the tall old-growth off in the distance that the Fischers owned.

Nicholas Fischer, Nicole's great-grandfather, built the inn with the spoils he reaped from the timber industry before the prices fell out of lumber during the Great Depression. It was designed by Richard Hunt, the leading architect of the time who became famous after designing the Biltmore House for the Vanderbilt family in nearby Asheville. The inn was built with the finest chestnut, oak, and maple to be found in the Appalachian region.

The Poplar Inn was both home and business for the Fischer family. With forty guest rooms, a large kitchen and dining room, and the family suite, the inn could comfortably accommodate one hundred people during the peak of the fall leaf season. When it first opened its doors for business, the rooms were available for only forty dollars a week.

Inside, a large stone fireplace that could handle eight-foot logs dominated the lobby, the first room to greet each guest as they entered the inn. It was built with the same stone that had been brought from the riverbed to make the foundation of the inn. French doors opened from the lobby onto the rocking chair porch. Returning guests often hung their coats on wooden pegs and stepped outside onto the rocking chair porch before checking in, eager to embrace the relaxed ambiance of the inn.

Nicholas Fischer spared little expense when building and decorating his inn, the place where his family and guests could count on "rejuvenating the spirit," as he liked to say. Doors made from rough-hewn planks held together by black wrought iron hinges opened from the wide hallways into the large guest rooms. Room numbers were engraved on brass plates fastened just above the iron knockers that adorned each door.

Wrought iron beds, small writing desks, deep pedestal bathtubs, lace-covered dressers, and curtains of country fabrics decorated the rooms. The large paned windows could be slid back into pockets in the chestnut paneled walls to let in the crisp mountain air and sounds of life from the surrounding woods.

The grounds around the inn were shaded by hemlock, dogwood, and poplar trees, and featured rhododendrons, azaleas, and ferns. English ivy draped the hillside and, in places, crawled up the wide girth of the tree trunks. Moss and flowering groundcovers filled in the areas where the shade was too dense for grass to grow. Large slate stones were fitted together to form a path all the way around the inn, and guests often strolled the grounds enjoying its beautiful landscape. Occasionally, mischievous children stepped from the path at the back of the inn and hid in the shadows of the towering trees to carve their initials into the bark shingles that covered the exterior walls.

Much had happened in the Poplar Inn over the years. Several babies had been born there, including Nicole's mother, and her great-grandmother and great-grandfather had died there. The inn struggled during the Great Depression, but rebounded near the end of that era to become the busiest lodging destination in western North Carolina, right up until the Second World War. Business eventually picked up again after the war and the inn did well once more until the late 1950s, when Nicholas Fischer suffered his first stroke. Ruth then took control of the business and slowly began to offer fewer reservations to guests, choosing to keep occupancy at just over half-full, which was just enough guests to pay the bills, and few enough to allow taking the extra time needed to care for her father. When he died at the age of seventy-three in 1964, she cleaned the rooms that had been temporarily closed, and began accepting more reservations.

The inn quickly regained its status as the overnight destination in the area, and Ruth was content busying herself with the tasks of keeping her guests comfortable. She continued to manage the inn and did much of the day-to-day work herself until she reached the age of seventy-three. Thinking of her father's health at that age, she hired a hotel management company to run the inn and then retired. She continued to live in the family suite and, from time to time, sat at the registration counter to greet guests, walked through the kitchen to sample the meals that were being prepared, or helped the gardeners to plan the spring flower beds. But what she enjoyed most was to mingle with the guests, some of who would ask her to autograph one of Joyce Kilmer's books of poetry. Otherwise, she spent her mornings drinking coffee and rocking in her chair on the porch, taking long naps in the afternoon, and waiting for her weekly phone call from Nicole.

Living in the inn since the day her father built it, Ruth knew all of its secrets—which boards on the stairs were loose, where on the property the morel mushrooms could be found, which plants grew best in the little sunlight that made its way to the ground on either side of the inn, and how to make the old furnace start when it didn't want to.

Finally reaching Brysonville and driving through the little town, Nicole turned onto the long, winding driveway that led up to the gravel parking lot of the inn. She could see the lights of the rocking chair porch through the branches of the trees that grew thick alongside the driveway. She glanced at her watch. It was almost nine-thirty and she hoped her grandmother was still awake. She parked near the stone stairs that led from the parking lot up a small grade to the base of the front steps that led to the main entrance of the inn. Neither the parking lot nor the steps were lit, her grandmother preferring to keep the inn as close to its original character as possible. She stepped from the car and into the night air.

A slight breeze felt chilly and moist against her skin. She hurried to gather her bag from the trunk and made her way to the steps. Mounting the first step, she grabbed the long cedar branch that had been fashioned into a handrail. As soon as she felt the knobby wood in her hand she pictured herself running up these same steps as a small child, bounding off the top one and into her grandmother's open arms. Tonight she climbed the steps briskly, counting off all seventeen as she went, just as she had always done.

All at once, she suddenly felt better, remembering back to a time when she was young and had not a worry in the world.

She reached the entrance stoop, which was lit by a simple chandelier made of deer antlers surrounding a single light bulb. The tall front doors were wide open, but a pair of screen doors kept the night bugs out. Nailed to the wall was a cedar plank. On it, her great-grandfather had carved a message for his guests: Welcome.

Nicole pushed on one of the screen doors and stepped inside. Over the tall back of a couch, she could see a low burning fire in the large stone fireplace. Although the days were still hot, the mountain air turned cool and nipped at you at night. She smiled; her grandmother claimed the chimney was so well built it could suck a cat right out of the room.

Nicole scanned the lobby. It was just as she remembered, it never changed. A long harvest table surrounded by ladder-back chairs dominated the middle of the room. On one end of the table, a small group of guests were playing cards, and at the other end, a couple quietly played chess. Club chairs and leather sofas held worn wool rugs in place on the wide plank floor. Antique lamps sat on the end tables and old books adorned the coffee tables. Beneath a bank of windows were low-slung bookcases that strained under the weight of years of issues of National Geographic, Reader's Digest, and Life magazines. One shelf held only her great-grandfather's collection of Zane Grey novels.

She went out another set of doors and onto the rocking chair porch on the overlook side of the inn, hoping to find her grandmother, but her rocker was empty. She must have already gone to bed, Nicole thought, disappointed, and stepped back into the lobby.

It was then she saw someone huddled in the corner of the couch in front of the fireplace, a woman wrapped in a crocheted blanket. Her arms were folded across her chest, her eyeglasses clutched in one hand, and her legs crossed at the ankles. Asleep, her head bobbed up and down with each breath.

Kneeling down, Nicole studied her grandmother's face. It was thin and deeply lined but flush with the color of health. Her lips bore a coat of pale pink lipstick, and her white hair was pulled back into a tidy bun with not a strand out of place.

Nicole gently tugged at the pair of eyeglasses.

Ruth woke up, confused at first, but her mind cleared quickly when she realized who had disturbed her. "Darling!" she said with a smile.

"Hi, Granna." They embraced.

"Did you just get here?" Ruth asked.

"Yes, ma'am, I did," Nicole answered.

"I tried to wait up for you, but I reckon I dozed off," Ruth apologized.

"I'm sorry I'm late," Nicole said, sitting back on the coffee table. "I didn't leave town as soon as I had hoped."

Ruth looked past Nicole and saw that she was alone. "Are you by yourself?" she asked.

Nicole looked down and did not answer.

"Your friend didn't come with you?" Ruth asked again.

"No, ma'am," Nicole said as she looked away from her grandmother's inquiring eyes.

"Is everything alright, darlin'?" Ruth asked.

"I know you're sleepy, and I am too," Nicole replied. "Let's talk about it tomorrow, okay?"

"That's fine, dear," Ruth said, leaning forward to touch her granddaughter's folded hands. She reached for Nicole's chin and lifted her face so that she could look into her granddaughter's eyes. She smiled affectionately at her. "Tomorrow then?" she said.

"Yes," Nicole answered. "I'll tell you everything in the morning. I'm an early riser, remember?"

"Oh hush," Ruth chuckled. "I'll be up for hours before you even realize it's morning." She started to push herself up from the couch, and Nicole took her outstretched hand and helped her to her feet. They walked arm in arm to the innkeeper's suite down the hall, passing by the guest registration counter unnoticed.

They entered the family suite, passed the antique furniture that filled the living room, and made their way to the bedrooms.

"You sure you don't want to sit and visit for a while?" Ruth asked as she approached the doorway of her bedroom.

"I'm sure," Nicole said. "I've had a long, hard day, and some sleep in my old room will do me good."

"We'll catch up in the morning then," Ruth said. "Now don't let the bed bugs bite." She pointed Nicole to the bedroom with windows that overlooked the rocking chair porch. "I had fresh sheets put on the bed for you," she said.

"You always spoil me, Granna," Nicole said. "Tomorrow, I want to spend the whole day with you," she said as she opened the bedroom door. "Let's have lunch somewhere nice, my treat. It's my turn to spoil you."

"You always were my favorite grandchild," Ruth said appreciatively.

"I'm your only grandchild," Nicole laughed.

Ruth grinned and kissed Nicole on the cheek, and then retired to her own bedroom right across the hall, her heart gladdened that her granddaughter had come home at last.

It is a pleasant thing to lie
Upon the meadow on the hill
With kindly fellowship near by
Of sheep and men of gentle will.

The Fourth Shepherd, 1914

Joyce Kilmer

CHAPTER 10

VIRGIL

Owen checked his watch. It was one o'clock in the morning. His mind was now muddled, and his notes had become illegible even to him.

The sound of keys jangled in the hallway. Virgil, pacing each floor to keep himself awake, saw light spill out from under the law office's main door. He let himself in and found Owen yawning over the thick law books, rubbing his eyes so hard his lids were red and wrinkled when he let his hands drop back to the table.

"It's none of my business, Mr. Montgomery," Virgil said, "but it seems you should get yourself home and go to sleep."

"I'll be out of here in a few minutes," Owen replied.

"Good night, then. See you next week." Virgil turned to leave.

"Virgil," Owen called out.

"Yes?" Virgil said, pivoting on his heels to face Owen again.

"Please call me Owen," Owen said.

"The Boss don't like that too much," Virgil frowned. "He says it ain't very professional."

"I won't tell him if you don't," Owen chuckled.

"All right then. I appreciate it. Now go home, Owen, and go to bed," Virgil said as he turned again to leave.

"Virgil, one more thing," Owen called out.

Virgil paused again and looked back over his shoulder. "May I ask you a personal question?" Owen asked.

"Don't see why not," Virgil answered.

"How are you doing?" Owen asked politely.

"Why do you ask?" Virgil questioned.

"Because of what you said earlier about getting left," Owen said. "I heard that your divorce went through; I'm just wondering if you're taking it well."

Virgil leaned his large frame against the open door, shoved one hand between his belly and his belt, and reached up to scratch his head with the other. His hair was cropped short, and his fingernails against his scalp sounded like scratching a two-day-old beard. "I miss my kids," he said.

"I bet it's hard on them, too," Owen said.

"She said I spent too much time away from the family, that she deserved someone who paid more attention to her," Virgil recalled painfully. "It don't seem fair, a man working two jobs to support his family, sleeping as little as he can and not destroying himself with long hours, but getting left for doing what he's supposed to do—provide for his family."

"I understand; I'm sure that hurts," Owen said.

"All men understand," Virgil said.

"Any chance you'll get back together?" Owen asked.

"I always say anything's possible, but right now, she won't even talk to me," Virgil said, "so I don't really know."

"Well, if it's any consolation to you, I'm impressed with how you keep your head up. Every day, you greet me with a smile and cheerful words," Owen encouraged him. "Not everyone is made like that, Virgil."

Virgil pulled out a chair and sat down at the conference table, comfortable and not needing an invitation now that he and Owen were on a first-name basis. "It ain't always easy to look up, but it's the best choice," he said.

"The best choice?" Owen asked.

"My granddaddy owned a farm down in Cordele, and he had some hogs," Virgil said. "I spent nearly every summer with him when I was a boy. One day, I was moping around 'cause some girl had put me down. My granddaddy, he says, 'You can wallow in it, like them hogs in their own shit, or you can pick yourself up and wash it off. It all depends on how close you want to get to other people. It's your choice.'"

"That's some analogy," Owen chuckled. "Farmer's logic, I guess."

"I knew what he meant," Virgil said. "I always wash myself off."

Curious, Owen leaned back in his chair. "Would you change anything if you and your wife could get back together?" he asked.

"If I could be at home every night, I would be, but I can't. This is what I do," Virgil said, pulling at the starched collar of his uniform shirt, his voice falling off to a near whisper. "I don't have much choice; can't do much of nothing else." He leaned back in the chair and slid his feet across the floor, his legs now sprawled out like he was sitting on his own sofa with a beer in hand and a championship game on the big screen. "Marriage is hard, Owen," Virgil said, "it is real work. But the more you put into it, the more you get out of it if you're married to the right woman. Sometimes you'll both feel like you're putting more in than the other, but in the end, you get plenty back." He wagged a cautionary finger. "But only if you marry the right woman."

"And how do you know who is the right woman?" Owen asked.

"I wish I knew," Virgil said with a grin. "Granddaddy never told me that." He pushed himself up to stand. "It's one of life's great mysteries, I reckon."

"Yes, I reckon it is," Owen agreed. He closed the law books, pushed his notes away, and stood to extend a handshake. "I bet I would have liked your grandfather. Good night, Virgil."

Virgil gripped Owen's hand hard and pumped it vigorously, and then released him and disappeared into the darkness beyond the library door. Owen quickly gathered his things, turned off the lights, and headed for his car.

Once in it, he dropped his head back against the headrest, and his eyes began to droop, adamantly refusing to cooperate with his will to stay alert. Emma was right, he thought, these seats are comfy. He looked at his watch. At this time of night, he could be home in less than fifteen minutes. He sat up, started the car, and opened the windows and sunroof again, hoping the cool night air would revive him. Uncounted blocks and a half dozen love song dedications later, he was driving through Virginia Highland. Relieved when he reached his driveway, he trudged through the darkness toward his front door. He should have left a message for Nicole, he thought; there is nothing difficult about leaving a voicemail. His chest started to hurt again.

He wondered if Nicole missed him that evening as she went to bed alone. He certainly missed her. He was accustomed to their careers keeping them apart during the business week, but he had come to depend on having her company during the weekend. They had learned how to make the most of being together for only two or three days at a time and could enjoy one another without the petty squabbles that could ruin a weekend. He craved her company and wanted to curl up to her when he fell asleep.

Reaching the front door, he was struck with regret that he had had to work this weekend, and he became even more determined to finish in time to drive to the inn on Sunday morning. He knew that if he did not, it would upset Nicole even more, and in spite of her reassurances to the contrary, she would not understand.

Finally, inside, he fumbled around in the dark living room, bumped into a chair, and reached over to find the lamp on the end table. He felt for its neck and then walked his fingers up until he reached the switch, and turned it on. He kicked off his shoes, removed his belt, and plopped down on the couch. Exhausted and asking himself if Nicole was the right one or not, he reached for the remote and began to randomly surf channels, looking for nothing in particular but hoping to find something to numb his mind. He settled on a late-night variety talk show and sank back to relax.

In spite of trying to listen to the teasing banter between the show's host and guests, his thoughts were preoccupied with second guesses. Should he ask another attorney at the firm to help him with the case? Maybe that would allow him to get away sooner. He wished that he had kissed Nicole more passionately before she had driven away and that he had tried to call her sooner than he did.

The conversation between the guests and host faded to blah-blah-blah, and his weary mind bounced from Nicole to Quinn and, finally, to trees.

Our minds are troubled and defiled
By study in a weary school.
O for the folly of a child!
The ready courage of the fool!

Folly, 1914

Joyce Kilmer

CHAPTER 11

STORIES

Nicole stirred when cheerful morning sounds spilled into her open window, rushing like a wave across the floor and up and over the handmade quilt her mother used to sleep under. Her body, sunken into the soft feather mattress pillow, was warm beneath the quilted remnants of old Easter dresses, checked gingham, summer denim, and curtain fabric stitched together not haphazardly but telling a life story if only you took an interest and the time to read it.

She stretched her legs as far as she could, pushing and pointing her bare toes downward until she could feel the grain of the old oak footboard. Crisp mountain air filled the room, and a chill ran past her ankles and up her legs. Bright streaks of sunlight wavered across the chestnut-paneled walls as the gentle breeze pushed the curtains into the path of the morning sun. The clean scent of the mountains filled her nostrils, and her ears gulped in the harmony of blue jays and robins singing in time with the rapid hammering of a nearby woodpecker. She grinned and turned her attention toward a rhythmic creaking sound, one she knew well, her grandmother's rocking chair. True to her word, the honorable matron of the inn had risen early and was already outside, probably having a cup of coffee while watching the sunrise.

Nicole climbed out of bed, quickly showered, and dressed for the day, not taking time to dry her hair or put on makeup, not caring about how she looked. She was in the mountains, after all, where everything was so beautiful that nothing else stood a chance by comparison. She was home. She stepped into her shoes and went to the dresser, where she had taken off her jewelry before going to bed.

Reaching for her watch, a framed photograph caught her attention instead. It was of her and her mother standing on either side of Ruth, who was sitting in her rocking chair. Nearly ten years old and taken on another of her grandmother's birthdays, the memory of that day was as fresh as mountain mornings. She picked it up and caressed her mother's face, but put it down as soon as a lump came to her throat.

But then after only a beat, she picked the photograph up again. Her fingertips caressed her mother's face again, and her eyes filled with tears as she was overcome with the stabbing pain of grief. She grabbed a tissue and dabbed her eyes dry. She sat the photograph back in its place, adjusting it so that she could see it from the bed, and decided not to wear her watch. It was going to be a day without a schedule, a day of singular focus, she thought, with no distractions to keep her from giving her grandmother a full day of fun and companionship.

She left the suite and headed toward the rocking chair porch. She approached the lobby and walked past the wide stairway leading to the rooms upstairs. At the first step was a ten-inch square wood newel post, deeply cracked with age. She reached out and brushed her fingers across it as she passed. It was worn smooth from the many hands that had rubbed over it during the years.

A small morning fire burned in the fireplace and warmed her legs as she walked past the couch where she found her grandmother asleep the night before. Several guests were already in the lobby, reading the morning paper, browsing the brochures of nearby tourist attractions, and chatting cheerfully about what a wonderful day it was going to be. Nicole pushed the screen door open and stepped outside onto the porch.

Ruth was the only one on the porch this chilly morning. Undisturbed by the sound of the screen door clapping shut, she continued to rock in the morning sunshine that poured over her shoulder and into the open window behind her, Nicole's room. Her hands were wrapped around a large steaming coffee mug balanced on her knees.

Nicole picked up a rocking chair and moved it closer to her grandmother. Taking a seat, she recognized the imperfect mug. She had made it herself in an art class back in elementary school and had given it to her grandmother as a birthday gift. Ruth always took her afternoon tea in a fine china cup and saucer, but would not drink coffee from anything but the clunky old mug with the extra-large handle. Nicole leaned forward, concentrated on the sway of Ruth's chair, and then leaned back and began to rock in unison.

"Good mornin', sleepy head," Ruth teased.

"I concede; you were right about me sleeping late," Nicole said.

"I'm always right, and when I'm not, you should let me think that I am," Ruth continued to tease. "It's a prerogative that comes with living to such an old age."

"You are not old, Granna; you've just been around a long, long time," Nicole said as she reached for Ruth's hand. They laced their fingers together.

"And I'll be here a bit longer, let's hope, the Lord and Mother Earth willing," Ruth chuckled.

They rocked with their hands clasped together between the arms of the rocking chairs, old and new intertwined, wisdom, and questions, hope and pain coursing past each other with each heartbeat. They continued to rock, swaying back and forth in time with one another. They remained quiet for a while, enjoying each other, loving each other, expressing it without having to say a word, the warmth within their clasped hands confirming it all for them.

"What have you been thinking about this morning?" Nicole eventually asked.

"Days gone by, your mother, what I want for lunch today. A little bit of everything," Ruth answered.

"I think of Mom nearly every day," Nicole said. "I was just looking at that picture of the three of us, the one on the dresser."

Ruth leaned closer to Nicole and smiled with curiosity. "What did you think about? Please tell me how you remember your mom."

Nicole looked into the mountains, searching for hikers on a trail or a small nook in a tree where she might have hidden treasures in her youth in hopes that one day they would be worth something, hoping the morning was not already about to take a serious turn of mood. She started to rock slower and dropped out of cadence. "Sometimes I'm reminded of things that we did together, and sometimes I find myself wishing I could tell her about how my life has turned out," she said. "But mostly I'm just conflicted about her. I can't help but wish we had more ups than we did downs."

"Why do you say 'conflicted'?" Ruth asked, her chair's rocking rhythm slowing down too.

"Granna, you know I loved my mother," Nicole began.

"And she loved you, too," Ruth interjected quickly.

Nicole nodded and picked her feet up off the porch to rest them on a rung of her chair. It came to a stop. "Yes, she did, but never as much as I loved her," she said.

"Your mother's heart was broken, Nicole, and she let it harden rather than heal," Ruth said. "Sometimes no amount of medicine can cure the infection a woman has let fester in her heart. But I know she loved you, Nicole. You were her greatest joy."

"She was more than heartbroken, Granna," Nicole said. "She was angry, and bitter, too." She blinked at an uncooperative tear.

"Maybe so, but don't you be bitter," Ruth said, her voice now stern yet somehow still sweet. She turned sideways to look into Nicole's eyes and she pulled her granddaughter toward her as she tightened her grip on her hand. "Your momma changed after your daddy left and she never got over it. It is hard to blame her, an unmarried woman with a new baby and a heart full of hopes and dreams, all dashed to pieces by a man who promised her everything but gave her nothing."

"I just wish she'd gotten over it," Nicole said in low spirits. "She spent her life doing everything she could to not love anybody ever again."

"She loved you, Nicole. Perhaps not openly, maybe not very affectionately, but nevertheless, she loved you," Ruth insisted.

Nicole looked into her grandmother's cloudless eyes. Pupils black as night, blue irises with flecks of brown, little pink veins, and the whites yellowed just a little, like between the pages of an old book in which is written the entire history of the world. Nicole bit her lip. "I know she did," she finally said.

"Good, I'm glad you know it," Ruth said. "And don't forget it. Now give me a kiss and smile for me."

"A kiss cures everything, doesn't it?" Nicole laughed.

"That's what I always say," Ruth answered.

Nicole leaned over, and Ruth kissed her on the cheek. Then, reaching around her neck, Ruth pulled her head down to kiss her forehead, too, leaving a red lipstick smudge just below the part in her hair. "Now," Ruth said, admiring the smudge, "everybody will know that you are loved. You've got the mark on you."

"I love you, Granna," Nicole said.

"I love you, too, my little Lady Bug," Ruth said, recalling a nickname she had given Nicole when she was a baby crawling on the floor, darting between the legs of the people who took care not to step on her.

Nicole's stomach growled. "Your Lady Bug is hungry," she said as she clutched her belly and managed to chuckle.

"I would be, too, if I slept as late in the day as you do," Ruth said, pushing herself up from her rocking chair. Taking Nicole's hand again, she led her back into the inn. The lobby was now nearly full of guests who had also risen and made their way into the common area. All the chairs and sofas were now occupied as people read the morning paper, drank coffee, or talked with one another about their observations after spending their first night as guests of the inn. A few looked up and watched the pair of women aged decades apart but who shared a similar appearance as they sauntered across the lobby floor.

"I've lived here essentially all of my life, you know," Ruth mused.

"I know. I love this place," Nicole said sentimentally, looking around the room.

"It's been a long time since you were here last," Ruth said.

"I know, I'm sorry," Nicole apologized.

"Please don't let it happen again. My time is short," Ruth said.

Nicole rubbed her grandmother's arm. "I won't," Nicole said. "And it isn't," she added.

They walked down the hallway toward the dining room. Nicole breathed in the unmistakable and irresistible aroma of buttermilk biscuits, smoked bacon, and just perked strong coffee. Like every guest encountering the smells of the Poplar Inn kitchen for the first time, her stomach leaped as if she had been given a chance to escape starvation.

Ruth stopped just outside the dining room and scanned a large bulletin board that hung on the wall. Framed and protected behind glass doors, it was a display of letters and postcards sent to the inn by former guests, newspaper clippings of stories about the inn's many festivities and visiting dignitaries of days long gone by, and faded photographs, including one of herself and her father, Nicholas Fischer. "I miss my Father," Ruth said. "He could be a handful of a rascal at times, and a curmudgeon at others, but I sure do miss him. Just like you miss your Momma, I hope."

Nicole nodded affirmatively. "I wish I had known him."

"You know you were named after him, don't you?" Ruth asked.

"I sure do. Hello there, Nicholas," Nicole said, smiling at the photograph.

"He would've been crazy about you, I know he would," Ruth said.

"Come on," Nicole said as she pulled Ruth into the dining room. "Those biscuits are calling my name."

They walked past the hostess who smiled and wished them a good morning, and took their seats at the table that was always reserved for Miss Ruth and her guests. It was about halfway into the dining room and against a window where Ruth could look outside and watch the arriving guests.

A young waiter with the profile and long jet-black hair of a Cherokee Indian came to their table carrying a steaming pot of coffee. "More coffee, Miss Ruth?" he asked even though he had already started to pour some into her mug.

"Yes, Martin, of course," Ruth responded. "Thank you."

He turned his attention to Nicole and was about to ask her the same question when he saw the lipstick smear on her forehead. "Are you sick, Ma'am?" he asked.

Nicole, suddenly embarrassed, grabbed a cloth napkin and wiped the lipstick from her forehead. "You must know about the kiss that cures all," she said.

"Anybody who knows Miss Ruth knows about the kiss," Martin said with a laugh. He reached down and turned up the coffee cup sitting next to Nicole's plate and filled it, certain that that was what she wanted. "The usual, Miss Ruth?" he asked.

"Yes, thank you," she answered.

"And you, Ma'am?" he asked, looking now to Nicole.

"Martin," Ruth interrupted, "you know her, she's Nicole, my granddaughter. Now don't go calling her 'Ma'am,' she's family."

"Ah, Nicole," the cheerful waiter said as he sat the coffee pot down and reached out to shake her hand. "I think I remember you, but I haven't seen you in a long while though."

Nicole, puzzled, looked up at him, her thoughts racing. Before she could speak, he did. "And what's it going to be for breakfast, Nicole?" He held his pen and pad ready.

"One poached egg, one biscuit but not a big one, no butter, and tomato juice, please," she answered promptly.

"Bacon, country ham, or pork or turkey sausage?" he asked expectingly.

"None, but thank you," Nicole answered.

"Grits? Sawmill gravy?" Martin continued.

"Neither, but thanks," Nicole answered.

Martin looked at Ruth with an explain this to me please expression on his face.

"She lives in Atlanta, dear. She's a city girl," Ruth offered as if everyone knew that city girls ate sparingly.

"Oh," Martin said, a bemused grin appearing on his face. "In that case, excellent choices, ladies. I'll have your breakfast right out." He picked up the coffee pot and walked briskly toward the kitchen, grabbing empty plates and glasses from the tables he passed along the way, somehow balancing it all without spilling a drop on the floor.

"Is he the little boy," Nicole held her hand out about three feet above the floor, "who used to come over here with the Indian Fischers? I can't believe he might be the one and same."

"Yes, he is a descendant of Bear," Ruth confirmed.

"Wonderful!" Nicole nearly shrieked. "Please tell me that story again; I haven't heard it in such a long time."

"Oh, you don't want to hear that old story again," Ruth protested.

"I most certainly do," Nicole insisted. "You always tell the best stories."

"I haven't told you a story since you were waist-high," Ruth said.

"Exactly, which is why I need you to repeat every one of them for me," Nicole pressed. "Tell me, Granna, please?"

"You don't want to hear all that ol' folklore when there is so much else we could talk about," Ruth resisted.

"Take me back, Granna," Nicole pleaded, "to when I was young and everything was simple and easy to understand."

"Oh, all right," Ruth conceded, and not unwillingly. "Well, you know how it begins. Most of the Cherokee Indians left the Appalachians a quarter-century before the War Between the States; the U.S. Army escorted them to the reservations in the west, whether they wanted to go or not, making them walk all the way to Oklahoma. Those poor Indians lost their homes, their land, and their way of life, and thousands of them died along the way, mostly children and the elderly. That's why they called the route the 'Trail of Tears'. But a few of them refused to leave forever, insisting this area was their home, and eventually, they made their way back and settled along the river in the valley just northeast of Brysonville. After much political turmoil, the government finally recognized the area as a Cherokee Nation reservation, giving the Indians title to the land that had originally been their own. You see, Bear's grandfather was among those who came back, and over the years, his family grew, and one day, my dear Bear was born. He was one of my father's first employees, and he was always really good to me. He was like a loving uncle, actually. He taught me about the Indian ways and the laws of nature, and he helped me look after Father after Mother died. He worked the gardens, took care of the repairs, and kept us well-stocked in chopped wood for the fireplace. Some people are too lazy to swallow boiled okra, but not Bear. He and Nathaniel truly were the hardest working members of the family."

"Now who was Nathaniel?" Nicole asked. "I don't remember him."

"Nathaniel Brooks, the first cook to work here at the inn. Those biscuits you like so much are still made like he used to make them."

"I wish I could have met Bear, and Nathaniel, too," Nicole said.

"I wish you could have too, honey, but Bear and Nathaniel are both long gone." Ruth paused and her mind wandered back to a time when she could walk all day without her feet hurting. "Oh, how my heart aches for the good old days when everyone was young and alive," she said at last.

Nicole sat back in her chair when she realized they had already talked about four deceased people and the dew hadn't even burned off the grass yet. "There's been a lot of people coming through and leaving their mark on this place," she said.

"You can't even count how many," Ruth agreed. "Babies had been born here, including your mother, and your great-grandmother and great-grandfather both died here."

"Tell me again about how Bear's family became Fischers. I want to know all the details," Nicole said. "Don't leave anything out."

"Are you testing my memory?" Ruth asked cheerfully.

"No, I'm not. Really, I'm not," Nicole laughed, "but I've forgotten everything. Tell me again, please. I like to hear you tell it."

"You like to indulge me," Ruth accused.

"I've got to indulge somebody," Nicole answered.

Ruth paused and looked at her granddaughter with an inquisitive eye, but chose not to change the topic of conversation. "We gave Bear some property near the reservation," she continued, "because he wanted his family to always have some of the land that once belonged to his ancestors. Because those acres were known then as Fischer land, everyone started calling them the Fischer Indians and, well, it just stuck. So, when they sent their children to public school they had to have a last name, and they asked if they could use ours. Of course, I agreed. So now, Fischer is the last name they all go by. Martin is a good boy and I'm happy to have him work here. He reminds me of Bear; he's his great-grandson."

"Fascinating," Nicole exclaimed. "And remind me of how you first met Bear."

"He just walked into our lives one day," Ruth recalled affectionately. "He came right up that driveway out there, but it was only dirt back then. Father was building the inn and this tall, big man with a ponytail strode up and told him he had to pray to the Creator if the inn was to prosper. It had to be blessed, Bear said. Without waiting for Father to agree, he prayed right then and there, just over there," Ruth pointed out a window, "and Father liked him so much he asked him to come to work for us. So he did."

"And why was he named Bear?" Nicole asked.

"I always thought it was because he was as big as a bear, but he said it was because he snored like one," Ruth cackled.

"And he prayed for the inn?" Nicole asked with a laugh.

"Oh yes. He used that prayer all the time," Ruth said.

"Do you remember the prayer?" Nicole asked, leaning forward.

"Of course I do, I'm not senile like you." Ruth lifted her hands into the air and looked up at the thick beams overhead holding up the roof. "Oh Great Creator, I come before you to pray to the Grandfather Sun, to the Grandmother Moon, to the Mother Earth, and to my ancestors. May this home be filled with peace and love." She reached for her coffee and paused in deep thought just before taking a swallow. "That's what he said."

"It's a beautiful prayer," Nicole said.

"It is, isn't it?" Ruth agreed.

Martin walked up to the table carrying a large tray balanced on his shoulder. "Hot plates," he cautioned. He set the tray on an empty table nearby and began to serve their breakfast, laying out silverware and cotton napkins first. Next, he put a heavy white ceramic plate with one poached egg and a steaming biscuit in front of Nicole, followed by small Blue Willow bowls filled with thick slices of almost cold butter, homemade orange marmalade, and cinnamon stewed apples that had been picked just yesterday from the nearby orchards. Finally, he laid a plate the size of a serving platter in front of Ruth. It hit the table with a thud. Unlike Nicole's scant serving, Ruth's was piled high with two fried eggs sunny side up, two biscuits, a heaping scoop of yellow course ground grits, and a pile of thick-cut bacon.

"Good Lord, Granna. What a breakfast!" Nicole said. "It's practically a heart attack on a plate. Are you going to eat all that?" she asked.

"She's been eating the same thing every morning for months now," Martin said. "I don't know how she does it."

"Nathaniel always said, 'Start your day on a full belly and everything else will be just fine,'" Ruth laughed, "and I've come to believe it's true. Besides, when you reach my age, there's no need to deny yourself anything you might enjoy."

"Obviously," Nicole laughed, shaking her head.

"Are you sure you don't want a breakfast meat?" Martin asked Nicole as he placed a chilled glass of tomato juice next to her plate.

Nicole looked across the table at her grandmother. She had split a biscuit with a knife, smeared butter on both halves, and inserted a folded slice of bacon. She smiled like a kid at Christmas as she put it back together and took her first bite. "What the hell," Nicole said, "sure. Bring me some bacon, please."

"Good," Martin said, pouring more coffee into Ruth's mug.

"Yes, very good," Ruth said as she chewed, thinking Martin had asked if she liked her breakfast. He smiled at Nicole, reached down and pushed the bowl of butter closer to Ruth, and left the table to return to the kitchen.

"Nathaniel ate this same breakfast every day," Ruth continued, "and he was the skinniest man I ever saw. When he turned sideways, he'd nearly disappear. I'm guessing if it didn't fatten him up, it won't fatten me, either."

"It hasn't seemed to hurt you," Nicole answered, "not yet. Now tell me about Nathaniel. I want to know everything about him, too."

"You act like you've never been here before," Ruth said.

"I told you," Nicole said, "I've forgotten so much."

"See, you should come here more often," Ruth asserted, "to keep your memories up. City living messes with your mind, I've heard." She gave Nicole a scolding glance.

"I said I'll come more often," Nicole reminded her.

"I'll believe it when I see it," Ruth said teasingly. And without missing a beat, she continued. "Now Nathaniel was twenty-two years old when he came to work here, and he stayed all of forty-six years. He died five years after your grandfather did. When he laughed, you could see that nearly all his bottom front teeth were silver. He always wore denim jeans and a starched white chef's tunic with the sleeves rolled up to his elbows. His pitch-black forearms bulged with muscles from kneading dough for so many years. When he made biscuits, he pinched off big wads of dough, placed them on a floured table, and flattened them with the back of his hand. 'No rollin' pin and fancy cut-out biscuit for me,' he said. 'I cook 'em thick, too, so they'll be a heap for soaking up pan gravy. Little thin biscuits are no good at all except for gummin' babies,' he used to say."

"I love these stories," Nicole said, piercing her egg yolk with a fork. The yolk ran out onto her plate and spread into a neat half-circle. "Even if I have heard them a hundred times before, I always want to hear them again." She used a knife to cut off a piece of biscuit, pushed it into the yolk, and then daintily lifted it to her mouth with the fork.

"My goodness, use your fingers, girl," Ruth scolded playfully. "You've got to feel a biscuit to know if it's made right."

"Something else Nathaniel used to say?" Nicole asked, putting her fork down. She picked up her biscuit, tore it with her fingers, and sopped up the yolk. "Like this?" She stuffed a large bite into her mouth. Her fingertips glistened with sticky, yellow goo.

"Well, not exactly. He didn't say to forget your manners," Ruth laughed, watching Nicole try to chew the mouthful, her cheeks bulging and a crumb trapped in the corner of her mouth. Now the time is right, Ruth judged. "When are you going to tell me about your fella?" she asked.

Nicole lowered her head and struggled to get the mouthful down in one swallow. She reached for her tomato juice and took a sip to help wash down the biscuit. "I will, but not now," she answered after a successful gulp. "I want to hear more of your stories first. Mine are boring."

"We must take turns," Ruth bargained. "I'll tell you a story and then you'll tell me one. Something about you that I don't already know. Agreed?"

"Agreed," Nicole nodded, stuffing another bite of biscuit, this time a smaller one, into her mouth. She licked her fingers and reached again for her tomato juice.

"Good; I'll go first," Ruth said, feeling accomplished. "You know my father was a lawyer, which made him a bit unusual in these parts. In those days, only a few of the local boys ever went to college. Most stayed here and became clerks in the stores, worked for the road department, or at the Lambert's sawmill. I think at least one person in every family around here worked at the sawmill. Even those boys who worked the family farms would eventually find themselves at the sawmill when the crop season was over. Lumberin', we called it."

"Did he ever work at the mill?" Nicole asked.

"He took his law courses at a night school in Winston-Salem during the early years of marriage, before I was born. He drove to his classes three nights a week and paid his tuition by working six days a week at the sawmill. He ran the conveyor belt that fed the logs into the saw. He wanted to be a lawyer so that he could help people and give my mother a good life, he told me. She was proud of him when he finally finished law school. At the beginning of his law career, he handled wills, contracts, a few damage suits, and the like. But what he made in fees just barely covered his incidental expenses, and pretty soon he thought he was going to have to go back to work at the sawmill. Like I've said, there was always work at the sawmill. You could hear the saw humming all day long, he once told me. That's when he realized there was money in timber, so he turned his law practice to handling land deeds and titles for the folks who were selling off their land for cutting. In his new wisdom, he demanded to be paid in parcels of virgin land instead of cash. Eventually, he accumulated a few thousand acres in the mountains. That's when he, too, began to sell timber. The business was good to him, and with his profits, he built this inn." Ruth slurped a bit of coffee after pausing to eat a bite of grits. "And that concludes my third story this morning. Now it's your turn," she said, tapping her knife on the butter dish.

"No, not now," Nicole pushed back. "I have to finish my egg before it gets cold. What did your mother do?"

"Don't I get to eat, too?" Ruth asked.

"Just tell me a little more, please," Nicole said, avoiding their agreement. "Besides, I haven't decided what to tell you yet." She looked around for Martin. "Where's my bacon?"

Ruth smiled at her granddaughter, their old affection beginning to rekindle, remembering summers that until this morning had seemed like a hundred years ago. Too big now to sit in her lap, too old to play silly games, but still young enough to be taught a thing or two, she thought. "Back then," she continued compliantly, "girls went to college to become teachers or nurses, or they married well and took up their places in the church or a social club. Those who couldn't get their education or didn't marry up became waitresses, beauticians, or cooks. Mother clerked at the dry goods store, and that's where she and Father met."

"Don't stop there," Nicole said. "Tell me how they started to date."

"How does anyone start to date?" Ruth asked with feigned sarcasm. "They are introduced to each other, the man asks the woman on a date, they go out, they kiss, and if you don't know about the rest I'm not going to be the one to tell it to you."

"Granna, come on, tell me. I want to know," Nicole begged.

"No, not until you tell me about you and Owen," Ruth strategically pushed back. "You haven't told me much of anything about you two. That's the story I want to hear."

Nicole's cheerful mood wilted noticeably, and she lowered her eyes and started to rearrange her food with her fork.

"Why did you come up here by yourself, honey?" Ruth asked, reaching across the table to rest her hand on Nicole's forearm. "I think it's time to tell me what's really going on."

"No story first, just skip right to the most difficult questions?" Nicole murmured.

"We don't talk as much as we should, Nicole," Ruth said.

"We talk every once in a while," Nicole answered apologetically.

"We chat now and then, but that's not the same thing as talking," Ruth said. "There's a big difference."

"I suppose," Nicole conceded.

"You can't run forever, Nicole," Ruth said.

"I'm not running," Nicole said unconvincingly.

Ruth's doubt went unspoken. After a pause, she shifted in her chair. "You don't have to tell me everything, Nicole, but you do have to tell me enough. I'm worried sick about you."

"I'm not sure where to begin," Nicole whispered.

"Just start at the beginning," Ruth urged, "that's always a good place."

The scented morning of the year
Is old and stale now ye are gone.
No friendly songs the children hear
Among the bushes on the lawn.

To a Blackbird and His Mate
Who Died in the Spring, 1914
Joyce Kilmer

Chapter 12

Reckoning

Owen woke up to the sound of a juicer and found himself still lying on the couch, his neck hurting from sleeping with his head crammed up against the armrest. His shirt was twisted around his belly as if he had been swaddled in a papoose. He uncinched himself and looked over at the television that had been on all night and watched two unbelievably cheerful women stuffing carrots, apples, ginger root, and fennel down the chute of the juicer. "It's so good for you!" one of them effused.

He reached for the remote, clicked off the television, slid down the couch to hang his feet off the other end, and straightened out his neck. The blades of the ceiling fan needed dusting, he observed. Outside, a lawnmower started. The late morning sunshine leaked through the spaces between the almost closed blinds on the windows on the east side of the house. Bright stripes of light sparkled across the hardwood floor.

He continued to look around the room, almost unsure if he was in his own home. His eyes landed on various reassurances, like his stereo and album collection, a short bookcase loaded heavy with southern novels and art books, and an antique clock collection spanning the width of his mantlepiece. Finally, his attention was drawn to a corner of the room where an electric guitar was resting on a stand next to an amplifier. It was his older brother's guitar. That corner of the room was a bit of a memorial to Joel. Alongside the amplifier was a pair of high-top Doc Martin boots, and on the wall hung a framed album cover, R.E.M's Reckoning. Joel had mastered the lead guitar parts on every song of the recording.

"Joel, oh, Joel," Owen groaned. "Why, why?" Tears filled his eyes as he remembered that early morning phone call from his father. "Have you heard from Joel?" the typically calm doctor had asked in a panic.

"No," Owen answered, "not since he stopped by here yesterday to chat for a little while."

"What did he have to say?" Dr. Montgomery almost demanded to know.

"Nothing serious," Owen answered. "He said he just felt like popping over to let me know that he loved me."

"Oh my God," his father said then.

There was a thump outside that interrupted Owen's recall of that painful morning two years ago. The Saturday paper arriving late, thrown onto the porch, perhaps? A car door slamming closed? Someone is using a hammer next door, he thought. No, that is knocking; someone is wearing out that knocker on my front door.

He swung his feet to the floor, ran his fingers through his hair, and stood up. His shirt was terribly wrinkled and he tried to iron it out with his hands before he reached the door. He didn't bother to look through the peephole and swung the door open wide.

A Jaguar was parked at the end of his driveway, and a late-fifty-something-year-old woman dressed in a tennis outfit stood there looking sternly at him. She was wearing expertly applied make-up, and her expensive blonde hair was pulled back in a tight ponytail. Her expression quickly morphed from maternal worry to annoyance as soon as she surveyed her son. "Owen, you look like hell," she said.

"Good morning, Mother," he said.

"Why didn't you answer your phone?" she demanded to know.

"It didn't ring," he said.

"I've been calling you all morning," she reported.

"I guess I slept through it," Owen said unapologetically. "I didn't hear it."

"I thought you were in a coma," she complained.

"Yet you took the time to get ready for tennis," Owen observed.

"Don't be so sarcastic," she protested. "I had to get dressed in something before leaving the house."

"Come in, I'll make some coffee," Owen offered, "if you have time." Please say you don't, he quickly thought, suddenly regretting his invitation.

"I hope you're drinking decaf, like the doctor said," she replied.

"Why'd you call?" Owen asked as he turned to go into the kitchen.

"Quinn called yesterday; she said you didn't look well," she answered as she followed him, half expecting the offer of coffee to be revoked at the mention of Quinn's name. "I wanted to check on you."

"Like I told Dad, I'm fine," Owen insisted. "Didn't he tell you that we talked?" He pulled a bag of coffee from a cupboard and poured dark roasted fully leaded brown beans from Guatemala into a grinder. "How many cups?"

"Just one, please. I don't want to be late for the match," she replied.

Thank God, Owen thought. "It's just as well; I need to get to the office," he said.

His mother gave him a discerning look over. "I hope you fix your hair first," she said. Blanche Adair Vandiver Montgomery had a way of putting things in as few words as possible, be they hurtful or not. She reached into the sink and lifted out the wine goblet Owen had used the night before. "Please tell me you're not having more than two of these per day," she said. Grabbing a paper towel, she quickly rinsed and wiped the goblet sparkling clean.

"Please don't badger me, Mother," Owen warned. "I don't need a nurse or a housekeeper."

"You know I'm an advocate for healthy living," she answered, "especially when you are concerned."

"How's Dad?", Owen inquired. "Is he still smoking?"

"Where does this go?" she asked, ignoring her son's question and holding up the goblet by its stem in the sunlight in search of lurking fingerprints.

"Over there, last door on the upper right," Owen said. He dumped the ground coffee beans into the cone filter and began to fill the reservoir with water. He looked over his shoulder to ask his mother to pull down two coffee mugs but saw that she was reading his calendar, which hung inside the cabinet door. "Aren't you nosey?" he said.

"Is this why Nicole isn't here?", she asked, her finger pointing to the circle around the dates of the long weekend. "Or did you finally break up with her?"

"She's in Brysonville, if you must know, Mother, visiting her grandmother."

"It looks like she had plans for you to go with her," his mother said.

"I'm going, just not as soon as we would have liked," Owen said.

"I thought you had that trial, something about some silly old trees," she said.

"Mother, you know more than you want me to think you do. Spare me, just cut to the chase." He flipped on the switch to start the coffee brewing, thinking for a moment he would almost rather be standing barefoot in a foot of snow than continue this conversation. He turned to face his mother, leaned against the counter, and crossed his arms over his chest. "Why are you really here?"

"Come play tennis with me," she requested.

"Like you just said, I've got work to do," Owen answered flatly. "For those silly old trees."

"I think you would really enjoy yourself," she tried to coax him, "a little exercise might relieve some stress. We could go to Neiman's for lunch afterward."

"Mom, you know I hate tennis," Owen said.

"Quinn will be there. I've invited her to come; we can play doubles," she said, "you and her against Colleen and me."

"I think you mean you, Quinn, and Colleen against me," Owen said, "plus whoever else you can prod into going along with your plan of attack."

"Must you be so difficult, Owen?" Blanche chided her son. She had begun to rearrange the glasses in the cupboard, sorting them by color and design, the tall ones in the back, the expensive ones within easy reach, and the cheap ones set aside on the counter to throw away later.

"Must you be so intrusive?" Owen pushed back.

"Must you be so disrespectful? I'm not intrusive, just interested." Blanche closed the cabinet door and faced her son. "I only want what every mother wants, for her child to be happy."

"Here we go again. Must we keep having the same argument? Don't you think by now I might be the authority on what makes me happy?" Owen retorted. The coffee pot beeped and he reached for the steaming carafe. One-hundred-eighty degrees, hot enough to burn the mouth, he remembered with a bit of dread. "Give me two mugs, will you?" he asked as he reached into the freezer and grabbed a few cubes of ice.

"You were so happy with Quinn, Colleen agrees completely," Blanche asserted as if her opinion was indisputable. She extended two mugs and when Owen looped his fingers in the handles to take them, she wouldn't let go. "She'd love for you two to get back together just as much as I would. We've always wanted our families to join."

"Mom, you're such a relic. It's almost 2001; no one thinks that way anymore."

"There's nothing improper about wanting to maintain our place in society, Owen, for the benefit of our future generations. Won't you at least consider it, for me?"

"Consider getting back together with Quinn?" Owen asked incredulously. "She almost killed me." He pulled the mugs free, just short of yanking them from his mother's hands.

"You know it was an accident," Blanche said quickly, "she would never have done that on purpose."

"Mother, I'm not talking about the rake."

"What are you talking about then?"

"You know what she did to me," he said.

"I'll grant you it was embarrassing, but that's in the past," Blanche acknowledged and rationalized. "You two can still make things work out; you ought to give it another try. Today is as good a day as any to give your relationship another chance."

"How long have you and Colleen been planning this little get-together?" Owen asked.

"You make it sound like we are co-conspirators," Blanche complained.

"Well, aren't you?" Owen asked sardonically.

"Colleen wants for her daughter no less than what I want for my son," Blanche asserted confidently. "We both have your best interests at heart. You two would make such beautiful babies."

"What's the dowry, Mother?" Owen asked. "Beachfront property, a herd of cattle?" He angrily poured coffee for her, dropped in the ice cubes, and sloshed coffee over the rim and onto the kitchen floor. He handed the mug to his mother and stooped down to wipe up the spill.

"Don't insult me, Owen," she said.

He looked up from where he knelt. From this vantage point, he saw her nostrils flare with each breath, the ligaments in her neck drawing taut, and that little clinching motion she does when she grinds her molars on the left side of her mouth.

"I don't mean to insult you, Mother," he said, meaning it.

"Then you should try harder not to," she said, moving to the sink and pouring out the coffee. "I'll tell the girls you were too busy for us." She marched toward the front door, the hem of her skirt bouncing on the back of her legs.

Owen stood and followed her. When he reached the front door, she had already crossed the brick walk and was headed down the driveway. "Nicole is the woman in my life, not Quinn," he called out. "Today is as good a day as any to accept that, Mother."

Blanche was at her car when she turned on her heels in a fury. "That Nicole," she shouted with propriety, "she'll embarrass us, Owen. She doesn't even know who her father is."

"So, you have finally reached your point," Owen sneered. "Momma didn't want any bastard woman soiling the family pedigree."

Blanche paused before getting into her car. She glared at her son and before thinking better of it, tossed one last hand grenade. "If I had asked Joel to join me, he would have said 'yes' right away," she snarled.

"Joel would have said yes to anything you demanded of him, Mother," Owen said. "He was scared shitless of you."

"He most certainly was not, Owen!" Blanche shot back. "How could you say such a thing?"

"Because it is absolutely true, Mother," Owen replied heartlessly. "He was so afraid of disappointing you that he would never say no to you. Hell, he even consented to seeing a psychiatrist even though he knew that having to disclose it on his medical school application would probably be the end of his dream of becoming a doctor."

Blanche dropped her head and began to openly and mournfully weep. "It wasn't my fault, Owen." She lifted her tear-stained face and begged her surviving son, "When are you going to stop blaming me, Owen?"

The song within your heart
Could never rise
Until love bade it spread
Its wings and soar.

In Memory, 1917

Joyce Kilmer

Chapter 13

Black Bird

Ruth and Nicole hardly noticed when Martin brought the plate of just-out-of-the-skillet bacon and a basket of extra biscuits to the table or when he refilled Ruth's coffee mug several times. Undisturbed by the noises of the staff cleaning the now empty tables around them, the women continued to talk long after the doors of the dining room had been closed and the last dishes were scraped and dunked into hot soapy water. The more Nicole told her grandmother about her relationship with Owen, the more relaxed she became. She even slathered butter on her last biscuit as she talked. "He always calls me his missing piece," she said. "At first, I was reluctant to get too close to him. I had my doubts about being in a long-term committed relationship, but he eventually wore me down. He seems so confident that our relationship will last. He can be so convincing. It's the lawyer in him, I suppose."

"It sounds like he's in love with you," Ruth observed cheerfully.

"That's what he tells me," Nicole replied.

"Do you love him?" Ruth asked.

Nicole hesitated. "Yes, I think so," she finally said.

"'I think so'? That's all you've got to say," Ruth asked. "That isn't much conviction."

"No, I love him," Nicole nodded, but only after a pause. "It shouldn't be such a hard thing to admit, but it is for me."

"What about it then?" Ruth pressed.

"What about what?" Nicole asked.

"You don't say, 'I think I might love you, but I'm not really sure.' You say, 'I love you like there's no tomorrow,' when you really love somebody," Ruth said.

Nicole's shoulders dropped. "I'm afraid of losing myself," she confessed, "if I let my guard down too soon."

"You don't lose yourself when you fall in love, my dear," Ruth said. "You discover more of who you really are."

"I don't know, Granna," Nicole said. "I don't know anything right now; I'm so torn up inside. We've been having trouble lately."

"Trouble? What kind of trouble, honey?" Ruth asked.

"We've been arguing a lot lately, and it's not like us," Nicole said.

Ruth leaned forward. "Two people can't spend much time together without arguing some every now and then, honey," she said. "Those who say they can, well, I think they just aren't saying that much to one another in the first place anyway."

"And that's yet another thing," Nicole continued. "We haven't been spending as much time together as we used to."

"Oh?" Ruth asked, raising her eyebrows.

"He's working longer hours," Nicole explained. She looked at her refilled juice glass; she had hardly touched it. "It's starting to bother me," she said.

"Why?" Ruth asked with concern.

Nicole sat back in her chair and slumped down deeper as if to hide under the table. "I tell him I'm upset that he spends less time with me. But the truth is," she said, looking away, "I'm upset with myself. I'm upset that it bothers me so much that he's not around as often as he was before."

"Go on, tell me about that," Ruth urged.

"I'm embarrassed," Nicole admitted. "It feels strange telling you all this stuff."

"Keep going, Nicole," Ruth urged. "You have already started."

Nicole lifted her hands from her lap, crossed her lean arms on the table, and leaned toward Ruth again. "I'm in love with him, and it scares the hell out of me. I'm so scared. I know it sounds juvenile, but for the first time in my life, I believe someone can hurt me, and I want to protect myself before he really does hurt me. I just want to turn and run sometimes."

"Why run from a man you love," Ruth asked as she reached across the table and rubbed Nicole's arm, "and who seems to love you in return?"

"To save myself before he hurts me," Nicole said, "before he can break my heart."

"What makes you think he would do that?" Ruth asked.

"Momma always told me, 'Never get attached to a man. It is just an invitation to heartache,'" Nicole said.

Ruth sat up, her eyes darting about. "She told you that?"

"I can't tell you how often," Nicole replied. "Whenever a boy showed an interest in me, she would spoil it. She would ruin it with her advice or one of her warnings. At first, it was, 'Boys are always up to no good; don't trust them,' and when I was older, it became, 'He doesn't want you; he wants something from you.' I began to believe two things, Granna. First, if I ever fell in love, it would only disappoint my mother."

"That's ridiculous," Ruth shot back. "Why would you believe such a thing?"

"Granna, in our house, standing on your own two feet was expected and demanded. Self-reliance was practically worshipped. Boyfriends were only a sign of my weakness."

"I'm sure she didn't mean for you to see it that way," Ruth said with sadness. "We aren't meant to be alone, darling."

"That's not what Momma said. 'Spending your life with somebody is unnatural; it's like trying to fly. We just aren't built for it,' she used to say," Nicole quoted her mother.

Ruth squinted, trying to see through the salty tears pooling in her eyes. "I didn't know she was still so hurt after all those years." She wiped her moist nose. "I should have insisted she come home to raise you, where she could enjoy the support of her family." Tears began to roll down her cheeks in heavy streams. "I'm so sorry, Nicole."

"Granna, don't cry." Nicole held out a dry napkin. "It's not that big a deal," she said.

"I don't know where your mother got such ideas," Ruth answered. She wiped her nose again and dabbed her eyes dry. "Had I known she was teaching you all this nonsense, I would've straightened her out good. I wouldn't have let her heart turn so stone cold. That's just not how I raised her. I would've made her understand that having the chance to be in love is a precious thing and that having your heart broken once was no excuse for refusing to fall in love again with someone else. I would have told her that we can all fly like a bird," Ruth continued, "if we just know where to find our wings."

"Now you've lost me, Grann," Nicole said. "What does 'find our wings' mean?"

"The song within your heart could never rise until love bade it spread its wings and soar," Ruth said.

"What?" Nicole asked.

"Joyce Kilmer wrote that", Ruth said.

"And who is Joyce Kilmer?" Nicole asked.

"Practically America's poet laureate!" Ruth exclaimed. "The poem means when two people are in love there's nothing that can keep them apart. Their love for one another lifts them above all else and brings them closer together. We can fly when we are in love. Life is not lived as it should be until you share it with someone. That's how I raised your mother; that's what I taught her."

"Frankly, I'm sort of shocked you say that, Granna. That's not how you raised her," Nicole shook her head. "You're the one who taught her that a woman doesn't need a man."

"I did no such thing," Ruth blurted out, hurt and disbelief thick on her tongue.

"I mean no disrespect, but yes, you did," Nicole continued. "You never married, you raised my mother by yourself, and you never let a man interfere with your life." Nicole struggled to maintain a calm disposition. "She learned everything about relationships from you, Granna," she said.

"Why would you say such a thing to me?" Ruth began to sob.

Nicole rose from her chair and went to her grandmother's side. She knelt down, gently took her hand, and kissed it tenderly. "I'm sorry, Granna, I didn't mean to upset you; I was just running off at the mouth, repeating what I was told. Maybe we should stop talking about it now."

"Obviously, we need to talk more," Ruth disagreed. "And obviously, your mother and I needed to talk more, too. A hell of a lot more."

"We talk, Granna," Nicole attempted to console her.

"I've already told you, chatting ain't talking," Ruth said. "All three of us chatted a great deal, but apparently, we didn't tell each other very much, now did we?"

"I'm sorry I upset you, Granna," Nicole said gently. "Please, let's change the subject."

"See what I mean?" Ruth pointed out. Her face pleaded for understanding.

"I'm just surprised by what you said; it's so unlike anything my mother ever said about you," Nicole responded.

"Just what did she say about me?" Ruth asked, her eyes penetrating, scaring off any notion Nicole might have of softening the truth.

"Mom saw you taking care of everything and everybody all by yourself, never asking for any help, and she thought you were the strongest woman she'd ever met," Nicole said. "She wanted to be just like you, completely self-reliant, not needing anybody. She got those traits from you, and I guess I got them from her."

"But I wasn't that at all," Ruth said. "I was just a young woman with a baby doing the best that I could."

"I'm so confused right now," Nicole said.

"Confused?" Ruth tilted her head.

"I've been struggling with how that part of me, our shared traits as Fischer women, survives in my relationship with Owen," Nicole confessed. "And now I am really confused, hearing you speak in such a heartfelt manner about spending your life with someone. I never thought of you like that. I thought the Fischer women were supposed to go it alone, that we proudly chose to be independent," Nicole explained. "It doesn't sound at all like you're saying that now."

"I never meant for your mother to think I didn't want her to get married," Ruth said. "Why would she think such a thing?"

"Because you never did get married," Nicole answered. "I suppose she assumed that's how it was supposed to be for her, too. Is that not how it was?"

Ruth clutched her napkin so tight her knuckles turned white and her nails dug into the palm of her hand. "I tried to tell her, but I see now that I waited much too long. Maybe that's why she wouldn't listen to me," she said.

"Listen to what?" Nicole pressed urgently.

At that moment, one of the hotel staff threw open the French doors and entered the dining room from the courtyard. The lingering smells of breakfast escaped outdoors, and a hungry blackbird leaped from a tree branch and flew inside to perch on a roof beam high over Ruth's table.

"My apologies, Miss Ruth," the man said. "I didn't know anyone was still in here. I'll get that bird out quick."

"No need," Ruth said, looking up at the bird. "He's here for a reason. He'll make his own way out when he's ready." She winked at the blackbird, certain it was looking back at her. She managed a weak smile.

"Whatever you say, ma'am," he said, leaving one of the doors open before heading to the kitchen.

"You said you believed two things, Nicole. What was the second?" Ruth asked, not taking her attention away from the bird.

Nicole sat silent.

"Tell me," Ruth insisted.

"I'm exhausted," Nicole dodged.

"Tell me, Nicole," Ruth pushed again.

The blackbird squawked as if to urge Nicole to speak.

"Men don't know how to love, they just know how to use," Nicole whispered, her head and shoulders heavy, bearing down and nearly pressing her body into the floor.

Ruth reached out, put her hand under her granddaughter's chin, and lifted her face so that she could look into her eyes. "Nicole, there is something I need to tell you. Something I should have told your mother years before I finally did. Something I haven't spoken of in so many years."

"You have a secret?" Nicole asked softly.

"Several, I'm afraid," Ruth confessed, "all of which I regret keeping hidden from the light of day. Your mother might have been easier on you had I told her everything when she first asked me to."

"What? What secrets?" Nicole asked, her eyes wide with alert curiosity.

"Not now," Ruth said. "We've been sitting here long enough. Shoot, it's almost lunchtime if you can believe that," she said, looking at her watch. "Come on, let's go for a ride first. I want to get some fresh air and take you somewhere."

Ah, if you will not take my hand
And bear me off across the land,
Then, traveler from Arcady,
Remain a while and comfort me.

Servant Girl and Grocer's Boy, 1914

Joyce Kilmer

Chapter 14

Family Plot

The women slowly pulled away from the Poplar Inn in Ruth's old Cadillac convertible, a red 1966 Eldorado. It was as wide as the Central Plains and so long that you had to nudge the front bumper against the back wall of the garage to ensure the garage door would close after you parked it. Ruth had insisted they take Big Red instead of Nicole's car. "That thing is too small to be safe," she warned and suggested Nicole would replace it with something larger.

The sun was high and had chased off the morning chill, so they put Big Red's canvas top down. Both welcomed the chance to feel the wind in their faces. It would dry their tears.

Ruth wore a scarf tied under her chin to hold her hair in place. Nicole wore only what she had put on that morning, and all that she carried with her was a purse. Her hair was dry, and she let it flap in the wind. She was steering with one hand and holding the other over her brow, shielding her eyes from the glare reflecting off all the chrome that surrounded her. She had forgotten her sunglasses; they lay in the passenger seat of her comparatively itty-bitty car, right next to her cell phone.

Rattling along, the front end of the Eldorado bobbing like a cork in rippling water, Nicole turned onto one street and then another, following the directions her grandmother doled out always at the last possible second.

"How about a little notice, Granna?" Nicole pleaded with a laugh, lurching into a turn.

"You don't always need to know where you're going, honey," Ruth said.

"I prefer it," Nicole said, "especially when driving this big old thing."

"Sometimes you just need to enjoy the ride. Now turn left here," Ruth pointed to a side street with one hand and held fast to the door handle with the other. "Besides, planning is often overrated, I think."

Nicole quickly slowed the car and turned onto the narrow street bordering the courthouse grounds.

"Stop there, just past the firehouse," Ruth pointed.

Nicole did as she was told and switched off the car, but the engine clanked for a few seconds, refusing to die quietly.

"Do you remember 'The Vault'?" Ruth asked.

"Who could forget it?" Nicole said excitedly.

The Vault, a café built inside an old bank, was one of Nicole's favorite Brysonville destinations because you had to walk through the safe door to get to the bathroom. It wasn't the kind of place you would go if you were on a diet. The tea was extra sweet, and they had never heard of skim milk. Nearly everything was cooked with butter and fatback, and chicken fried steak with white gravy was always one of the daily specials.

"I haven't been here in I don't know how long," Nicole said, looking through the big plate glass windows at the townsfolk resting their elbows on the tables inside.

"I know, that's why I brought you," Ruth said.

"I can't wait to go inside. But first," she reached across the expansive red leather seat and patted her grandmother's arm, "when are you going to tell me about your secret?"

"Patience, child, patience. Everything has its time and place. Right now, it's time to go inside."

Nicole smiled and shrugged, glad her grandmother seemed happy again and feeling a bit better herself, too. She got out of the car and went to help Ruth get to her feet. She grabbed the car door and, surprised by its weight, used two hands to pull it open. With Ruth standing at her side, she let the door swing back shut. It sounded like a can of nuts and bolts when it slammed into place.

"Is this thing going to fall apart, Granna?"

"I should give Big Red to you; you would be much better protected if I did," Ruth answered. "That tiny car of yours is a death trap." She took Nicole's arm, and they walked toward The Vault. Nicole pushed the door open and then stood back to let Ruth enter first. A bell above the door announced their arrival. "Look who I've got," Ruth called out as she stepped onto the worn black and white checked linoleum tile floor.

The owner of the café, a pudgy man who sampled the specials every day, wrapped in a white apron stained with coffee and gravy spills, stood behind the counter near the cash register. No Cussin' and No Fartin' signs hung on the wall behind him, over the chalkboard where the daily specials were written. Chicken-fried Steak, Pulled Pork Butt, or Trout Almondine, two sides and a drink, $6.95. He looked up from his newspaper and smiled as the women walked in. "Well, well, if it isn't the famous Miss Ruth," he said. "And who comes in here with you today?"

"It's Nicole, Elizabeth's daughter," Ruth said. "Put your glasses on, Garland. You're as blind as a bat."

"You don't say, Elizabeth's daughter?" he asked as he reached over the counter and extended his hand to Nicole. "Garland Oliver," he said. "Very nice to meet you."

"I'm pleased to meet you too," Nicole said, "again," enthusiastically clasping his handshake with both of her hands.

"Again? Have I had this pleasure before?" he asked.

"You remember me," Nicole protested. "You offered me a quarter to take a bite of pickled pig foot. I think I was ten years old at the time."

"That little girl can't be you," he said with a knowing laugh, pulling her closer so he could kiss her on the cheek. "How are you, Angel?"

"I'm fine; how are you?" Nicole answered.

"Not yet returned to dust, praise the Lord. Look, we still have those feet if you want one," Garland said, pointing to a glass gallon jar sitting on the other end of the counter.

"No thanks," Nicole answered, her nose scrunched up.

"I'll give you a dollar this time," Garland offered with a laugh.

"Not for a hundred dollars," Nicole said.

"She's got champagne taste, Ruth," Garland said.

"No she doesn't," Ruth snorted. "If she did we wouldn't be here to buy some of your day-old cake."

"Day old cake!" Garland barked.

"Just hush and give us two of your largest pieces to go, please," Ruth said.

Garland grinned, reached into the dessert case, and pulled out a large cake stand piled high with thick slices of sour cream pound cake, each wrapped tightly in plastic wrap. "They're still warm," he said. "I just cut it about fifteen minutes ago."

"Just the way I like it," Nicole said, selecting two slices. "How much?"

"On the house, in memory of your mother," Garland said.

"Oh, don't do that," Nicole responded appreciatively. "Let me pay for them."

"No, it's my desire to give them to you and to that old goat you're dragging around," Garland nodded toward Ruth.

Nicole said, "Thank you," while attempting to subdue a grin.

"Don't turn your back, Garland," Ruth warned. She tugged on Nicole's arm and led her toward the door. Moments later, back in the car, she unwrapped the cake and put both slices between them on the seat. "Don't you think this cake is going to taste better now, when it is a surprise to you, rather than if you knew all along we were coming here to get some?" Ruth asked.

Nicole nodded in agreement and asked, "Are we eating dessert before we have lunch?"

"It's not dessert; it's a special occasion treat," Ruth explained. "Besides, sugar is good for you. It takes the bitterness out of life. Have a bite," she said, pushing a slice toward Nicole.

"Where to next?" Nicole asked, breaking off a piece of the cake.

"Drive over to the church, please," Ruth answered.

"The church?" Nicole asked with amusement.

"It's not such a bad place to go," Ruth said, popping a morsel of cake into her mouth.

"Come on now," Nicole coaxed her grandmother, "what secret are you going to tell me, Granna?"

"Just park under the big tree out in front of the church," Ruth instructed. "It'll shade us while we finish this old cake."

Another span of moments later, they sat parked beneath the shade tree at the Hillside Baptist Church, its far-reaching limbs saving them from the burn of the midday sun. Except for its white-painted doors, window frames, and tall clapboard steeple, the church was built completely of stone. The steeple was repainted every year and could be seen piercing the treetops from the rocking chair porch of the Poplar Inn.

"Okay, we're here," Nicole announced. "Now tell me, Granna. The suspense is killing me."

"Calm down, child. It's my story," Ruth said, "and if you don't mind, I'll let it unfold according to my own comfort and inclination."

"Yes, ma'am," Nicole said.

"Now, first, I want to tell you more about our family," Ruth began.

"More about our family?" Nicole asked. "I thought you'd already told me everything?"

"Not everything, child," Ruth said, "not everything."

Nicole rolled her eyes none too discreetly and turned in her seat to lean against the door in an effort to shore up her patience.

"Did you know my father built that steeple?" Ruth asked, pointing toward the church's spire.

"No, I didn't. If you've told me before, I forgot," Nicole said.

"There used to be a smaller one, only about half as tall," Ruth explained. "After Mother died, Father gave the church the money to build this taller one, provided it was dedicated to her memory. He, Joshua, and Paul painted it once it was built; wouldn't let anybody help them. Paul was just a little thing, so he stayed on the ground and mixed the paint. Joshua was thirteen and quite brave for a young boy. He climbed the scaffolding with Father and painted right alongside him. Working a little at a time, it took them nearly a month to finish it."

"I remember Uncle Paul," Nicole interjected, "but I was too young to get to know him very well. I do remember that he had a funny middle name."

"Oh my gracious, child, if Mother heard you say that, you would be switched good," Ruth guffawed. "All us children were named after one of the books or great characters in the Bible. Me, Esther Ruth, then Joshua David, and after him, Paul Obadiah. Father wanted his children to have good English names, nothing German sounding like Boris or Leopold. We are descendants of German stock, for sure. Our ancestors came over from Germany around seventeen-hundred-something and settled in North Carolina, but Father was a proud American and wanted everyone to know it by the names he had given his children. It was Mother who insisted our names be plainly Biblical, so God-fearing she was. Father didn't like that much either at the time, him not being as devoted to the

Lord as Mother was, but she got her way. I remember how Mother used to sit in an armchair with one child in her lap, and others gathered around where we could all look at the pictures in the book she was reading to us, many times from the Bible, but sometimes from other books suitable for our ages, like Mother Goose and Peter Rabbit. Not every child could be in her lap at the same time, but she worked out a good compromise, letting us take turns at the beginning of each new chapter. She spoiled us good, Father used to say."

Ruth paused, slid forward, and leaned her head back against the car seat. She looked into the leaves moving gently in the wind. "Who knows how old the wind is or how far it reaches," she said.

"Granna, don't go and change the subject," Nicole scolded, wagging a finger.

Ruth smiled and continued. "You know, other than him fussing about her spoiling us too much, I never heard my parents argue, not once. If there were ever any disagreements between them, they settled it out of our sight and hearing distance. We always only heard about the decision they had made together. That's why I used to think discussions and explanations weren't necessary; I had never heard any while growing up."

"I don't know how you functioned without explanations," Nicole said. "Weren't you ever curious?"

"I was sixteen when she died," Ruth carried on without detouring away from her story. "I became a grown woman that day." She paused again, closed her eyes, and turned solemn. "It was the influenza that took her. She was mad with the fever in her last few days. I always said she died because she didn't get proper medical attention, no medicine until the last minute, and by then, it was too late. Like most good country doctors, ours did not keep abreast of changes in medical theory and practice but relied on the oft-repeated skills he acquired through trial and error, thankfully without too many errors and only two untimely deaths in his long career. Unfortunately, Mother was one of them. She's buried out back of the church."

"I want to go see her grave," Nicole said. "It's been such a long time since I was last here." She curled her fingers around the car door handle.

"Not yet, honey," Ruth protested. "Let me tell you a little more about Father first." She untied the scarf still wrapped around her head and folded it neatly into a square the size of a dinner napkin before placing it across her knee. "I'm afraid I'll start crying again," she said, stroking the scarf like a lap cat. She cleared her throat and swallowed hard, her gaze still fixed on the leaves. "Father was a man of strong emotions and sometimes downright bull-headed, but he was kind, too. He always told me that a man's primary duty is to serve and protect his womenfolk and that bravery in their defense was among the highest virtues. That was his most deeply held philosophy. He looked after me like that; he sure did. Perhaps a bit too much, but then how are you to know your father loves you if he ain't overprotective at times?"

"I wouldn't know," Nicole groaned.

"Oh, child," Ruth said quickly, reaching out to touch Nicole. "I'm so sorry. I'm not thinking as fast as I'm talking."

"It's a habit we have in common, Granna," Nicole said. "He's never tried to contact me," she muttered nearly inaudibly.

Ruth's heart ached. "I'm sure if he knew what he has missed, if he knew how wonderful you are," she said, "he would regret every minute he wasn't here for you."

"You're the only one who has ever really been here for me, Granna," Nicole said weakly.

Words wouldn't come to Ruth. As much as she wanted the two of them to talk more about things of substance, she had to admit that it could be a struggle for her, too. She rubbed Nicole's arm apologetically.

"I don't want to talk about him, Granna. Now, please, take me away with your stories."

Ruth smiled as best she could, and proceeded cautiously. "My father was a man's man. Regardless of the place or the size of the gathering, you could not help but notice Nicholas Fischer. He was very handsome and sturdy at six-foot-three; you could tell he didn't spend all his time behind a desk. He was well proportioned with his two-hundred-twenty pounds, and he was a powerful man, but it was his peaceful demeanor that held one's attention. That heartfelt serenity seemed to just reach out and take hold of you, and when you were with him, you felt the comfort of security come over you." Her eyes went downcast. "Everyone knew him, but everyone failed to grasp the weight of loneliness and guilt he carried. He simply couldn't forgive himself."

"Forgive himself? For what?" Nicole asked.

"He wasn't saved when Mother died," Ruth answered. "He went to church with us, but religion wasn't in his heart like it was for Mother, not until after she died. He believed his not loving the Lord sooner than he did was the reason she died so young. He said the Lord took her away from him because she was such a good Christian, and he was such a terrible sinner. 'God thought better of taking any chances I'd make a backslider out of her,' he told me." She dabbed her eyes with the scarf. "I'll never forget the day he got baptized. He was crying like a baby when the preacher brought him back up out of the water. People were yelling 'Hallelujah!' and 'Praise Jesus!' because they thought he was crying for joy. But I knew it was grief that had a hold of him. He was crying because the grief did not wash away with his sins."

"He's buried next to her back there, right?" Nicole asked.

"Oh yes, yes he is, right there with Joshua and Paul, too," Ruth said.

"Come on," Nicole said, reaching for her door handle again. "Let's go visit them now."

"No, wait." Ruth reached out and grabbed Nicole by the shirt sleeve. "I'm not finished. Eat some more cake and let an old woman talk. I've got still more to tell you."

"Are we finally getting to the secret you've been keeping from everybody?" Nicole asked.

"No, no, not yet. I want to tell you more about the family plot first," Ruth said. "There are things you still don't know or remember."

"What don't I know, Granna?" Nicole asked.

"There's more of our folk back there," Ruth answered.

"Who?" Nicole asked.

"Nathaniel," Ruth said.

"Nathaniel?" Nicole exclaimed.

"Yes, Nathaniel," Ruth said. "The cook, the biscuit maker."

"In the family plot?" Nicole asked, still surprised. "I mean, that's great, but I didn't know that."

"That was one of Father's last wishes; he loved ol' Nate," Ruth said. "In the early mornings, the kitchen was quiet except for the wooden bowl Nathaniel used when he kneaded his biscuit dough. It was always thumping against the table. That and the big tin coffee kettle perking a little song when the coffee bubbled up. That's when he and Father talked; they did every morning until Father had his first stroke. Bear and Nathaniel stayed with us all those years, helping to make the inn what it is and helping me look after Father. They were part of our family, pure and simple, he figured."

"Well, I guess I would have expected him to be buried at a black church, given the times, that's all," Nicole said.

"You know Brysonville is a different kind of place," Ruth said. "It always has been. Prejudice of any kind, racial, political, or social class, was not particularly tolerated here. We all had to work together to keep the town going after the Depression and what it did to business at the sawmill. Prejudice against the Yankees survived to a small extent, I guess, but only as a faint echo heard mostly by the elders in the community. Prejudice based on religion was not known either because everyone was either a Baptist or didn't attend church at all. Those who didn't attend gave a righteous purpose to those who did."

"So no one objected to him being buried here?" Nicole asked.

"Not a soul," Ruth said.

"Is Bear buried here too?" Nicole asked.

"Oh no," Ruth answered, "but he could have been if he had wanted it that way. He died the same year Joshua was killed in Europe during the war. When my brother's personal belongings came home on the train, Bear helped Father bring them to the inn, where we all gathered to see them and pay our respects. It wasn't but three months after that when Bear died of pneumonia. He knew it was coming, and he told me he wanted to be buried in the traditional Indian way, alongside the river, near the apple orchard at the reservation."

"How'd he know he was going to die?" Nicole asked, no longer so eager to get out of the car.

"He saw the signs," Ruth said. "Nature communicates, he used to say, everything has a meaning. The woodpecker is a sign of good luck; when you see one, you're supposed to clap your hands three times and make a wish. Once, he warned everyone living by the river to move to higher ground just because he saw a momma fox take her pups out of her den and run up a hill. That night a storm came and flooded the river by eight feet. There's no telling how many lives he saved. A bird flying into the house is a sign of death. The day he told me how he wanted to be buried, a blackbird was flitting around in the lobby of the inn, just over the place where we sat."

Nicole shivered, frozen in place, her mind abuzz. "You don't believe that stuff, do you?" she asked hesitantly.

"Sure I do," Ruth responded without an ounce of doubt.

"There was that blackbird this morning, the one in the dining room," Nicole recalled fearfully.

"Don't worry. I don't think today is my day," Ruth said.

"You can't leave me, Granna," Nicole pleaded, "not for a long time yet."

"Nicole, we all leave each other eventually," Ruth said. "And that is what family plots are for, to give us something to remember each other by."

"So now we can go see them?" Nicole nearly begged.

"I have to tell you about one more person," Ruth said as she sank even lower into her seat, her knees pressed against the glove box.

"You've mentioned everybody, haven't you?" Nicole asked.

Ruth extended her arm and laid her open palm on the seat. "Give me your hands, darling." Nicole complied, and Ruth held fast to both of her hands. They stared at one another. Nicole waited patiently, and Ruth delayed tirelessly. Ruth's neck and what little of her chest showed beneath her blouse soon turned red and splotchy.

"Who is it, Granna?" Nicole asked carefully, leaning closer. "Who else is buried back there?" Her eyebrows peaked with curiosity.

"Please don't be upset with me," Ruth nearly begged.

"Why would I get upset?" Nicole asked.

"Your mother is here, too," Ruth confessed in a weak whisper, nearly unable to speak over the clinching sensation in her chest. She could barely breathe.

Nicole stiffened and withdrew her hands. "What do you mean?"

"Your mother is here, Nicole. I buried her here."

"No, she was cremated, and you scattered her ashes in the mountains as you promised me you would," Nicole snapped, incredulous. "I brought the urn to the inn to decide with you where to spread the ashes."

"You did," Ruth acknowledged, "and I asked you to let me keep them for a while. It was winter then, and my daughter's memory would be better recalled if her remains were scattered during the spring when the mountains were being reborn rather than in the bleak gray of winter when the trees were naked, and the ground was cold."

"And I agreed," Nicole said, "because, as much as I tried to hide it, I was not ready to face the finality of scattering Mom's ashes."

"I just couldn't do it, Nicole. I couldn't. I know why your mother wanted to be cremated; she thought she was a disappointment to us," Ruth said, her voice halting, breaking between words. "She withdrew from us in life, and she thought by having her ashes thrown across the ground, she could withdraw from us in death, too, leaving no trace behind. Once the rain washed the ashes away, Nicole, there'd be nothing left of her. It'd be as if she never existed."

Her scarf was now soaked through, and her hands trembled as she fingered the hem along its edges.

"She was my only child, Nicole; she was somebody to me," Ruth continued. "I had to have something to keep, somewhere to go, a place to visit and to remember her by. Something to apologize to. Please try to understand."

Nicole sucked in deep breaths, determined not to sob, afraid if she broke down, she could never pull herself back together again. "I'm in shock," she said and looked away. "It's been nearly two years." She looked back at her grandmother. "Why did you wait so long to tell me?"

"I should've told you before now, I know," Ruth admitted. "But at one point in time, it was too soon to tell you; you were so despondent and all, and then, well, one day, I guess I thought it was too late to tell you unless it was in person." She tried to offer a smile. "I do that sometimes, not tell people what I should, when I should." Her lips trembled, and her eyes pleaded for forgiveness. "I thought the least I owed you was a chance to look me in the eye and tell me if you were disappointed or not."

Seeing that her grandmother was about to crumble under the weight of remorse and fear, Nicole opened her arms wide. The women moved toward one another and into a tearful but loving and relieving embrace.

"You need your mother, Nicole," Ruth said, "and she's here for you."

"I haven't cried over her in so long, Granna." Nicole sat up and wiped her eyes dry. "And I don't know why."

Ruth pushed Nicole's hair behind her ears and then brushed her moist cheeks with the back of her fingers. "You hold too much in, my little Lady Bug. You and your mother both got that curse from me. But I've learned that you have got to let yourself feel on the outside what you feel on the inside. You've got to learn that lesson too, Nicole."

"I've been so mad at her," Nicole said mournfully. "Mad for dying so young, mad for not encouraging me more, just plain damn mad at her."

"You've got to let it go, darlin', before it ruins you," Ruth urged.

"I can't get those memories out of my mind," Nicole said. She looked down and pulled on the loose thread of a shirt button.

"You can't choose what you forget about someone, but you can choose how you remember them, Nicole. You have to decide how you want to remember your Momma," Ruth said. "Now come on, it's time for us to go visit everyone."

The women exited the car, stepped onto the lush grass of the church grounds, and walked arm in arm to the small cemetery in the back. It was surrounded by a waist-high wrought-iron fence, and the old gate creaked as Ruth pushed it open. She gingerly led Nicole toward the center of the cemetery to a plot outlined with a thick granite border that rose above the grass. As they approached, Nicole noticed writing etched into the border.

"Unlock the door this evening, and let your gate swing wide. Let all who ask for shelter come speedily inside," she read out loud. "I've no idea where that comes from. What does it mean?"

"It's more of Joyce Kilmer's poetry," Ruth said. "As an innkeeper, I thought Father wouldn't mind these words. They fairly capture the way he ran the inn."

"Is that Momma's?" Nicole pointed to the newest of the six granite headstones that stood in the plot.

"Yes," Ruth said as she pulled Nicole past the headstones of her father and mother. "That's her," she said, standing before her daughter's marker, clutching her granddaughter's arm.

Nicole studied the headstone's details and then read out loud its inscription. "Esther Elizabeth Fischer. Beloved daughter and mother. 1937 – 1999." She paused, her eyes on the smaller inscription near the base of the headstone. "Remain awhile and comfort me," she whispered.

"It was my way of making sure she didn't spend time in eternity as alone as she did in life," Ruth said, her voice stronger. "It reminds me to sit with her awhile when I visit. I talk to her; I tell her how things are with me and with the inn. I like to think she's listening and likes what she hears."

"Why did you say you need to apologize to her?" Nicole asked.

"Parents don't always know the darker aspects of what they teach their children," Ruth said softly. "If we could know how our children would eventually cope with the legacies of their parents, we would have been better parents than we were. When I realized what I'd done, I needed to make amends."

"What could you have possibly done wrong?" Nicole asked.

"I'm telling you everything as fast as I can, Nicole," Ruth said. "This isn't easy for me."

"I'm sorry," Nicole responded. "I'm trying to be patient, but my head is spinning with so many questions."

"Do you like her stone?" Ruth asked.

"It's perfect," Nicole said.

"Are you sure?" Ruth sought reassurance and forgiveness.

"Yes, I'm sure. I'm so glad you did this," Nicole said. "It's really so much better this way, isn't it?"

Ruth, breathing easy again, her eyes beginning to brighten, nodded in agreement. They stood quietly, leaning against one another and looking at the markers. Finally, Ruth broke the silence. "I'm tired, honey, very tired. All this has worn me out. Besides, it's getting close to my nap time."

Nicole looked at her watch; it was almost three o'clock. She felt compassion for her grandmother and decided that the secrets could wait a while longer. "I'll take you home," she said, taking her grandmother by the arm to lead her back to the car, but the old woman planted her feet firmly in the gravel.

"Are you sure this is okay with you?" Ruth asked.

"It means more to me than you know, Granna," Nicole said. "More than I can explain."

Unlock the door this evening
And let your gate swing wide,
Let all who ask for shelter
Come speedily inside.

Gates and Doors, 1917
Joyce Kilmer

CHAPTER 15

REVELATIONS

They strolled back to Big Red hand in hand and in silence, soaking in the comfort offered by the peace and serenity of the church grounds and allowing new revelations to sink in. When they reached the car, Nicole opened the door for Ruth. "Thank you, sweetheart," Ruth said as she slid back into the passenger seat. Tired and emotionally spent, she suddenly felt much older than she had that morning.

Nicole watched to make sure Ruth was comfortable before shutting the door, this time not letting it slam. Then, she leaned down and kissed her grandmother on the top of her head. "Thank you, Granna," she said.

"What on earth for?" Ruth asked.

"For everything," Nicole said. As she walked to her door of the car, she saw that Ruth was reaching for the last bite of cake.

Noticing that she was being watched, Ruth smiled and held the chunk of cake up in the air. "It's so good," she managed to say through a mouthful of cake and icing.

"Some lunch, huh?" Nicole said as she slid into her seat.

"Better than pig feet," Ruth chimed.

"What isn't?" Nicole agreed with laughter.

"We'll eat smart tonight," Ruth said. "I promise."

"We certainly should. Now, let's get you home for your beauty nap," Nicole said.

"Yes, let's," Ruth agreed with a yawn.

The car engine shuddered at the turn of the key, and Nicole laughed. "It's safe because it won't go anywhere." Ruth laughed through another, bigger yawn. Her scarf was too moist to put back on her head, so she stuffed it in her pants pocket and let her hair fend for itself. Nicole drove the Cadillac back to the inn without the help of Ruth's directions. The women did not speak much to one another during the brief ride. Instead, they held hands over the place in the seat where the cake had been, and shortly, Ruth fell asleep before they were halfway to the inn.

Nicole drove slowly and entered turns at a snail's pace, trying not to toss her passenger about and not overthink all that had been revealed to her. The latter effort was without much benefit.

She glanced at Ruth and shook her head, the details of everything that had been disclosed still sorting out and sinking into her mind. There were so many more questions to ask, she thought. And a few old unanswered ones, too, long thought forgotten, that had dusted themselves off and demanded to be considered again.

Nicole knew her grandmother had remained at the inn after her child was born, helped her father run the business, kept her brothers out of trouble, and raised her daughter as a single parent. And she never married. In fact, Nicole couldn't remember in her lifetime when her grandmother had shown even the slightest interest in a man. It never occurred to her why. She had blindly accepted that that was the way Fischer women lived out their lives.

Ruth mumbled.

"Granna?" Nicole reached for her.

"Michael," Ruth said softly in the nearly unintelligible speech of deep sleep.

"Who?" Nicole asked.

Ruth opened her eyes and looked around, groggy and confused. "Did you say something?" she asked.

"You did," Nicole said. "I think you said someone's name."

"Oh, good. We're home," Ruth said, rising higher in her seat when she saw the inn's mailbox alongside the road ahead.

Nicole turned into the driveway and let the conversation drop. She drove to the front entrance of the inn to let Ruth out and then waited and watched as she climbed up the front steps.

Ruth turned and waved when she reached the front door. "I'm going to lie down for a while," she called out. Nicole nodded, returned the wave, and then drove to the garage. She lined up the old barge for docking and pulled it in slowly, inching forward until she felt the chrome bumpers contact the back wall. Not another inch, or the headlights might crack. She brushed the cake crumbs from the seat into her hand and scattered them on the ground as she walked back to the inn.

Before going inside, she looked down the bluff into the heart of Brysonville and saw the church steeple jutting out of the treetops. She smiled, her heart lifting as a breeze tossed errant strands of hair across her forehead.

Back inside, Nicole grabbed the doorknob of the family suite and found it locked. Reluctant to knock, sure that Ruth was already asleep again, she returned to the lobby and stopped at the registration counter.

"Pardon me. Have you seen Miss Fischer?" she asked.

"Yes," answered a young woman in a pantsuit and wearing a name badge who stood up from behind her desk. "She just went into her suite." The woman looked at her watch. "It's her naptime; she'll be out again around dinner time. If you come back then, I'm sure she will be delighted to meet you."

"I'm her granddaughter," Nicole replied.

"You're Nicole?" the woman asked.

"Yes, I am, and I'm locked out of the suite. You know my name?"

"Anyone who knows Miss Ruth knows about you. She talks about you all the time." The woman walked to the counter and extended her hand, smiling warmly. "I'm Susan Hilliard; I'm somewhat new around here. I work for the company that now manages the place for your grandmother."

"Hi," Nicole said as she shook Susan's hand. "I'm pleased to meet you."

"You're from Atlanta, right?" Susan asked.

"Yes, that's me," Nicole confirmed.

"And you're in consulting, right?" Susan asked.

"Right again," Nicole said. "I'm a human resources consultant."

"That's advising about insurance, hiring and firing, company policy, and stuff like that?" Susan asked.

"Well, yes, that, and I help companies figure out how to treat their people better and keep them happy so they will stay longer with the company," Nicole said.

"Like a workplace marriage and family counselor," Susan remarked, "helping people sort things out and stay together. I get it."

"Well, not exactly that," Nicole started to answer but changed her mind. "But then again, yes, something like that," she said.

"We were expecting you yesterday and had a nice room prepared for you, but we have already let it out," Susan said, "since you didn't check in."

"Oh, I stayed with Granna last night," Nicole explained. "I guess I should have canceled the room. I'm sorry."

"Oh, not to worry, it's okay," Susan replied. "Martin told us this morning that you were here. We were waiting to see where you wanted to sleep tonight."

"I'm going to stay with Granna again tonight," Nicole said, "but right now I'm locked out. Can you give me a key?"

"Sure, just a minute." Susan leaned down, rummaged around in a large drawer under the registration counter, and eventually produced a key. "Here it is," she said, holding up a key.

"Do you want to see my ID?" Nicole asked.

"No. I trust you are who you say you are," Susan said.

"How can you be so sure?" Nicole asked, struck by the woman's seemingly misplaced confidence.

"You look just like the picture," Susan said, turning around and pointing to a photo hanging on the back wall of the registration area, just above a small desk. It was Ruth's workspace.

Nicole stared at the photograph. It was her standing in front of the inn with her mother and grandmother. She remembered the day it was taken, just four months before her mother died. She had never seen it until now. "Why is a family photo hanging out here?" she asked.

"I'm sure you already know that's Miss Ruth's desk," Susan pointed behind her. "She likes to look at the photo occasionally while she works. She still clocks in once in a while. I've learned that she likes to keep a close eye on the business."

"May I see it?" Nicole asked, eyeing the photograph.

"Of course!" Susan said as she took it down and handed it to Nicole.

Nicole moved over to a nook at the end of the check-in counter and studied the photo. Her mother's face was gaunt and tired, and she was trying to smile. She wore a turban to hide her loss of hair. Ruth's hands were placed firmly on her daughter, one on her arm and the other around her waist, pulling Elizabeth toward her, and she was smiling wide. Nicole saw rhododendrons in bloom in the rueful gap separating her and her mother. There was only a weak smile on her own face, the kind you squeeze out for a photograph you don't want to be in. Her heart sank, and old regrets came back to life in her mind.

"Here," Susan said, reaching for a box of tissue and sliding it to Nicole.

"I'm sorry; I didn't even know I was crying," Nicole said.

"No bother. I'd be lost without my mother, too," Susan sympathized.

Nicole wiped her nose, her hands shaking more than she wanted them to.

"But you're not lost; you've still got Miss Ruth," Susan added.

"I don't know what to do," Nicole said impulsively, surprising herself. Before she could refrain, she said it again. "I just don't know what to do."

Susan struggled for words, and she felt awkward simply standing there looking at Nicole. All she could think of doing was reaching out and clasping her hands. Squeezing gently, she offered Nicole a comforting smile, just as she had always imagined an older sister would. "Whatever it is," Susan reassured, "it'll work itself out. Everything always works out in the end."

"That would be nice if that were true," Nicole said.

"Here's the extra key to your grandmother's suite." Susan turned Nicole's palm up and dropped the key into her open hand. "Go on in and take a nap yourself. It'll make you feel better."

"Sounds like a good idea," Nicole said agreeably, touched by Susan's kindness. She smiled weakly and gave back the photograph, grabbed a few more tissues, and headed back to the family suite.

"Oh, wait a minute. I forgot something," Susan called out. Nicole turned to find her leaning over the counter and waving a piece of paper in the air. "I've got a message for you," she said.

Nicole took it and scanned the slip of paper. Owen Montgomery called, it read.

"He called this morning," Susan explained, "but didn't say much. He just wanted to make sure you had arrived safely and knew that he had called."

Nicole searched in her purse for her phone and only then remembered that she had left it in her car. "Thank you," she said, folding the message and stuffing it in her pants pocket.

She let herself quietly into the suite and slipped down the hall to Ruth's bedroom. The door was ajar. She pushed it open just enough to peek inside. There she was, atop the bed covers, sleeping soundly. Nicole watched for a moment, listening for more names to be called out or perhaps the secret to be revealed. Hearing neither, she retreated and pulled the door closed.

She then crossed the hall and entered her room. She went to the dresser where she had dropped her car keys and glanced at the family photo once again before leaving the room to go back outside.

She walked into the living room and past Ruth's armchair, the place where she sat to watch television or read, a button tufted Queen Anne upholstered in chintz, the arms protected with broomstick lace doilies. Next to it was a small end table, and on it was a well-worn book. Nicole picked it up. The words "Trees and Other Poems, by Joyce Kilmer" adorned the cover. She smiled and remembered the phrase, "Let your gate swing wide." She gripped her car keys and slipped out of the suite, closing the door with a soft click as the latch slipped into place.

She waved to Susan as she made her way outside. The sun was halfway between tea time and dusk, and long shadows spread across the walkway, pointing the way to the steps that led to her car. She reached for the handrail and practically skipped down the steps, wanting to return Owen's call as soon as possible but in privacy. She jumped into her car and found her phone lying in the passenger seat. Eager and hopeful, she flipped it open - one missed call. She checked her voicemail.

Nothing. It was just like him, such a technophobe, she miffed.

Disappointed, she dropped the phone in her lap and, shaking her head, looked out the window and watched clouds drift over Brysonville. She sighed and wished she could see the future, to know what was going to happen before she made any more important decisions.

After a moment, she started the car and slowly approached the end of the driveway. After sitting with her turn signal blinking for a long pause of indecision, she finally rolled onto the street and headed toward the church.

His world has narrow walls, it seems:
By counters is his soul confined;
His wares are all his hopes and dreams,
They are the fabric of his mind.

Delicatessen, 1914

Joyce Kilmer

CHAPTER 16

GARLAND

Walking slowly toward the cemetery, Nicole resisted the temptation to turn around, race back to the inn, and throw herself under the bedcovers. Her chest rose nervously with each breath as if she were about to crest the first hill on a rollercoaster. She stepped across the granite border and into the family plot and, three paces later, was standing over her mother's grave. Grass flattened beneath her feet as she shifted her weight from one leg onto the other. In the distance, she heard the faint sounds of a small city closing up for the day, and male crickets were beginning to warm up to play their courtship songs. Her hair lifted in the occasional breeze, and goosebumps suddenly marched across her arms.

Still struggling to talk herself into doing what she had come to do, she pulled a crumbled tissue from her pocket and wiped her nose as she sat down on crossed legs. She landed close enough to her mother's headstone that she could reach out and touch it.

A half-hour passed, and the crickets' noise grew to a roar, and courage and words still eluded her.

And then everything but the drum roll of her beating heart fell silent as she cautiously reached out and touched the rough edges of the headstone. Her fingers traced tenderly over the letters of her mother's first name, Esther.

It was her first name, too, as was her grandmother's. Esther, a biblical heroine, she remembered from her days of Vacation Bible School. Esther was an orphan but a woman of strength.

Sucking in a deep breath and straightening her back, words began to tumble out of Nicole's mouth. Awkwardly and haltingly at first, but eventually with calm and liberating freedom. And the more she spoke, the farther her anger drifted away from her like thunder disappearing over the horizon.

She told her mother about her career, life in Atlanta, Granna and the inn, and finally, Owen. "I love him," she said, pausing when she realized her pulse had slowed to a steady, cleansing, replenishing drizzle after a storm. She reached for a few pebbles and shook them in her hand like dice. "But I haven't told him how much," she confessed and tossed the stones into the grass. "Not like I should."

Her attention was suddenly drawn to movement at the edge of the trees and shrubs growing at the back of the cemetery. A figure was leaning against a tree, watching her.

"Hello," she called out.

"I didn't mean to disturb your private time," a man said, moving out of the shadows. It was Garland Oliver.

"May I sit with you," he asked, approaching tentatively.

Nicole nodded and scooted over. "How long have you been watching me?"

"Not long," Garland said. "And don't worry, I didn't hear anything."

"You have someone buried here, too?" Nicole asked.

"Yes, I do. And I visit her every once in a while," he answered. He slowly lifted a finger and pointed to Elizabeth's headstone. "Seeing you today made me want to come visit her again."

"You visit my Mom?" Nicole asked, somewhat shocked.

Garland reached into the grass and plucked a few yellow dandelion flowers. He placed them on top of Elizabeth's headstone. "I do," he said.

"Well, that's very nice of you," Nicole offered, "but why?"

"To tell you the honest truth, I was in love with your mother, Nicole," Garland answered.

"Excuse me?" Nicole responded in even more shock.

"I was crazy about her'" Garland said. "I always was."

"You had a relationship with my mom?" Nicole asked.

"I wouldn't exactly call it a relationship," Garland said. "But I was smitten with her alright; she knew that I was." His shoulders wilted. "She was always very nice to me but otherwise never gave me much hope that something more could happen between us. I waited for her anyway, hoping she would one day change her mind."

Nicole put a gentle hand on his shoulder. "I didn't know," she said after a pause. "Will you tell me about her, please?"

"You don't want to hear my sad, unrequited love story," Garland said.

"I want to know more about my mother, Garland, and no topic is off limits." Nicole dropped her head and looked at her mother's headstone again. "Sometimes, I think I never really knew her."

"A lot of people would say the same thing," Garland answered. "But I knew her well."

Nicole rubbed her hands over her folded thighs, and sadness filled her eyes.

"She was afraid of relationships, that's all," Garland offered, "but most folks confused it with something else entirely."

"You mean anger, don't you?" Nicole said.

Garland nodded. His eyes were heavy, weary with hopeless longing. "She took it pretty hard when your father left; it changed her." He rearranged the dandelion flowers and added a few more. "You don't want to hear this ol' stuff," he said.

"I promise you, I do. Please go on," Nicole said, her eyes begging his.

He ran his fingers through his hair and looked off into the distance. "We met in high school. She was happy about everything back then. Dew on the grass, tulips pushing up in the spring, watching trout dart about in the river. I remember her laugh so well," he said.

"I can think of only a few times when I heard her laugh," Nicole recalled heavily.

"I wish you remembered her like I do, back before everything turned out the way it did," Garland said.

"I've always felt responsible, like it was me who ruined her life," Nicole said.

"That's crazy talk, Nicole. Don't think such things," Garland said. "You were the only thing that kept her going. Without you, I don't know what she would have done."

"She never told me anything about my father. I think about him sometimes, wondering who he is, wondering if he ever thinks about me. I've thought about looking for him."

"Why would you go out in search of someone who has never come looking for you?" Garland asked hesitantly.

"To try to understand why he left, to understand why he never wanted to see his own child," Nicole moaned. She clasped her hands together to stop them from shaking.

"There's nothing good that would come of that conversation, Nicole. Some things aren't worth knowing. He wasn't ready for the responsibility of marriage and fatherhood, that's all, leave it at that." Garland dropped his head. "It's best, I've come to believe, to invest your interest in someone who is interested in you."

"Did you know him?" Nicole asked gently.

"No," Garland lied.

"Granna never spoke of him either," Nicole said. She leaned back and stretched her legs out. "Why didn't she love you, Garland, if you were there to help make her pain go away?"

"We'd been friends for so long," he said. "I suppose it was hard for her to see me as much more than that. It goes that way sometimes."

"I'm not sure she ever loved anybody after him," Nicole said.

"She loved you," Garland retorted swiftly.

Nicole tried to smile.

"Now tell me about that man of yours," Garland diverted, putting his hand on her shoulder and shaking her, hoping not to delve deeper into his lingering heartache.

"So you were listening," Nicole said with a chuckle.

"Why don't you tell him that you love him if you really do?" Garland asked.

"I'm afraid to, I guess. You might have noticed we Fischer women don't do so well with love." She dropped her head back and looked up into the sky. "I haven't seen many examples of how well love rewards people, you know."

"You have to believe in love before it can work out, Nicole," Garland said. "If you don't believe in it, you can't surrender to it." He pulled up more dandelion flowers and gave them to Elizabeth. "There's no proof of the afterlife, honey, but I'm pretty certain you can't get there if you don't believe in it. Love's the same way; you have to believe two imperfect people can come together and make each other happy before you can really experience that kind of love for yourself. If you don't have that faith, you can't ever be as happy as you ought to be."

"You think that's what bothered Mom, that she stopped believing in love?" Nicole asked.

Garland averted his reddening eyes and nodded. "No matter how hard I tried, I just couldn't talk her into opening up again."

Nicole reached for him and hugged him, resting her chin on his shoulder. She rubbed his back. "I never knew," she whispered. "Thank you for telling me." She kissed his cheek. "I bet you could've made her very happy."

He nodded appreciatively. "I should leave you alone; let you finish your visit in private," he said, moving to stand.

Nicole let him break away from her hug but wouldn't take her hands off him, sliding her grasp down his arms until she held his hands. "Why didn't you find someone else, Garland?" she asked.

"Some people believe, I know I do, there's only one person for each of us," he answered. "Your mom was the one for me." He wiped his eyes and brushed his pants off. "Come by and see me again before you leave town. Lunch on me, anything you want." He turned to walk away but then called over his shoulder. "Maybe have another slice of cake, too," he laughed. He put his hands in his pockets and strolled across the cemetery grounds, back toward the center of town, where he could fall back in step with the life he had made for himself.

Nicole watched him, his shoulders still drooping, until he turned a corner and disappeared.

She turned back to her mother's headstone again. The wind had blown a few dandelions onto the ground.

"Garland loved you, Momma. I can see it in his eyes," she whispered.

Her throat tightened, and she fought back a sob about to leap from her chest. "I'm so sorry you were hurt, and I'm sorry you never gave love a chance again. But more than anything else, I'm sorry I've been mad at you for so long." The sob finally won. "I shouldn't have blamed you for everything," she finally blubbered as tears streamed down her face and dripped steadily onto her jeans. She wiped her nose with the back of her hand. After a while, she could breathe easily again.

"I don't want to be angry anymore, Momma. I want to be happy when I think of you," she said.

She leaned forward until she came close enough to kiss the headstone. Touching her lips to the granite, still warm from spending the day in the sun, she threw her arms around it, resting her cheek on the smooth surface where her mother's name was engraved.

By now, the crickets' courtship songs drowned out the sounds of passing cars and leaves rustling in the wind. Only the sound of the single thought on Nicole's mind rose above it all.

"I forgive you, Momma," she said as she sat up, "and I miss you so very much."

She reached down and pulled up a few blades of grass. Then, she reached for the fallen dandelion flowers and tied them together with the blades of grass, making a little bouquet. She returned Garland's gift to the headstone, and a broad smile came across her face.

"I love you, Momma. And I know that you loved me, too," she finally said.

She remained there in the shade of the tree and enjoyed recalled memories of childhood fun, heart-shaped sugar cookies, and goodnight lullabies, memories she hadn't let see the light of day in years. She then heard the happy music of wind chimes sounding from somewhere nearby.

Slender your hands soft and white
As petals of moon-kissed roses;
Yet the grasp of your fingers slight
My passionate heart encloses.

Slender Your Hands, 1911

Joyce Kilmer

Chapter 17

Confessions

Owen was still agitated. Wads of legal pad paper covered in scrawl, lobbed at a nearby trash can but falling short, littered a corner of the library. Nearly a whole shelf of the law books was now on the conference table, half of them sprawled out and open to pages of undetermined interest while the rest, already found to be keepers, were in a tidy stack with Post-it Notes hanging out from between the closed pages. A half-eaten egg and cheese bagel grabbed at a drive-thru window hours ago sat near the edge of the table alongside an empty take-out box of Pad Thai that came from the hole-in-the-wall place down the street. It was only a matter of time before another precious book was found useless and shoved away. Surely, something was soon going to fall off the messy table.

His shirt sleeves rolled up and his bite-marked pen in hand, he glanced at his watch. I'm running out of time, so skip dinner and push ahead, he decided. He rubbed his eyes, scratched his head with both hands, his hair already in a state of disorder, and once again scanned the pages of notes he had thought better of than to throw away. He pinched his lips between his teeth and shook his head. "Not a damn thing," he muttered, drumming the top of his pen on a clean sheet of paper. Ludlow Stovall hadn't called him back either. Where do tree huggers go during holiday weekends, he thought. "I'm eager to see how well you perform," Quinn's courtroom remark taunted him still, just like other hurtful statements she had made in the past. "I need an equal partner, Owen," she had said to him more than once.

"I'm every bit as good a lawyer as you are," he answered, his sulking expression not convincing anyone.

"Really? I earn three times as much as you do; it's embarrassing," she minimized him.

"I'm not ashamed of what I do," he said. "One of us must be the compassionate one."

"You're wasting your potential," she said. "Even some of your friends are laughing behind your back."

"Are you laughing at me, Quinn?" he had asked.

"I think it's clear we want very different things in life," she said unapologetically.

The engagement ring was a family heirloom. When he gave it back to his mother, she nearly snorted as she took it from him. He was making a mistake letting Quinn go, she said. And what would Colleen think now? "I didn't know you could be so foolish, Owen," she growled when she marched out of the room with the engagement ring buried in her clutched fist.

Owen pushed his chair away from the conference table and walked to a bulletin board where he'd pinned two aerial photos he'd found on the Internet. Taken just three years apart, they clearly demonstrated the loss of green space in Atlanta and the direct impact of aggressive development. A bad thing for the environment, some said.

Frustrated, he laced his fingers together and rested his hands on top of his head. Quinn had always been the competitive one, he thought, the aggressor. She knew how to make him feel like a fool.

His cell phone rang. He raced back to the table and grabbed it. Looking at it, he saw Nicole's name.

"Did you get my message?" he asked right away when he answered her call.

"Yes, just a little while ago. I thought you would have called last night," she said flatly.

"I tried but couldn't get you," he fumbled, regretting that he had not left a message. "I was buried under notes and law books until after one in the morning."

"So you did work last night?" Nicole said.

"You doubted me?" Owen asked.

"Maybe a little," Nicole answered after a short hesitation. "I'm sorry."

"You need to have a little more faith in me," Owen said.

"You must be tired," Nicole said.

"I miss you," Owen replied.

"Do you think you can make it up here?" Nicole asked.

"I thought you were leaving me," Owen said.

"I guess we both need a little more faith in each other," Nicole replied softly.

Owen sat down heavily in the conference room chair, his faith wearing thin, his words of affection too often left unrewarded. "It bothers me when you ignore some of the things I say to you," he said.

"I'm so sorry, Owen," Nicole answered. "That's really terrible of me. I haven't been as kind to you as you have been to me."

"Is everything okay?" Owen asked.

"Yeah, everything's okay. It's just that I've been thinking about things that I haven't thought about in such a long time," Nicole said.

"Things? What things?" he asked.

She sighed. "My mother."

Owen pushed the laptop away, sending it into an open book, and then a chain reaction set into motion. The last swigs of cold coffee in his cup on the edge of the table spilled onto some notes and then dripped onto the carpet. "What about her?" he asked, reaching for napkins and throwing them at the spill, missing it.

"I'm finally being honest with myself and realizing that I have a lot of unresolved issues with her," Nicole admitted. "I never stood up to her, and now that she's gone, I can't. I always bent to her will. I let her tell me what was best for me, and I resented her for it." She hesitated again. "But the truth is," she continued, "I'm not so sure I know what is best for me. I can't make a decision even now without worrying about whether she would approve of it. It wears me out, Owen."

"Your mother," he confessed, "has always scared me. I know that sounds silly, but she does. I never know what kind of mood you'll be in when she is on your mind."

"I understand. Sometimes she scared me, too," Nicole said.

"You can't go on trying to please your mother, Nicole," Owen said. He braced for a second chain reaction, but it didn't happen. He inched forward. "You have to start living for yourself and worrying about what you think."

"I found out that her ashes are buried here," Nicole said. "Granna didn't scatter them like I thought she did."

"You found out what?" Owen asked.

"She's buried in the family plot; I saw her grave today. And I've been thinking about all that's wrong between you and me."

Here it comes, Owen thought. He stiffened in his chair. "What do you think is wrong?" he asked carefully.

"I wish you were here," she said.

"I'm going to be there tomorrow," he said as he relaxed appreciatively and slumped down. "I've gotten a lot done and what's left should only keep me here a few more hours."

"So you're coming?" Nicole asked.

"Yes, of course I am," Owen answered.

"I'm so glad," she said. "You'll get to meet Granna."

"I told you I would get there," he said.

"I know, but after our fight, I thought you might decide not to come," Nicole admitted.

"I'd rather talk about this when we are together," Owen said as he fished around in his briefcase, looking for that picture he had taken at the beach, "when we can look at each other and feel the moment." He found the photograph and pulled it out. "From now on, I am going to work less and get my schedule back to what it used to be. I promise you that, Nicole, and it's a promise I'll keep." His thumb caressed her belly. "You'll see."

"What about the new practice you want?" she asked.

"It's becoming difficult for me to believe I could get such an opportunity out of this case. I think Whitaker just said that to get the extra hours out of me. He's using me to pay back some favor he owes," Owen said.

"That doesn't keep you from wanting it," Nicole said.

"What I want is to be happy," Owen almost whispered into the phone.

"Ditto," Nicole answered softly. "I mean, I want you to be happy, too," she said quickly.

"You make me happy, Nicole," he said.

"I don't know how," she replied. "I'm such a pain in the ass sometimes."

"Well, that's true," he said with a snicker.

Nicole let out an agreeable laugh.

"I'll be there tomorrow before lunch," he said.

"Drive carefully," she said.

"Aren't you going to tell me what you think is wrong between us?" Owen asked, bracing for what she might say.

"It can wait until tomorrow," she said, sighing with some relief. After a moment, she continued. "You know, Owen, although we don't give ourselves much credit, there are things that are right between us, too. Now finish your work and get up here."

No iron bars, nor flashing spears,
Not land, nor sky, nor sea,
Nor loves artillery of tears
Can keep mine own from me.

Madness, 1914

Joyce Kilmer

CHAPTER 18

DISCOVERY

Owen resumed his work with vigor, determined to complete his case preparation so that he could leave for Brysonville no later than seven o'clock the following morning. He looked at his watch. He decided to press ahead an extra hour or so.

He had found several precedents among the many planning and zoning decisions he had reviewed, and examples of case law in other states that he thought he could use in his arguments. He had prepared a few charts representing the loss of green space in Atlanta and other evidence of the negative impact of aggressive development. What he lacked was a compelling emotional hook, something that he could use to appeal to the judge's sentimentalities as well as his reason. He had initially planned to pit the small, minority neighborhood against the well-heeled developer, a David and Goliath story of sorts, but the comparison rang hollow for him, and he feared the judge would find it amateurish or even offensive. He searched his mind for something, anything, he could use for emotional impact. He found nothing.

But he kept going back to the newspaper article about Ludlow Stovall that Vanessa had found for him.

Ludlow Stovall, who worked as the city's chief arborist and who helped write the Tree Protection Ordinance five years ago, aggressively enforced the law and bristled when others overlooked obvious violations. When he was called into the office, Stovall thought his bosses wanted to talk about the possible misconduct he had alleged in the agency that was formed solely to enforce the Tree Protective Ordinance. Instead, they fired him, claiming he had filed numerous complaints against other employees. In reaction, he accused other arborists of routinely looking the other way when developers illegally removed healthy trees, approving construction sites when violations of the Ordinance were clearly obvious, and failing to regularly impose fines even after blatant disregard of the law. "It smelled funny to me," he told the newspaper reporter. It was documented that Stovall rubbed his thumb and fingertips together on a pretend stack of cash as he made that comment.

Stovall promptly appealed his termination, and the Human Resources representative told the reporter that the case was now under Executive review and that a decision could take weeks or months.

In the meantime, Stovall was nowhere to be found. Earlier in the day, Owen had located the arborist's address and driven over to his home where he found newspapers scattered in the driveway and an employment attorney's business card wedged between the front door and its frame. Owen pounded on the door for ten minutes before he gave up and then tried his neighbors' doors. Stovall hadn't been seen in days, they reported.

Before leaving, Owen looked around the house and discovered a covered motorcycle in the carport and a nice bass boat parked under a pole barn in the backyard. Nice toys for a civil servant, he thought as he climbed back into his car.

Owen snapped back into the present, opened his laptop, browsed the list of questions he had planned to ask Stovall when he got him on the stand, and deleted it.

He got up to stretch his legs and walked into his office, wishing he kept a bottle of scotch in a drawer like he'd seen so many other lawyers do in the movies.

He scanned the wall behind his desk and admired his diplomas and bar license, and then turned to his credenza to survey his trinkets, a small collection of outdated cameras, the heavy porcelain coffee mug his grandfather used for as long as he could remember, and a spinning globe his father had given him. He reached out to spin the globe, closed his eyes, and poised his finger above the rotating Earth, ready to poke it. Wherever it stopped, he thought, he would go where his finger landed and start over after he lost this damn case.

Before he could figure out where that was, he heard his cell phone ring again and realized he'd left it in the library. He ran in that direction. When he grabbed it, he was nearly out of breath. "Hello?" he managed to say.

"Are you okay?" the caller asked.

"Yes, Dad, I'm fine" Owen replied. "I just ran to get the phone before it went to voicemail, that's all."

"You're sure you're okay?" his father asked again.

"I'm fine," Owen insisted.

"Your mother's not doing so well," his father said.

"Oh? What's wrong?" Owen asked.

"Don't be coy, Owen. You know you upset her."

Owen waited.

His father did too.

"I'm sorry," Owen finally spoke first.

"You should be telling her, not me," his father said.

"I know," Owen said. "I'll call her soon, I promise."

"That will mean a lot to her. And to me, too," his father said.

Owen waited again.

"So how's your chest?" the doctor asked.

"Dad?" Owen began.

"Yes, son?"

"You work a lot of hours; you always have."

"I do," his father admitted.

"Did it ever get in the way, I mean, between you and Mom?" Owen asked.

Dr. Montgomery cleared his throat.

Owen sat down. "Dad?"

"We've had our disagreements about the hours I keep," the doctor confessed.

"How do you handle it," Owen asked. "How do you make it work?"

The doctor, father, and husband sighed heavily. "We've both had our disappointments about how things have turned out, Owen, but we also still love each other in spite of our disappointments and each other's shortcomings. We just make it work." A long pause passed slowly. "We just make it work," he repeated.

"So you still think she's the right woman for you?" Owen asked.

"Even at my worst, Owen, your mother always remembers who I can be when I'm at my best. It's hard to ask for more than that."

"I'll call her in the morning," Owen said again.

"Owen, there is something you should know," his father's voice turned more serious. "You think Joel ended his life because your mother took him to a psychiatrist. That's not why, not at all why. Your brother

153

was dying, Owen, and he couldn't bear to have us see him go through what he would have if he had endured the disease until the end."

"What are you saying?" Owen asked, stunned.

"Do you remember that Sunday when there was a blood drive after church?" his father asked.

"Yes, of course," Owen answered. "That's when we found out Joel was afraid of the sight of blood."

"No, he wasn't," Dr. Montgomery pushed back. "It was the questionnaire that made him back out of donating blood."

"The questionnaire? Owen asked. "Dad, I don't understand what you are telling me."

"One of the questions for male donors was, 'Have you ever had sex with a man?' That's what made Joel stop. He knew if he told the truth, he would be disqualified as a donor."

"Because he was gay?" Owen asked.

"Yes, because of the fear of AIDS-contaminated blood," his father explained.

"But Joel didn't have AIDS," Owen said.

Doctor Montgomery hesitated.

"Dad?" Owen prodded.

"He didn't know it at the time," Doctor Montgomery said, "but Joel was a very responsible person, so he chose not to donate. Later, we agreed that I would order the tests for him."

"And?" Owen pressed.

"Unfortunately," his father said, "his caution was warranted. That's why Joel did what he did, Owen. He wanted to avoid the shame and humiliation he had convinced himself he would bring to us. He wouldn't listen to me tell him it would not be that way."

"Doctor Montgomery, dial extension 1104, stat," a voice blasted out from the hospital's overhead intercom.

"I've got to go, Owen."

"I know," Owen said, choking back tears.

"But first, I want to tell you that your mother needs you, Owen. She is not responsible for what happened. Call your mother, son," he said just before he hung up.

Because my Love has eyes that taste glory,
That breathe of love, that are as red as wine,
My days and nights are a pleasant story
Told in a valley sweet with rose and wine.

Tribute, 1911

Joyce Kilmer

CHAPTER 19

SECRETS

Ruth stirred from her nap and arose, feeling rested and spry but annoyed that she'd slept much later than she had meant to. It was dark in her room. She turned on a lamp and checked the alarm clock. It was nearly dinner time. Standing before a mirror, she tried to smooth out the wrinkles in her clothes and combed her hair back into place with her fingers. Thinking for a minute that she should change clothes but then decided it wasn't necessary, she went from room to room searching for Nicole. She wasn't in the guest bedroom or the living room, and no answer came when her name was called.

Ruth moved on and searched the lobby and then the rocking chair porch, but still found no sign of her grandchild.

"She left a while ago, Miss Ruth," Susan called out, seeing Ruth pace the floor.

"Oh? Where'd she go?" Ruth asked.

Susan shrugged. "She didn't say, but I know she is coming back. She said she was staying with you again tonight."

"She'll be back alright; she'll be hungry soon," Ruth chuckled. Susan nodded with an agreeable smile and returned to her work. Ruth decided to sit in her rocker and wait for Nicole's return, but not before returning to the family suite to retrieve her Joyce Kilmer book of poems.

She had cherished that book for more than sixty years, and although it was well worn, the pages yellowed and tattered along the edges, and the spine cracked from being opened so often, she would not consider replacing it with a new edition. It was a priceless treasure, a possession she had kept longer than any other.

Book in hand, she took her place on the rocking chair porch and began to read. Although it was late and the events of the afternoon had

156

drained her, the nap proved restorative and she didn't yawn even once as she carefully turned each page. She was nearly halfway through the poems when Nicole finally stepped out onto the porch.

"Curled up with something good, I hope," Nicole said.

"Just some sweet little poems," Ruth answered. She closed the book and looked up. "Where have you been? I woke up and couldn't find you."

Nicole knelt down in front of her grandmother's rocker. "I went back to the church to visit Momma and talk with her for a while," she said.

"You did what?" Ruth asked with surprise.

"I went to visit Momma to talk with her for a while," Nicole repeated.

"What on earth possessed you to do that?" Ruth asked, surprise still thick in her voice.

"Well, the phrase you put on the marker beckoned me for one thing," Nicole said, "and then you telling me I can choose how I remember her, for another."

"So you went to get reconciled," Ruth concluded.

"Yes, I guess I did."

"Did the two of you work it out?" Ruth asked.

"I know I look like a mess," Nicole said. "I cried a good bit but I feel much better now."

"Are you still mad at her?" Ruth asked.

"No," Nicole smiled. "Not anymore."

"Good. I'm so glad." Ruth reached out to touch Nicole's cheek. "That makes me happy. Did any good memories come to mind?"

"Yes," Nicole laughed. "A good one indeed."

"Well, go on, tell me. I want to hear it," Ruth urged.

Nicole sat down on the porch and leaned back on the support of her outstretched arms and hands. She looked into the darkening sky and saw the moon rising just above the mountains. It was encircled in a halo, diamond dust, she remembered her mother told her once. "You'll probably think I'm silly," she said.

"What if I do?" Ruth asked. "Old women like me need things to laugh about now and then."

"I remembered a day when I was twelve years old," Nicole began, "and about to get braces. I was upset about having to give up crunchy and chewy things to eat. Momma felt sorry for me, and said I could eat anything I wanted one last time before the braces went on. That day, I chewed a whole pack of gum and a handful of saltwater taffy. Then, we went to a movie and I ate an entire box of Cracker Jack all by myself."

"Glory, you ought to have been sick," Ruth laughed, holding her belly.

"Oh, I haven't gotten to the good part yet," Nicole continued. "Next, I wanted a slice of red velvet cake with butter cream icing from Melvin's, a little diner in Atlanta. Even though I could've still eaten that with braces, she took me anyway and we sat at the counter and each ordered a slice. When it came I decided I wanted ice cream, too. The waitress told me no one eats ice cream on red velvet cake. That's when Momma told her to give me two scoops."

"What kind did you get," Ruth asked, her eyes twinkling.

"Chocolate fudge!" Nicole rubbed her stomach and licked her lips as if she could still taste the sweet abomination.

"Oh my, please stop. My stomach's turning over," Ruth protested.

"Mine did!" Nicole laughed. "Alongside the road on the way home. After that, I was begging for those braces. I never wanted to eat dessert again!"

"So," Ruth, her laughter trailing off, turned serious with her question, "what does that story mean to you?"

Nicole looked to the moon again and her smile never left her face. "Mom wanted me to be happy," she said.

"She did, darlin', I know she did," Ruth agreed.

"I told her I loved her," Nicole went on.

"She loved you, too, little Lady Bug," Ruth said.

"I know," Nicole said, beginning to believe it.

Ruth began to rock nervously. "I should have told her that myself more often than I did," she said.

"She knew you loved her," Nicole reassured her grandmother.

"Perhaps, but knowing it doesn't keep one from wanting to hear it every now and then," Ruth stammered.

"What really happened between you two?" Nicole asked. "It's time that I know."

"I was stubborn," Ruth said with a heavy sigh. "I wouldn't tell her who her father was. It turned her against me. In later years, after she moved to Atlanta, your mother would come with the Williams family whenever they visited the inn, but she spent most of her time with them instead of me. In her own way, she was letting me know she had found for herself a new family. I always suspected they visited so often out of compassion for me. They were good people providing a way for me to see you. I'll always be grateful to them for doing that."

"I'm so glad that none of this is very familiar to me," Nicole said.

"So am I," Ruth agreed quickly. "You being too young at the time to remember those goings-on is probably what gave the two of us a fighting chance to be friends."

"We're much more than friends," Nicole reassured, "we're family."

"Praise the Lord," Ruth said, "for he is merciful!"

"Why wouldn't you tell her about her father?" Nicole sat upright, her ears tilted forward.

"I thought I was protecting her somehow," Ruth began, "that keeping her from knowing that she had a good daddy but lost him. You can tell yourself something so many times that it somehow becomes what you really believe. It was really shameful of me. I guess not knowing about her father, and then with what happened with my father, was too much for her to deal with. No wonder she was so unhappy."

"I don't understand," Nicole said. "How could that protect her? It seems like it would only hurt her more."

"I was already being ostracized for being pregnant out of wedlock, so at the time it seemed that to add to it that her father was a Catholic would have only resulted in even more condemnation of my child," Ruth said. "It seems so petty today, but back then it was regarded as a serious matter."

"What, that he was Catholic?" Nicole asked.

"Yes," Ruth answered. "No one wanted to see the Pope get a foothold in the U.S. of A."

"Good grief," Nicole groaned.

"Be merciful, Nicole," Ruth insisted. "I'm trying to help you understand the times, hoping it will help you to understand my choices."

"That's a fair request," Nicole said. "Please go on and I'll keep my lips zipped."

"Thank you," Ruth said. "Now, everyone eventually knew the man who was my beau was a Catholic. So, to refuse to acknowledge who fathered my child was the only way I could think of to save Elizabeth from at least one of the reasons people might look down on her. As time wore on, the matter had been kept private for so long that it eventually became a well-guarded secret." Ruth hesitated a moment. "The longer you stay quiet about something," she continued, "the harder it is to bring it back out into the open, I suppose. Once I had decided not to confirm his identity, I just continued to keep his name a secret. I was constructing a reality that was less painful for her, and for me, too. My secret protected me as well if you want to know the truth about it."

"I still don't understand," Nicole said.

"I simply could not imagine living every day bearing the pain of losing him," she abruptly stopped rocking in her chair. "It nearly killed me several times."

"What are you saying, Granna?"

"You know what I'm saying," she admonished Nicole. "Don't make me admit it out loud."

"You thought about…" Nicole began to ask carefully.

"I hung on only by a thread for years. It was the inn that kept me going," Ruth answered quickly.

Nicole fell back onto the porch and draped her arms over her eyes. "There's been so much loss and grief in this family." She exhaled deeply.

"Yes. We've all suffered one way or another," Ruth admitted.

"I wish you had told Mom about her father," Nicole said mournfully.

"I started to tell her about him after you were born," Ruth said, "but by then, she had already closed her heart and ears to me; she just wouldn't listen."

Nicole bolted upright and grabbed the armrests of Ruth's rocker. "So you did tell her?" she asked.

"Yes, at least as much as I could before she refused to listen any longer. Eventually, she dismissed me as a wacky, irrational, old woman, so we stopped talking to one another for pleasure. If it were not for her boss, that doctor, keeping me informed, I would have missed out on a lot of good news back then."

"She never told me that she knew," Nicole said.

"Sweet Jesus. I kept a secret from her, and she kept one from you. Dear Lord, please forgive me." Ruth buried her face in her hands and her body trembled as she wept.

Nicole took her grandmother into her arms, rubbed her back, and whispered all the soothing words she could think of. They took effect, but slowly.

The tears soon subsided and Ruth sat up. "I'm sorry for squalling so much," she said.

"We've both cried our share today," Nicole said.

They looked at each other and smiled awkwardly.

"While I was there, Garland showed up," Nicole volunteered. "He told me he was in love with Mother."

"He was, poor thing," Ruth confirmed. "He pined for her affections for so many years."

"Why didn't she love him," Nicole asked.

"Nicole, your mother had decided she would never love anyone again," Ruth said.

"Why didn't I know about Garland before now? Why are there so many secrets around here?" Nicole asked.

"Sometimes the heart just isn't strong enough to admit to what the eyes have seen, Lady Bug," Ruth said. "Besides, he wouldn't want anyone to have pity for him."

"You say we don't talk enough", Nicole said. "How can we really talk to one another if we're always so careful about what we say?"

"I'm not feeling well, Nicole," Ruth said. "I think all that sugar went to my head. I should eat some real food. Please help me up," she asked, reaching for Nicole's hand. "I got stiff sitting here waiting for you to drag in."

Nicole frowned at the avoidance of her question but acquiesced and gently pulled her grandmother up from the rocking chair.

With the book in hand, Ruth looped her arm around Nicole's and together they headed into the lobby. "Let's talk about it over a good meal," she said.

"I spoke to Owen," Nicole said. "I think he'll be here tomorrow."

Ruth slowed their pace and looked into her granddaughter's gaze. "You never did tell me why you came up here by yourself last night," she said.

"He's obsessed with a case that's going before a judge on Tuesday," Nicole explained. "He claimed he needed more time to get ready. We had a bit of a tiff about it. I think he works too much. But now I'm glad he couldn't make it because I got the chance to be alone with you, and then with Momma, plus learn all these things you've told me. These conversations probably wouldn't have happened if he were here."

"Fightin's not good," Ruth said.

"It's not like he has a murder case," Nicole answered. "It's just about some trees."

"Some trees?" Ruth inquired.

"Yes. There's an old neighborhood in Atlanta where, years ago, the residents planted trees on Arbor Day. Now a developer wants to cut them down to make room for a parking garage. Owen is trying to stop him."

"You're kidding," Ruth said, stopping in her tracks.

"See, I told you it wasn't that big of a deal, but to him, you'd think it was the end of the world." Nicole heard herself and, ashamed, looked down at her feet. "I should try to be more understanding. He's got a lot on him."

Ruth, her eyes open wide, unlaced their arms and then shook Nicole. "Lady Bug, your Owen is my Michael."

"Michael? Who's Michael?" Nicole asked.

"Michael Kirkpatrick. He gave me this book way back in nineteen hundred and thirty-six," Ruth said. "He was your Momma's daddy and your granddaddy."

Because the road was steep and long
And through a dark and lonely land,
God set upon my lips a song, and
And put a lantern in my hand.

Love's Lantern, 1914

Joyce Kilmer

CHAPTER 20

MICHAEL

"Dear Lord, we are thankful for what we are about to receive, and for all the blessings we receive at thy hand. In Jesus' name, we pray, Amen." Ruth squeezed Nicole's fingers as she finished the blessing and then, with just as much purpose, reached out to pick up a bowl of vegetables and began to load her plate.

The meal was served family-style, with crockery bowls filled with fried buttermilk chicken, field peas, creamed corn, sliced tomatoes and onion, and fried okra. Ruth asked that a pitcher of tea be left on the table so they could talk without interruption by the wait staff. She reached across the table to reposition her book, making sure it was well out of the way of anything that might spill on it.

Nicole sat patiently, pushing her okra around on her plate, waiting for her grandmother to tell her about Michael Kirkpatrick, a man and another story she had never heard. She watched Ruth chew a few bites of chicken thigh and wash it down with what started as a dainty sip but became a big gulp of tea.

Finally, Ruth wiped her fingers clean, adjusted her glasses, and faced Nicole. "As I have said all along," she began, "you must start at the beginning. It was nineteen-thirty-six, and I was twenty years old. Mother had been in heaven for nearly four years by then. The Olympic games were in Berlin that summer. I remember how Nathaniel was particularly interested in the Negro athlete Jesse Owens. You could hear him in the kitchen hollering at the radio every time that man ran. Gene Autry, and Bob Wills and His Texas Playboys were who people usually listened to on the radio around these parts. Gone With the Wind was the popular novel of the times, and nearly everybody had a subscription to Reader's

164

Digest. My little brothers wouldn't read anything but Captain Marvel and Lone Ranger comic books. It was a historic time, right in the middle of the Great Depression. Even though times were hard in those years, big things were happening. The Empire State Building was dedicated, Charles Lindbergh's son was kidnapped, and Bonnie and Clyde were shot to death on a dirt road. It was a hard time, but yes, ma'am, a lot was happening everywhere you looked."

"All this is leading up to Michael?" Nicole asked, "Or are you just stalling?"

"Be patient, Nicole, my goodness," Ruth answered. "You need to understand the times in order for the rest of the story to make any sense to you. It was a different time back then. Everything was different, nothing like today. Now hush, eat something, and let me talk."

"Yes, ma'am," Nicole said, trying to muster patience.

"Go on, eat," Ruth urged. "You said you were hungry."

"Yes, ma'am," Nicole said again, this time picking her chicken up with her fingers and taking a bite.

"Now remember, for many years before then, lumber had been the chief moneymaker around here," Ruth said. "The Brysonville Land and Timber Company bought the rights to several large parcels of land in the mountains, and it bought trees from farmers clearing their land to make way for more tobacco and corn crops. The company cut down trees and then hauled them down the mountain to the sawmill for milling. The sawmill bought the fallen trees and made boards out of them. Some lumber stayed here for furniture making or was milled into fancy paneling and the rest went to places all over the country. Brysonville paneling went far and wide to cover the walls of libraries and billiard rooms of the well-to-do all across America. As long as you could hear the sawmill singing, as they used to say, you knew there was work in Brysonville. But that all changed when the Depression came."

"What changed?" Nicole asked, trying not to roll her eyes, eager for the storyteller to get to the point.

"People stopped building," Ruth went on. "Nobody was buying furniture or paneling billiard rooms at that time. The sawmill couldn't sell what lumber they had on hand, and it had started to buckle from the sun and rain, so the mill had to let a lot of folks go. It was hard for everyone, even the inn. We still had guests but not as many, and the dining room wasn't full of locals anymore."

"How'd you get by?" Nicole asked. "It sounds like the situation was pretty dire."

"Oh, it was. We started to do most of the work around here ourselves to keep expenses down," Ruth explained, "and for a while, only Bear and Nathaniel worked for us until we started getting busy again. Like I said, Father had made good money in the past by selling timber, so we had some savings tucked away, thank goodness. You know, it was the timber that first set me and Father against one another."

"I've never heard that you two didn't get along," Nicole said. "If this is the big secret, please tell me more."

"We got along famously, always did until the evening the Lamberts came here to visit," Ruth recalled. "They're the people who owned the mill."

Nicole leaned forward on her crossed arms, uninterested in what food remained on her plate. "What happened then?"

"Father still owned thousands of uncut acres on the mountain; it was Mother's favorite spot in the world. She loved that land and the trees that stood on it. She felt close to God there, she used to say. Father promised he wouldn't sell it off, so she would always have a special place of her own to go to. But Mother was gone by then, and lots of people we knew weren't working. The Lamberts were worried about keeping the sawmill; they still owed money on it. So they visited Father one night and convinced him to sell the timber. They said they had some buyers up North looking for good lumber and that it would be good for the whole town if he would let them cut the trees. I think he gave in to them because they reminded him that they had helped him by giving him a job while he was in law school, and later, when he was building his legal practice, they sent people to him for land title work. I guess they did help him to some extent, but not so much that he owed them anything they asked for, or at least I didn't think so. But he felt like he had to do it, with everyone in so desperate a situation."

"It sounds like he had noble intentions," Nicole observed. "You have to give him credit for that. So why, then, did you have a spat with him?"

"He promised Mother he would leave that land be, and I felt like those were words he had to keep."

"So he agreed to sell the trees, your mother's favorite place?"

"Yes, and I was furious with him," Ruth said.

"How does all this lead to Michael?" Nicole blurted out, unable to refrain herself a moment longer.

"I'm getting there, Nicole. Now hush; this is my story, and I'll tell it like I want to." Ruth drank more tea and waved at guests seated nearby. "I begged him not to sell," she continued after a moment. "I was stubborn and prideful at the time, and I thought I was the woman of the house. I let it get to my head, I guess, because I expected Father to respect my wishes like I had a say in the matter. He wouldn't listen to me. He said it was the right thing to do: good Christian generosity. I think that's another reason he agreed to sell the timber; he said it was a test. Either keep the trees or do something sacrificial for the struggling people of Brysonville. He made up his mind that Mother would have approved of him helping everybody."

"What did you do next? Get to the good part," Nicole pleaded. "Please, get to Michael. I can't wait another minute."

Because my Love has hair that smells of flowers,
That is as soft and cool as forest shade,
Therefore the tale of all my blissful hours
Be writ in gold and at her footstool laid.

Tribute, 1911

Joyce Kilmer

CHAPTER 21

THE LETTER

"I have been reading Joyce Kilmer's poems since grade school," Ruth said, pointing to the book. "He's my favorite poet. He was a big hero in the First World War, and the Veterans had been petitioning the government to set aside some forest land to honor him."

"Why a forest? Why not a statue somewhere or a federal building named after him?" Nicole asked.

"Where did you go to school, Bug?" Ruth teased. "He wrote 'Trees.' We all had to learn it and recite it on Arbor Day. Only a stand of majestic trees like those poplars up on the mountain at Mother's place would be a fitting memorial to Joyce Kilmer."

"You're right," Nicole said as convincingly as she could, scarcely succeeding. She didn't know the poem. "What was I thinking?"

"Too much television and fast living, that's what I think happened to you," Ruth said, tilting her head back and eyeing her granddaughter with suspicion. "Now listen and learn something. I read in the paper one morning that the U.S. Forest Service was looking to purchase some land to appease the veterans. I wrote a letter and sent it to Washington, telling them that if they wanted to buy some land, they should come down here. I told them it was urgent, that they had to come to Brysonville as soon as possible."

"And they came down just like that?" Nicole asked.

"Well, I had to lie a little to get their attention," Ruth confessed.

Nicole shook her head and chuckled. "You did what?"

"I told them the Lambert's were going to destroy Indian burial grounds so they could get to the timber, and if somebody didn't come quick, there was going to be an uprising at the reservation," Ruth said plainly.

"You did not," Nicole grinned.

169

"Bear helped me think of that," Ruth said. "Well, they believed it, and that's when he came."

"Who, Momma's daddy?" Nicole asked, motioning with her hand for Ruth to hurry, and nearly knocked over her glass of tea.

"Yes, Michael Kirkpatrick," Ruth said, her face all aglow. "I remember the day he walked into my life. I knew he was special as soon as I laid eyes on him. He came up the steps and knocked on the door; he was too polite to walk into the place without permission. I went to the door to greet him. 'It's okay to come in, sir; it's a hotel,' I said as I pushed the door open for him. It embarrassed him, but I didn't mean it to. I was taken with his good looks right away. He was tall, had reddish blonde hair, a nice square jaw, and wore wire-rimmed glasses just like Teddy Roosevelt. And he was wearing a uniform; it was all starched and pressed crisp and showed off his broad shoulders. His back was as straight as a ruler. A fine-looking man, he was. 'I'm here to see Miss Fischer,' he said, 'on official U.S. Government business.' I reached out to shake his hand and it thrilled me when our fingers touched. 'I'm the one who wrote the letter,' I said. I don't know what he was thinking at the time, but he kept staring at me like he didn't believe me."

"Or maybe he'd never seen such a pretty mountain gal before," Nicole teased, enthralled. She loved how her grandmother's eyes sparkled when she mentioned Michael. "I remember what a fresh, natural beauty you were in all of the old family photographs I've seen," she said.

"Maybe," Ruth grinned. "About that time, Father entered the lobby, and he overheard us talking. 'What letter?' he wanted to know right away. I hadn't told him what I'd done, and at that moment, I wasn't inclined to confess I had lied to the government. 'Just a letter I sent to the Forest Service asking them to stay with us when they came to North Carolina, that's all. Just doing my part to help the business,' I said.

'I'm here for the...,' Michael started to say, but I interrupted him. 'He's here for the weekend,' I told Father, all the while giving Michael the side eye to let him know that he should be quiet and go along with me. Thank goodness he did.

Father walked up and introduced himself. 'Nicholas Fischer, proprietor,' he said, shaking Michael's hand. 'And this is my daughter, Ruth Fischer.'

'Yes, we've just met,' Michael said, a bit perplexed. 'I'm Michael Kirkpatrick, sir, and I'm very pleased to meet you and your daughter,' he said, turning his attention back to me.

'Kirkpatrick, that's Irish, isn't it?' Father asked.

'Yes, sir, it is; a full-blooded Irishman, I am,' Michael answered. Well, that didn't please Father very much," Ruth said.

"Good Lord, what was wrong with him being Irish?" Nicole asked.

"Like I said, Nicole, it was a different time," Ruth said. "Al Capone was in the papers all the time back then. Everyone was saying that he was such a brutal criminal because he was a Sicilian, and he was quoted saying that if you think the Sicilians were bad people, you ought to meet the Irish."

"And your father took the word of Al Capone that the Irish were not good people?" Nicole asked with teasing sarcasm.

"It wasn't just that," Ruth replied. "Most of them being Catholic was what it was really all about. Father really disliked the Catholics."

"I'm sorry, I'm trying to keep this in perspective, but that just seems silly," Nicole remarked.

"Lots of people thought the same way back then," Ruth explained. "Especially in the south. Some folks thought they were spies for the Pope, traitorous scoundrels coming into the U.S. to overthrow our system and install the Pope in power, but most people were just against them for religious reasons. Father called them theological abominations. Baptists, and mind you, the only folks here in Brysonville were either Baptists or heathens, didn't understand the saints and the Virgin Mary at all, and especially not their statues in the church. 'Idolatry,' I heard the preacher say more than once."

"So you lied to your father about why Michael was here, and he despised Michael's nationality and religion. Sounds like a great start, Granna," Nicole said. "How did you get past the Indian burial ground thing, and how did you change your father's mind about the forest?"

"I had to confess everything to Michael because I needed him to help me with my plan," Ruth said. "I had no choice but to confess to the lie. Father never knew of it, but I had to tell Michael if I was going to get him to cooperate with me on the real reason why I had brought him here."

"And how did you get him to agree to help?" Nicole asked, arching her eyebrows flirtatiously.

"Are you suggesting I can't be persuasive?" Ruth teased.

"Not at all," Nicole laughed, "now that I realize you are a con artist at heart. Now, tell me how you did it?"

"I told him about the deal Father had made with the Lamberts and that I just couldn't let the trees be cut down. That was Mother's piece of heaven; it had to be saved. I just begged him to help me. I knew the government was going to buy some land somewhere anyhow and saw no reason that it couldn't be right here in Brysonville, North Carolina."

"If he got the Forest Service to buy the land, it would save the trees from the Lambert's sawmill. How did that benefit anybody but the Fischers?" Nicole asked, trying to fit the pieces of the puzzle together. "I still don't get it."

"Father just wanted to help get money into the pockets of the people in Brysonville," Ruth said. "I thought if I could figure out another way for that to happen, then everybody would get what they wanted, and the trees would be left alone. I realized if people were going to visit the forest, there would have to be a road, and roads need bridges, signs, guardrails, and the like. And tourists would come to see the forest. All that added up to jobs. If I could get the government, the Lamberts, and Father to agree about the land and the trees, everybody would get a piece of the pie."

"I'm very, very impressed," Nicole said. "I didn't know you were so shrewd."

"You flatter me," Ruth chuckled.

"Well, obviously, you were able to get everyone to reach that agreement," Nicole said. "I'm very impressed."

"I did, although it took me a good while. The Lamberts were reluctant at first; they didn't think they would benefit as much, but Father reassured them he would make sure they prospered as much as anyone else."

"And what did you get out of the deal?" Nicole asked carefully.

"I got a man," Ruth said with a sly grin. "I charmed myself a man."

"I've got to hear this. What do you mean, you 'charmed' him?" Nicole asked with delight.

"Honey, I knew what I was doing. It took nearly all summer to put all the arrangements together, to get everybody satisfied with the deal, and to get Washington to actually spend the money. But it came together all right. During that summer, I kept by Michael's side, helping him all

I could, telling him what he needed to know about the people around here so he could make his negotiations go the right way. We became quite attached to one another during all those meetings and discussions," Ruth blushed. "Some held in public, some in private."

"This is so romantic," Nicole marveled, surprised at her growing excitement. "I love this side of you; I never knew it existed." She had almost become giddy. "It's funny," she said, "I had always assumed there wasn't a drop of romantic blood in your veins."

"There are plenty of romantic notions in me, Nicole," Ruth scolded. "And it was very romantic, but it was a secret courtship. Father wouldn't have stood for it if he knew what was going on between us. No daughter of his was going to be tarnished by an Irish Catholic." Ruth paused, and her smile drooped. "I reckon you're right. We've always had too many secrets and wrongheaded ways of looking at things." She lifted her glasses and dabbed her eyes. "Father wouldn't have stood for it if he knew what was going on between Michael and me. We had to sneak around to see each other once we realized we couldn't stand being apart."

"Granna, I'm having a hard time imagining you sneaking around. What did you do?" Nicole asked.

"We were talking about a lot of land, over thirty-eight hundred acres, and it all had to be surveyed. There was plenty of opportunity for us to be in the forest together, setting out markers, choosing the right path for the road, and picking the spot where the dedication plaque would go. Eventually, there were lots of men working on the surveying project, and it got more and more difficult to keep our little rendezvous a secret, but Bear helped us to see each other."

We owe no gratitude to wanton chance,
For not through him does heart cleave fast to heart.
Not time nor place nor any circumstance,
Could keep our lips, our breasts, our souls, apart.

Wherever, Whenever, 1911

Joyce Kilmer

CHAPTER 22

CHEROKEE WAYS

"That surprises me," Nicole said. "I expected Bear to be loyal to your father."

"He would have been if Michael hadn't also won his heart." She put her napkin down, and her hand showed a slight tremor. "It wasn't a matter of loyalty for Bear, Nicole; it was about doing the right thing."

"I didn't mean to imply anything negative; I just wasn't expecting to hear that Bear was a part of your plan," Nicole said. "How did Michael get him to go along?"

"We were all in here talking around the dinner table one night and Father was goading Michael about his religion. He said he couldn't see how one could be an American and a Catholic at the same time. He said he thought that when push came to shove, all Catholics would be more beholding to the Pope than the Constitution. 'Of course, I am a loyal American,' Michael said. 'I was born in Ohio. But sir, you must agree no man can be a pure American in blood unless he is an Indian, like this gentleman here,' he said, slapping Bear's shoulder. After that, he and Bear were like twin brothers."

"I bet that raised the hair on the back of ol' Nicholas' neck," Nicole said.

"Oh, Father was mad enough but he knew Michael was right, what with us having our own roots elsewhere. Nevertheless, Father was stubborn; it was the German coming out in him. Things got touchy after that."

"What happened next?" Nicole leaned forward. "Keep it coming, please."

"Father caught on that I was rather impressed with Michael, and started watching us real close," Ruth said. "He did his best to keep me away from Michael. He never directly told me not to spend any time with him, but he did his best to keep me busy and away from him. Once I thought he was going to call off the whole thing."

"Call off the sale? Why would he have done that?" Nicole asked urgently.

"He saw Michael and me together one evening. We were walking around the grounds after dinner. It was getting dark, and we thought we were out of sight of everyone, but I reckon not. We were making plans about how we would see each other after all the business was done, and he leaned over to kiss me. Father saw it and was pretty upset about it. He told Michael that he was changing his mind, that he wanted him to leave the inn as soon as possible. But they talked a lot the next day, and Michael saved the deal by promising he wouldn't see me anymore if Father would just go through with the sale."

"Wait a minute. Are you saying he wanted the land, the trees, more than you?" Nicole asked. She sat back in her chair and shook her head.

"That's not what I'm saying; hold your horses and listen to me," Ruth said. "Michael loved me. We were already married by then." Ruth's voice cracked, and she grabbed the napkin again to wipe her eyes before tears could stream down her cheeks. "He was my one and only true love. He was my dear husband."

Nicole's eyes opened wide, and momentarily, her mouth dropped open. "Your husband? You were never married," she almost shouted.

"I wasn't married in the traditional way," Ruth went on, "at least not according to the laws of North Carolina, but I was on the reservation where it was legal according to Cherokee law. One night, we stood by a ceremonial fire, surrounded by all of Bear's people who kept the flames going by tossing in handfuls of sage, tobacco, corn, and dry grass." She paused and looked over her shoulder toward her suite. "Do you remember that Indian vase I keep on my hutch cabinet?"

"Yes, ma'am, I do," Nicole said.

"Well, during a Cherokee wedding, there is a sacred vase ritual when the couple tries to drink out of a vase together at the same time. If they're successful, without spilling a single drop of water, they can expect to experience mutual love and understanding throughout their marriage. We didn't spill a single drop," Ruth said with great pride.

"I'm sure you didn't," Nicole smiled.

"And then Bear sang a Cherokee wedding song for us," Ruth continued, "he blessed us and then covered us in a blanket. He said it symbolized the beginning of our new life together."

"So you never really married, then, right?" Nicole asked.

"Like I said, not legally in the eyes of North Carolina, if that's what you want to know," Ruth said. "But we believed that if we made love, it would make us married. After the ceremony, we believed ourselves to be married, and it wasn't a sin to consummate our love for the purpose of committing ourselves to each other, not just to please the flesh."

Nicole put her spinning head down on the table. "Oh, my God, he was my grandfather, wasn't he?"

"Yes," Ruth replied. "He certainly was."

"I'm in shock," Nicole said. "Obviously, I knew you had been with a man at least once in your life, but I didn't know it was with your husband. All this time, I thought you just wanted a child, not a husband, too."

"Of course, I wanted a husband; I never wanted to live alone," Ruth said. "Certainly not for this long."

"This is so hard to believe," Nicole said. "I'm not sure I do believe it; it's so fantastic."

"Oh, it was fantastic alright," Ruth assured Nicole. "It certainly was."

"If you loved once, Granna, why didn't you love again?" Nicole asked. "Why didn't you ever have a relationship with another man?"

"That's exactly why I should've told your momma all this much sooner than I did," Ruth said, "so she would know why I never took another man and gave her a father. It was never because I didn't want love in my life or that I meant to deny her a father. I did love someone, and I loved him beyond measure. I loved him too much to let someone else try to take his place."

Nicole sat back up in her chair and stared at her grandmother in disbelief.

"In fact," Ruth continued, "I still love him to this very day. I never took up with another man because I promised Michael there would be no one else for me, no matter how long it might take us to reunite." Her lips trembled, and her neck turned splotchy again. "Dear Lord, what a mistake it has been to remain silent about him for so long. He must be so ashamed of me."

Nicole shifted uncomfortably in her chair, not sure what to say. Finally, "Why did you keep him a secret? You've spent a lifetime hiding this story. Why, Granna?"

"It disappointed Father that I was pregnant; he said I'd brought embarrassment to my mother's memory," Ruth said reluctantly. "I didn't want to make matters worse by confirming that Michael, an Irish Catholic, was the father. I thought that news would send Father into an evangelical rage, and I wanted no chance that my baby would be unwelcome in our home, so I eventually stopped speaking of Michael altogether. Looking back, I reckon Father knew the truth anyway, but it was never spoken out loud. I chose to raise your momma by myself, with the help of my brothers. It took a while, but Father finally came around to her. He couldn't help but love your momma, with her always reaching out for him and calling him. 'Nicky' was what she always called him."

"Wow," Nicole said, amazed and trying to absorb the details of her family history. "This is all so complex, so entangled, and yet so astonishing at the same time." She paused, studied her grandmother's face, and proceeded cautiously. "But tell me, why didn't you and Michael get together? Didn't he come back? What kept you two apart if you loved each other so much and you were carrying his baby?" She softened and reached across the table to take Ruth's nervous hand. "What happened to him?"

"The Lord took him, honey," Ruth answered, her voice choked with pain. She picked at the napkin again, it now moist with tears and chicken fat, and released a bottomless sigh that seemed to cause her to shrink as bottled-up grief escaped from her body. "It was an unfortunate accident. He died that summer."

Careless you speed over fields of stars,
Darting through Heaven swift and free;
Nothing your arrowy passage bars
Back to the earth and back to me.

White Bird of Love, 1911
Joyce Kilmer

CHAPTER 23

QUINN

It was almost 10:00 P.M., and Owen couldn't think about trees a moment longer without becoming tempted to cut them down himself. The details of the Ordinance, Department of Agriculture and Environmental Protection Agency reports, and research findings published by the Forestry Department at the University of Georgia and the National Institute on Environmental Health Sciences had all run together and formed one big blob of sap where his brain used to be. All that data someone had lovingly collected, crunched, and written about using terms like urban canopy heterogeneity, plant hydraulic architecture, stomata, transgenic hybrids, epicormic branching, and trichloroethylene, terms all too scientific and boring as hell to him and over the heads of most. He smacked his open palm on the table. "No one is going to understand this stuff," he snorted. To hell with big corporate law and partnerships, he thought with anger. He wanted a simple life and always had. He was pissed about his lack of progress. He knew he had spent too much time searching the Internet for very little profit, except for the laugh he got after stumbling across an article about an activist chaining herself to a walnut tree in Los Angeles. Feeling himself beginning to rage, he threw in the towel for the evening, returned the law books to their respective places on the shelves just as Florence would have wanted him to do, stuffed everything else into the trash can or his briefcase, and headed for home.

On the way, he pulled over at a crowded diner in Virginia Highland that stayed open late and ordered a club sandwich, hold the fries, to go. He stood at the counter near the front window, yawning and waiting and browsing the rack of independent newspapers and magazines that promised interesting restaurant and theater reviews and only the hottest personal ads of singles in search of erotic adventures disguised as short-lasting romances. When his sandwich was finally presented in a brown paper bag, he was reading about a woman who, calling herself Desiree, promised the thrill of a lifetime in a no-strings-attached relationship to any man willing to demonstrate his appreciative generosity first. "Well, maybe just one string," he said in a chuckling whisper.

He worried Emma would not forgive him if he lost the case. If not for the promise he had made to Emma, she had extracted it from him so easily, he would leave Atlanta behind right now. He imagined himself running off with Nicole, if she'd still have him, to do something else for a living. Something with less stress and regular hours. Something that wouldn't prevent him from attending his children's birthday parties, that would allow him to be home at night to answer their urgent questions, and tuck them in with a kiss after their worried minds had been put to rest. That was why he refused to attend medical school, no matter how much his mother had fumed about it.

Leaving with the sandwich bag in hand, he walked to his car, thinking about relationships with and without strings attached, and he didn't notice the faces of people who passed him on the sidewalk or the band of teenagers doing their best to imitate the Allman Brothers in a bar across the street, or the black Mercedes that slowed as it passed him and turned around at the end of the block.

He reached into his pocket for his keys. "Owen," he heard just then. He looked in the direction of the voice and found Quinn creeping along in her car, her window down, with one hand on the wheel and the other waving at him. "Got a minute? Can we talk?" she asked.

"You're going to cause an accident," he said, pointing to the car behind her. She pulled over to let the car pass, got out, and crossed the street. "It's late, Quinn; I'm going home," he said as she drew near.

"I just need a minute, that's all," she insisted.

"What do you want?" he asked.

She was dressed in Ferragamo heels, a Prada miniskirt, and a white silk blouse that, just like the suit she had on yesterday, didn't leave you guessing about what and how much was hidden underneath. "Why are you so angry with me?" she almost pleaded to know.

"I'm not angry with you, Quinn," he answered.

"It sure seems like it," she pushed back. "Even your mother thinks so."

"What are you doing here?" Owen asked.

"I'm on my way to a party in Druid Hills. I just came this way to see how the neighborhood has changed," she said. "I drove by your house."

"What for?" he asked.

"I wanted to see if you were home," she answered. "Like I said, I would like to talk."

"I really don't think we have anything to talk about unless this is a business call and you want to negotiate a compromise," Owen said with tension in every word.

"It isn't a business call; it's a personal matter. Can we sit in your car?" Quinn asked.

"I'd rather not," he answered quickly.

"Please, it's so noisy and unpleasant out here," Quinn protested. "You used to be such a gentleman."

"I am a gentleman unless a confrontation is at hand," he said.

"Never mind." Quinn turned around, hurt, and started stomping toward her car.

"Quinn," Owen called out after quickly changing his mind, knowing word of this exchange would get back to his mother, and the last thing he wanted was a phone call from her first thing in the morning asking who was he to make her look like she hadn't trained him properly. "Wait, I'm sorry," he said before he clicked the remote and unlocked his car. "I can chat for a few minutes."

They climbed in, and when he reached behind his seat to put the sandwich on the floorboard he saw that she had already crossed her legs toward him and folded her arms together under her chest, giving her bosom an intentional upward push. His eyes involuntarily drifted and scanned his former lover's legs, the ones that used to wrap around his hips and hold him in place. Against his will, he remembered how freely she once offered herself to him. There were no guessing games between them about whether or not their weekend getaways would include lovemaking. He turned forward in his seat and attempted to distract himself by reading the advertisements taped in the windows of the drugstore just ahead.

Batteries were on sale. Milk $2.76 a gallon. Transfer your prescriptions for free. ATM inside. "Now, what is this all about?" he finally asked.

"Seeing you in court brought back a lot of memories," Quinn admitted, "and, to be truthful, some old feelings. I…."

"Quinn, don't," Owen interrupted.

"Can't I reminisce for a moment?" she whined. "Be kind. I'm having a regretted decision crisis."

"A what?" Owen asked tersely.

"You know, as in realizing that sometimes the things you throw away are bound to become the very things you wish you still had," Quinn answered.

"There's no going back; I've told you that," Owen said firmly. "And you know that I'm involved with someone else now."

"I know, your mother told me," Quinn said.

"I'm sure she told you plenty," Owen said, annoyed at the thought of his mother oversharing his business.

"She wants you to be happy, Owen, that's all," Quinn said.

"Of course she does, as long as she's happy with what makes me happy," Owen responded. He immediately regretted his words, knowing that if his father were listening right now, he'd be disappointed. He remembered his promise to call his mother to offer an apology.

"I saw you rubbing your chest," Quinn interrupted his thoughts. "It made me worry about you," she said.

"I'm fine," Owen insisted. "There's nothing to worry about." Quinn placed her hand on his arm, and he turned in his seat to pull free from her grasp.

"I wish you would forgive me," she said.

"There's nothing to forgive; I know it was an accident," he said politely.

"I'm talking about me calling off the wedding," she said.

His lower eyelid started to twitch, and he glanced at himself in the rearview mirror. He looked like hell, sporting bleary eyes and day-old stubble. He looked around and wished a policeman would come along and ask him to move his car. "It was for the best," he said. "I can see that now. It really was."

"I'm not so sure," Quinn replied. "We had a lot of good times."

"We were too different for it to last, Quinn," he said.

"I know, I was the get-it-done-in-a-hurry over-achiever, and you were the philosophical laidback one," Quinn said.

"More honestly," Owen responded, "you were the brash and bold one, and I was more even-tempered and compassionate."

"Like oil and water, we were," Quinn said with a grin. "You know that is why I had to be the go-getter. You can't pay the bills with compassion, Owen. But you balanced me out, and I miss that. You kept me from being consumed by my own ambition."

"Funny hearing you say that," Owen said, turning to look at her.

"What do you mean?" she asked.

"As I recall, our problem, at least from your perspective," Owen said, "was never that you had too much ambition. It was that I didn't have enough. At least not enough to impress you."

"There you go again," Quinn shook her head. "So, are you angry at me or not?" she cross-examined him.

"If you want to hear me say I forgive you, then I forgive you," Owen said. "If you want something else, please just say what that might be. It's getting late, and we need to wrap this up."

"You sound so certain that we can't give it another try," Quinn complained. She turned more in the seat and pointed her knees at him. Her skirt was too short for the shift in position and it pulled up to show off more of her long legs. Seeing that he noticed, she smiled and winked at him, taking advantage of the moment as all good lawyers should. "Why don't we go to your place?" she suggested. "We can talk more there where we can be more comfortable." She placed her arm on the center console and let her fingertips brush against his thigh.

With both hands on the wheel, he looked straight ahead, unphased by her seductive gestures. He remembered the photo of Nicole in his briefcase, reached down to Quinn's hand, and removed it from his leg. "Like I said, I'm seeing someone," he said firmly.

"I thought she was out of town," Quinn cooed suggestively.

Owen quickly reached across to her side of the car, taking care not to bring his face too close to hers. "Like I said, I am a gentleman," he said as he pulled the handle to open her door and then pushed it open. "Have fun at the party."

Bitter and selfish sorrow,
Poverty, strife and ruth,
Fear of the dreadful morrow,
These take away our youth.

To J.B.Y., 1911
Joyce Kilmer

Chapter 24

The Year 1936

"It was the day of the dedication ceremony, the thirtieth of July, a Thursday," Ruth said. "It had been raining for several days, and everything was soaked to the core. But I didn't care; it couldn't dampen my mood. I was excited that the big day was upon us and the forest was going to remain untouched forever. Even Father was excited. The newspapers had arrived to cover the event, and the inn was full of people who had come for the ceremony. I hadn't heard that many footsteps on these floors in a long time. Father was running around here busier than a moth in a mitten, making sure everybody was comfortable. He was pouring coffee and answering questions as fast as he could without being overwhelmed by it all.

What we had pulled off, selling the land to the government, was indeed good for everyone; even the Lamberts said so. The veterans and the Kilmer family were happy; the inn was full and getting priceless advertisement, the people of Brysonville were working, and more jobs would be created as the real roadwork got underway. They were going to widen and pave the old dirt road to make the forest accessible year-round, no matter what the weather.

Michael and I were happy, too. We were going to be together again soon. The papers had been signed, and the money had changed hands, so there was no threat of Father changing his mind again. We could finally be together, Michael and me, when the time was right. We kept our distance from one another until a few weeks after the ceremony to give the appearance that Michael was good on his word, even though we were secretly planning to be together again as soon as possible. As I said, he was going to leave Washington and come to Brysonville. He had already arranged to be the forest overseer once he set up housekeeping here. I was betting that the good results of all our plans had enough merit to make up for our being dishonest and that Father would eventually decide that he would rather me be happy than not. I thought he would accept Michael one day because he loved me."

"Of course, he would," Nicole said. "I don't believe for a minute anyone ever could resist you."

"You are as precious as a peach for thinking that," Ruth said, smiling. "Now, let me continue, darlin'. Michael had moved out of the inn and was staying at a boarding house in town. It was a condition of his agreement with Father, who did not yet know about our wedding. We had not been alone together in over three weeks, and I was nearly busting inside with the desire to touch him. I simply could not restrain myself when he came to the door that morning. He had come to join us for breakfast before the ceremony. Everybody involved was to sit around the same table, toast the morning, and then leave together to go up the mountain. He came through the door, still wearing his hat and raincoat. Even though he had shaken off the water outside on the porch, he was still dripping wet. He looked like a boy at that moment, handsome, fresh, and innocently careless. He pulled his coat off to hang it on the wall, and I watched him with great desire as he slid it off his shoulders. He was dry underneath and, oh, so handsome in that uniform. I walked right up to him and hugged him. I just couldn't help it. I had missed him so much. I just needed to feel myself pressed against him, even if only for a moment. He smiled at me, and said, 'Hello, Sunny.' He called me Sunny, because I made him feel warm all over, he used to tell me."

"I have something for you," he smiled, reached into his coat, and pulled out a package.

"What was it? A ring?" Nicole asked in a rush of excitement.

"No, silly. It was this book." Ruth pointed to her beloved treasure. "As much as I loved Joyce Kilmer's poetry, learning it in school and reading it in the magazines, I'd never owned one of his books until then." She opened the book and tenderly turned a few pages until she found the one she was looking for. "He wrote a lovely note for me on one of the inside pages."

"Oh, please read it for me," Nicole begged.

"I am; hold your horses, child. Give an old woman a minute to breathe," Ruth said with a chuckle. She first read the note to herself, remembering the moment she had read it for the first time. "Reading this that morning was the moment when I realized how much Michael really loved me. His words touched my heart and ever since have given me comfort when I sit alone in the family suite, thinking of him and the days we had spent together." She cleared her throat, adjusted her glasses, and held the book up in the best light. She began reading it to Nicole.

My dearest Sunny, you are my greatest blessing and most cherished gift in this life. In Heaven, you will be my eternal comfort and joy. This I know, for a love like ours will have no end. I am yours forever, Michael.

When she finished, she closed the book and set it back in its safe place on the table, letting her fingers rest on the cover before slowly moving her hand away. She took off her glasses and wiped them clean, and when she looked across the table, she found Nicole using her napkin, too.

"That is the most beautiful thing I've ever heard," Nicole said, dabbing her eyes.

"It is, isn't it?" Ruth agreed. "And he said he wasn't good with words."

"Did you open it, the present, right then and there?" Nicole asked.

"Of course, I opened it. A girl loves gifts, now don't we? I opened it and read the note to myself right there in the lobby in front of everyone. I was so overcome I couldn't help myself. I set the book down, then reached up, took his face in my hands, and kissed him," Ruth recalled.

"In front of your father?" Nicole nearly gasped.

"I sure did. What could he say there in front of everyone? He wasn't one to make a scene. He was angry, though, as mad as a wet hen. I could read it in his expression when I turned around and saw him standing by the fireplace, watching us. He motioned for me and then kept me right by his side for the rest of the morning." Ruth paused, and sadness drew the corners of her mouth into a frown. "That was our last kiss."

"Oh my God, my heart is breaking," Nicole said, clutching her shirt over her heart. "I don't know if I can bear to hear the rest of this." She stood and slid her chair around the table to be closer to her grandmother. "But please, carry on."

"He grabbed my hand that morning," Ruth nearly whispered, her eyes gazing into a world only she could see, "just as I was letting him go. 'Do not let another man kiss you until I come back for you,' he winked. 'I won't,' I said. 'I promise,' I told him. I've never forgotten his words and always kept my promise. Sometimes I told myself it was easy, that keeping that promise was how I kept his memory alive. The truth is, I was so heartbroken I just withdrew into my own thoughts. I was blinded by grief, numbed by my pain."

"You mean you have never kissed another man, not since that day?" an astonished Nicole asked.

"Not an intimate kiss, no ma'am. Sure, I've kissed men kinfolks when greeting them or when saying good-bye, but I have never kissed a man like you would when you love someone," Ruth explained.

Nicole cradled Ruth's hand between hers. "What happened to him, Granna?"

"An accident took him from me that very day," Ruth said, grief choking her voice.

"Oh, my God!" Nicole exclaimed. "What happened?"

"Hundreds of people were coming to attend the ceremony." Ruth continued. "Most of the morning, cars and trucks had been making their way up the mountain to the dedication site. The road was a narrow one, unpaved and barely wide enough for two cars. It was still a dirt road at the time, and in places, it was quite muddy where the ground had been scraped, and ditches were being dug. They weren't finished with it yet, only the beginning of the road right outside of Brysonville, and the end of it, near the heart of the forest where that memorial plaque was to be placed. Everything in the middle was a complete muddy mess. Pretty soon, cars were getting stuck, and they had to bring in tractors to haul them out. Some were even pulled all the way to the spot where the ceremony was to take place. People had come in from all over the country, the ceremony couldn't be called off, and so we went ahead with it in spite of the rain. I remember it like it just happened a moment ago."

*****

Nicholas momentarily flipped open his pocket watch and then shoved it back in his pants pocket. "Let's load up," he ordered, spreading

189

his arms wide as if to sweep everyone from the lobby and outside. His family, the Lamberts, a few guests, and Washington dignitaries began to shuffle out the door and down the steps toward their cars.

"You're riding with me and your brothers," Nicholas said, taking Ruth by the elbow and guiding her toward the big blue Buick parked nearby.

Joshua and Paul, laughing at something, raced past and jumped on the running boards of the family car. They turned and bounced up and down, directed their puckered lips at Ruth, and made loud kissing noises.

"Stop it!" Ruth shouted just before her brothers grabbed each other in a melodramatic embrace. Paul slipped on the running board, and both boys tumbled onto the wet ground.

"Get up and shut up," Nicholas barked, reaching down to take his boys by their suspenders. "Now wipe yourselves off and get in." They obeyed immediately but sat still only a few seconds before seeing who could bounce highest in the back seat. Joshua still puckered his lips but knew better than to make another kissing sound.

"See what you've started," Nicholas turned angrily to Ruth.

"I didn't mean to embarrass you, Father," she said sheepishly.

"You embarrassed yourself. Now get in." He practically slammed Ruth's door shut once she had pulled her skirt into the car. He smacked both swooping fenders, the second one much harder, with the palm of his hand as he walked around the front of the car toward his own door. Water spattered onto his coat. The Buick fired up, and he shoved it into gear, and his passengers' heads tossed backward as the car lurched forward.

Bear and Nathaniel jumped into the Forestry truck with Michael and followed the Buick. Michael gripped the steering wheel with the white knuckles of one hand and nervously scratched his chin with the other.

"Mr. Fischer will calm down in a jiffy," Nathaniel predicted confidently. "He ain't never stayed mad at that girl for long."

A large city-slicker sedan filled with the men from Washington followed close behind Michael's truck.

"Sit still, boys!" Nicholas shouted after a few miles.

Paul immediately turned his face into the seat back and started to whimper.

"Don't be mad at them, Father," Ruth pleaded, "It's me you're upset with."

"What's that dagnabit book about?" he growled.

"It's just poems. Mr. Kilmer wrote them," she answered quietly.

Nicholas huffed and turned off the pavement onto the muddy road leading to the dedication site. The Buick bounced in the ruts left by the cars that had gone ahead of them, and once, it tried to slip sideways. Ruth uttered a startled cry, and Nicholas instinctively reached across the seat to steady his only daughter.

"Thank you Father," Ruth said after Nicholas regained control of the car.

"Don't leave that book lying around," he warned, though without anger. "I don't want to see it."

*****

"We finally made it to the site but were well behind schedule," Ruth explained. "People waited patiently for us, standing under droopy umbrellas, trying to stay dry. There was a small stage set up next to a large boulder where a plaque had been placed. It was covered with a fabric drape until the official unveiling. Michael, Father, a few of the officials, and I went to the stage. Father and I sat on one side of the podium, and Michael on the other.

One of the veterans who served with Joyce Kilmer opened the ceremony with some words about their war experiences and Mr. Kilmer's heroism, patriotism, and deep faith. He was a Catholic. I don't think Father knew it until that moment. I saw him raise his eyebrows when that news reached his ears. Sweet irony, I thought. Then it was my turn.

I paced to the podium to read one of Mr. Kilmer's poems. The rain was pelting my umbrella, and I remembered that I'd left the piece of paper the poem was written on at the inn. That morning, I had decided to read from the book Michael had given me, but heeding my father's request, I left the book in the car, carefully tucked under my seat.

I remember how badly my knees were shaking. Before I began, I stole a glance at Michael, who smiled at me and dared a quick wink. That calmed my nerves, so I drew a deep breath, lifted my hand to gesture toward the overhead canopy of the poplars, and accidentally pushed back my umbrella. Rain fell on my face, but it made me laugh and feel even better, and I began to recite the poem from memory. 'I think I shall never see a poem as lovely as a tree....'

When I finished, there was respectful applause, even Father joined in, and then a high-ranking official from the Forest Service stood up to read the dedication. I still remember what he said. 'The United States Forest Service herewith reserves this forest as a primitive area and dedicates it to the spirit of Joyce Kilmer and the use of the people for their enjoyment and inspiration until time shall be no more.' He motioned for the drape to be removed and then everybody clapped when they saw the plaque. Then he read a letter that had been sent by President Roosevelt. 'It is particularly fitting that a poet who will always be remembered for the tribute he embodied in "Trees" should be honored by this living monument,' he wrote. The man then folded the letter and gave it to Father, who proudly accepted it. I still have it."

"But what happened to Michael?" Nicole asked again.

Nay, since ye loved ye cannot die.
Above the stars is set your nest.
Through Heaven's fields ye sing
And fly and in the trees
Of Heaven rest.

To a Blackbird and His Mate
Who Dies in the Spring, 1912
Joyce Kilmer

CHAPTER 25

TRAGEDY

"It rained hard all through the whole ceremony," Ruth went on, determined to tell the story in her own way. "Folks were tired of being in the rain. As soon as it was over, everybody piled into their cars and headed back down the mountain to Brysonville. Nathaniel, Bear, and Michael followed the car carrying the officials from Washington. Those men, I guess they had never driven on a muddy road before. Bear said they were sliding all over the place. Somehow, they managed to get their car nearly sideways, and the rear wheels went off the road. It was a dangerous spot along a steep slope where the guard rails hadn't been put up yet. The driver kept giving it gas, but instead of helping, it only made matters worse. The back of the car kept sliding further down the shoulder.

Bear said that Michael jumped out and ran up to the driver's window, where he stood leaning down, yelling at the man to shut off the engine. At that moment, the front passenger opened his door and jumped out of the sedan. The front end popped up even higher, lifting both tires off the ground, and before anyone else could move, the sedan slid off the shoulder and down the slope, coming to a crashing stop against a tree.

Those still inside were bounced around but no one was hurt much. Except Michael, that is. Bear saw him first. He fell to his knees in the mud when he spotted a twisted arm clothed in a muddy tan sleeve sticking out from under the car. Somehow Michael had gotten pulled under the damned thing, and it dragged him all the way down the slope." Ruth exhaled and then didn't breathe again for what Nicole thought was far too long a time. Finally, Ruth drew a shallow breath and looked at the book. "It killed him instantly."

"Oh my God," Nicole exclaimed again, this time more loudly. "That's horrible. How did you go on?" she asked. "I don't think I could have. It's nearly killing me just to hear about it."

"I was heartsick in the worst way. Couldn't eat or sleep. I just cried and cried," Ruth said. "Father was so worried he kept having the doctor come by and check on me. He had a hard time accepting that there was no medicine that would make my misery go away. I had to grieve until there was no grief left in me, the doctor said. There was plenty of grief in me, all right, until two months later when I discovered I was pregnant. That was when I finally began to perk up. I didn't have Michael, but I had a life growing inside of me that we had made together. Knowing I would still have a part of him in my child brought me back to my senses. Father was so relieved to see me returning to my old self; he dared not chastise me for my condition. I guess he figured I might be fragile, so he let me be. If he was embarrassed or ashamed, he didn't let on. He never asked me who the father was because he already knew. But to keep the peace, Michael's name remained unspoken."

"Granna, forgive me, but I have to ask," Nicole interrupted. "It baffles me that you would not talk about Michael all this time. I know that you loved him, I can tell that, but it seems like you just let him go. Were you trying to forget him? Why did you keep this a secret for so many years?"

"No, child, gosh, no. I could never forget the only true love of my life," Ruth said. "I've already told you about the ruckus that was stirred up just because he was an Irish Catholic. All that is true, but there is a little bit more to it than I've told you. First of all, and this is so very shameful and regrettable, Father insisted that Michael's family not know about your mother because he was convinced they would come to try and take her and make her into a Catholic, so we were intentional about mentioning him as little as possible to avoid that risk. Today, I don't even know where his people are. May God forgive me."

"So that's why mom grew up knowing only half her family," Nicole concluded, fitting more pieces of the puzzle together. "She always thought it was because everyone on the other side wanted nothing to do with her."

"It wasn't that at all," Ruth said, "it was simply paranoia on our part. Father had lost the love of his life, and he thought he was losing me to depression, so he was determined to make sure your mother was always with us to help keep my spirits up and his, too, to be honest about it."

"Oprah would have a field day sorting through this much dysfunction," Nicole said, meaning it sincerely. "But still, if you loved him so much, how could you manage to suppress his memory so successfully?"

"Lady Bug, this may make no sense to you," Ruth continued after collecting her thoughts, "but try to understand. Let's say you have a favorite shirt. If you wear it all the time, it will eventually wear out and one day you discard it. But if that shirt were a wedding dress instead, you would save it, protect it, and go to it only on special occasions. And each time you held it up to your breast and looked at yourself in the mirror, you would be a bride again. I keep Michael to myself kind of like that, and I hold him to my breast when I want to see him." Her lips quivered.

Nicole gave her a dry napkin. "Are you okay?" she asked tenderly.

"Yes, child, I'm fine," Ruth said. "I'm just happy to finally be telling all this to someone, to bring Michael into the light of day, that's all. I'm glad it's you who's listening."

"Me too," Nicole said.

"When I want to see him, I close my eyes, and I wrap my arms across my chest like I'm hugging him, and I squeeze real tight." Ruth demonstrated the embrace. "And when I open my eyes, he is standing right there in my arms, looking down at me."

"I do that sometimes," Nicole, sheepish, said, "when I miss Owen. I close my eyes and think of something that we've done together, and I play it over again in my mind."

"If you love that man," Ruth leaned forward, "you best take hold of him and love him without restraint. Get the most you can out of being together, and be good to one another every day. Nicole, you have got to decide what means more to you, embracing your happiness or avoiding your pain."

"You are so right," Nicole whispered. "I've never thought of it like that before."

"Then make up your mind about how it's going to be," Ruth said. "You never know when you'll spend your last minute together."

"Don't say that," Nicole protested, "it scares me. I can't bear to think of something happening to one of you, you or Owen, and all of us not being together again."

"Both of you will live a long life, Lady Bug," Ruth said. "And even if you didn't, you'll be together again one day. Bear used to say that the spirits of people who loved one another on earth will find each other again when they get to Heaven. He told me that the day we put Michael's body on the train and sent him back to his family."

"That's a sweet notion," Nicole said. "I hope it's true."

"It is," Ruth said confidently. "Between that and what Mother taught me, I'm confident that I will open my eyes one day, and Michael really will be in my arms again."

"What did she teach you?" Nicole asked.

"She said to live every day like it was your last so you would have no regrets when you meet your Maker. She said if you tried to live right and love the Lord, anything you missed on earth would be made up to you tenfold when you get to Heaven," Ruth explained. "Mother feared the Lord, she certainly did, but in a good, respectful kind of way. She loved church, and she took all of us every Sunday, no exceptions. Well, I've tried to live by her words, hoping that by doing so, they will get me into Heaven, where I know he is waiting for me. He's there, of that I am sure. He was a good man, a gentleman, and a God-fearing man, too. That's why I know he is up there, and he is waiting for me. I like to think he is watching me, and that helps to keep me honest. If he's looking down on me, seeing everything I am doing, I want to behave myself and do him right. Sure, I've done things I wish I hadn't, but nothing so bad that he would be disappointed in me. Living right is the least I can do for him after all that he did for me. After all that he gave me."

"So you've been waiting all this time, saving yourself for the day you will see him again in Heaven?" Nicole asked.

"Yes, that's it, I sure have. I wanted no other man to come between us, so I saved myself for him. You can only feel that way about one person in your life. Anybody else, well, it just wouldn't be fair to them." Ruth looked at Nicole and managed a smile, hoping the girl was absorbing everything she was trying to tell her. "Michael's waiting for me in Heaven," she continued. "I am sure he's looking down on me right now, listening to everything I've been saying." She looked away. "And yet I've done things I wish I hadn't, like keeping him hidden from his own child. I just hope he can forgive me for that and that your mother can, too."

"They would understand if you could only explain it to them just like you explained everything to me," Nicole reassured her.

"I pray for forgiveness every night," Ruth confessed.

"It's terrible that he died so young, but at least he had you for a while," Nicole said, reaching out to console her grandmother with a gentle touch.

"If a man has to die young," Ruth waxed on, "then it's a blessing that it is not before he has had the chance to do something good for the world. Michael did his share of good; yes, he did. If a man has to die young, it's also a blessing when it happens quickly, unexpectedly, like how it happened to him. The doctor said his neck broke. The Lord took him before he could feel any pain. I've always been thankful for that. Bear said he didn't see it coming, so I guess he wouldn't have been scared, either. I like to think that anyway." Ruth, her cheeks chapped, looked up at the ceiling to hold back the tears that were about to brim over. "I'm going to meet him again in heaven one day. We'll have our sweet reunion, and then there'll be no more parting. No parting ever again."

"Don't talk about dying, Granna; you have to live forever," Nicole said.

"You can't ask that of me after what I just told you, Nicole," Ruth scolded. "I won't live forever, honey, and I don't want to, either. It would cheat Micheal and me out of our reunion."

"Still, I don't want to think about losing you," Nicole said.

"You know you are going to someday, honey," Ruth said. "But when I go, don't grieve too much. Remember this night and this conversation, and know that I'll be happy then, getting what I have been waiting for during all these long years."

Nicole looked into her grandmother's eyes and nodded. "It has been an emotional day, hasn't it?" she said.

"Yes, it has been. All this crying has worn me slap out," Ruth said. "We should go to bed and get our beauty rest. I'm sure we are a pitiful sight right now."

The women returned to the family suite, hugged one another, said goodnight, and then went their separate ways. Nicole undressed quickly and jumped into bed. Though physically and emotionally exhausted, her mind raced and she tossed fitfully before finally falling asleep.

Ruth got into bed and read Michael's note once more. When she finished, she put the book on her nightstand and within easy reach should she want to read it a fourth time. She looked out her window at the night sky for a long while, watching moths flutter about the porch lights and listening to the tree frogs, a Barred Owl, and the call of a Whippoorwill. She closed her eyes and thought of Michael until she fell asleep and then began to dream about him, just as she had hoped she would.

God be thanked for the Milky Way
That runs across the sky,
That's the path my feet would tread
Whenever I have to die.
Some folks call it a Silver Sword,
And some a Pearly Crown,
But the only thing I think is,
Is Main Street, Heaventown.

Main Street, 1917

Joyce Kilmer

Chapter 26

Remembering

Their breathing quickened as they climbed the ridge toward its summit. Under the thick canopy of overhead branches and leaves, which held in the warmth of the afternoon sun, it was humid. Sweat ran down his strong arms and legs. She was sweating, too; her muslin blouse clung to her back, and a hint of her creamy skin and the outline of her undergarments showed through.

When they reached the top, she smiled and turned around to face him. He saw beads of sweat the size of dew drops on her upper lip. More sweat ran down the nape of her neck and puddled in the small divot just above her collarbone until it filled to its limit and then broke loose and ran farther down her bosom. It followed the curve of her breast and disappeared behind the buttons of her blouse.

He stepped closer to her. "It's beautiful here," he said.

"I told you so," she said, still smiling at him.

"You are beautiful," he admired.

"You make me feel beautiful," she said. She reached out and caressed his forearm with the tips of her long slender fingers.

He moved even closer to her, close enough to put one hand behind her in the small of her back and the other on her hip. He gently pulled her toward him. Her body pressed against his, and she brought her hands up to his big shoulders and leaned back just enough to look into his eyes.

He moved his hand from her hip and brought it up to her delicate chin, lifting her face near to his. He pushed his fingers into her hair, pulled her closer to him, and leaned down to meet her lips with his own. He kissed her gently, barely brushing his lips against hers.

She moaned to invite him to continue.

He kissed her solidly and quickly, and their lips parted. They tasted each other's passion and felt each other's urgent breaths on their faces. She moved her arms as far around him as she could reach and pressed her fingers into the muscles of his back.

"Is this a good place?" he asked.

"Of course it is. That's why I brought you here," she teased.

"That's what I was hoping," he answered. He reached for the strand of twine that ran across his chest, grabbed it, and pulled it over his head, taking off the rolled bundle that he carried on his back. He knelt down, untied the twine, and unrolled an Indian blanket to make a bed on top of the fallen leaves. He looked up at her; she was unbuttoning her blouse. "I love you," he said.

She slipped the blouse off her shoulders. "I love you, too," she said.

The road is wide and the stars are out
And the breath of night is sweet,
And this is the time when wanderlust
Should seize upon my feet.

Roofs, 1917

Joyce Kilmer

Chapter 27

The Next Morning

Nicole opened her eyes before the alarm clock buzzed. The sound of her grandmother's rocking chair creaking on the porch had awakened her. Not usually a light sleeper, she had been restless most of the night and aware of even the faintest nocturnal sounds coming from outside her open window. Her mind had refused to rest, skipping around instead from one imagined scene in life to another, each featuring her mother or grandmother in leading roles. New questions came to her a mile a minute, and she couldn't decide which to investigate first. She remembered Garland had said some things aren't worth knowing. How would she know which weren't, she wondered. He didn't tell her that. She reached for the alarm clock and turned it off, wishing she could just as easily flip a switch and still her restless mind.

She stayed in bed, stretching and listening to the steady rhythm of the rocking chair. Against the background of the birds' morning songs and the laughter of children already running in the halls, she was tempted to close her eyes and snooze some more, but she knew she couldn't. She had to prepare for Owen, to look her best for him when he arrived.

She kicked the covers to the foot of the bed. Exposed to the cool morning mountain air, she shivered as goose bumps sprang up all over her body. Every centimeter of her body responded to the chill. She jumped up, scurried to the dresser, and dug out a flannel shirt and sweatpants. She threw them on, stuffed her hair under a baseball cap and her feet into terrycloth slippers, and headed to the porch to say good morning.

Ruth had not risen as early as usual but was still among the early birds of the inn that morning. She had brought out a carafe of coffee and sat in her rocker with the beloved mug in hand and a blanket across her lap. She continued to rock back and forth in a steady rhythm. She watched the mist floating over the treetops disappear as the sun rose higher above the distant tree-lined ridge.

"Good morning, Granna," Nicole said when she stepped onto the porch and leaned down to kiss her.

"Good mornin' to you, Lady Bug," Ruth said.

"Have you been up long?" Nicole inquired.

"Not really, a half-hour maybe."

"Did you sleep well?" Nicole asked as she seated herself in a rocker next to Ruth.

"Well, enough. How about you?" Ruth asked.

"I tossed and turned a bit, but I slept enough, I think," Nicole answered.

"Why couldn't you sleep?" Ruth asked.

"I kept thinking about everything you told me yesterday," Nicole said. "My mind just wouldn't settle down."

"It is a lot to absorb," Ruth confessed, "I'll grant you that."

"Indeed," Nicole agreed. She reached over to pat Ruth's hand. "Not to worry though, I have enough nervous energy to keep me going all day."

"Why would you be nervous, dear?" Ruth asked.

"You're going to meet Owen," Nicole said, "and I have so much to tell him. And I'm nervous about what you might think of him." She folded her legs in the chair. "I hope you will like him."

"You like him, don't you?" Ruth said.

"Yes, I do," Nicole said.

"Then I like him, too," Ruth insisted. "I don't even need to meet him to know that."

Nicole laced her fingers between her grandmother's, noting how their hands were nearly the same size. "You watch him today, Granna, watch him close," Nicole implored. "And then tonight, you tell me if you think he loves me. Will you do that for me?"

"You don't need any reassurance from me, Nicole. Your heart already knows the truth," Ruth said.

"I'm not looking for your reassurance, Granna," Nicole said softly. "I want your blessing."

Ruth looked at her granddaughter and pondered her request as she watched her sitting there, looking back into her eyes. Though the question was unasked, she understood what her granddaughter needed. It touched her, yet at the same time, it deeply saddened her to see that the young woman before her needed to hear someone give her permission to be in love. "You don't need my permission to fall in love, Bug," she said gently. "But if you wish, I'll watch him good and then tell you what I think."

"I do wish. Thank you, Granna," Nicole whispered.

"I asked Susan to watch for you and have the kitchen bring out breakfast for us once you got up," Ruth said.

They rocked side by side in unison, engaged in small talk. Soon, a serving table carrying a basket of biscuits stuffed with country ham and two bowls of fresh berries was brought to the porch.

"I thought we would eat light this morning," Ruth said, "so we could enjoy a nice picnic lunch in the mountains at Mother's place."

"We're going into the forest today?" Nicole asked.

"Yes, if you don't object," Ruth said. "I thought it would be nice for us to go see what Michael and I accomplished together."

"Owen will like that. He enjoys being outside," Nicole said. "He says working in the yard and driving around with all the windows down helps him to relax."

"I told you," Ruth smiled, "he's just like my Michael."

After finishing their breakfast, they returned to the family suite to prepare for the day. "Wear something comfortable," Ruth advised as she entered her room and shut the door.

Nicole sat on her bed to slip off her shoes and sweatpants but left the flannel shirt on. The morning chill still filled the room. She reached down to feel her legs and realized she hadn't shaved them in three days. She walked over to the dresser mirror and looked at her face. Her eyes were clear, but she looked worried and tired. She went to the bathroom mirror over the pedestal sink, turned on the bright vanity light, and studied her face more closely. A pair of tweezers and a few plucks later, and the stray eyebrows were gone.

She reached into the white porcelain claw-foot bathtub, turned the two faucets on, poured in a handful of bath salts, and stirred the warm water until it foamed. The scent of vanilla and oatmeal reached her nostrils.

She took off the flannel shirt and let it fall to the tile floor, wondering how many others had stood in the very same spot. Just how many conversations had other people had with themselves in here, she thought?

She turned to the full-length mirror hung on the back of the bathroom door and looked at her nakedness. Turning first one way and then the other, she frowned at her legs and then her butt. Age will always outrun the number of miles I can jog or squats I can do, she thought. She passed her hands over her flat stomach and thanked herself for not getting her naval pierced that time in Panama City when she went there with a few girlfriends the weekend after they'd gotten drunk together and planned the trip during their high school reunion. She then brought her hands up beneath her breasts and lifted them. "I'm not twenty years old anymore," she said out loud. She turned away from the mirror and climbed into the bathtub.

The water was hot; her skin tingled and quickly turned an angry pink. She stayed in it anyway, her body grateful for the warmth. Her goosebumps retreated, and she laid back to soak for a while, wondering if she stayed there long enough, would she eventually smell like oatmeal.

She reached for the bar of soap and razor and began shaving her legs. She thought of how Owen liked to sit on the side of the tub and watch her shave her legs. He sometimes did it for her or washed her back with a sponge.

"You remind me of a Degas painting," he said once, "one of the bathers," she remembered his words with a smile.

Sometimes, he reached into the water, ran his fingers along the length of her thigh, and touched her. There have been plenty of times since she had put the brakes on sex that she had lusted for him, yet never let temptation materialize beyond his hand exploring her under the water. Suddenly, even though the walls of the old inn were too thin to afford any privacy and her grandmother with good ears was just right across the hall, she wished he were there with her right then when she was willing to give herself to him again.

She sat up in the water, finished shaving her legs and underarms, and rubbed the soap over the rest of her body. When she had washed all over except for that spot on her back she couldn't reach, she lay back in the water and slipped under to get her hair wet. While working in the shampoo, she pictured Owen working in the flower bed that recent Saturday.

His shirt was wet with sweat and plastered to his back from spading the Georgia clay to amend it with sand, peat moss, and plant food. This made the bed fertile before burying the tulips, hyacinths, and daffodil bulbs that would sleep there through the winter. She had the easy job of putting in a border of pint-sized tufts of variegated liriope.

She reached into the water and touched herself but changed her mind, deciding to save the pleasure for Owen. She pulled the plug from the drain, watched the water run out until the bathtub was empty, and then turned the water back on again. She splashed the clean water all over to rinse off the soap suds and then leaned forward to put her head into the stream of water to soak her hair. It ran around her ears and down her neck and slithered in between her breasts, and she remembered the first time Owen had tried to make love to her.

It started with a kiss at the door when they returned to her apartment after a dinner date. They had kissed before, but on that night, it was different. Maybe it was how he held her face with both hands or drew a quick breath just before their lips met. Maybe it was the way he kept kissing her gently, passionately, deeply, and then gently again, standing there after midnight on the Welcome mat of her little concrete porch under the light above her door, not caring who was watching, pretending they were the only ones in the world at that moment, sharing a hunger even though their bellies were full, acting like they had never done this before yet knowing exactly how it could turn out. That kiss got him inside, she remembered, and down the hall and into her bed.

She was hesitant when he first pulled her blouse out of her pants and then overwhelmingly nervous when his hand crept underneath and caressed her stomach. She knew where he was headed and wanted him to go there. It had been so long since she had let anyone touch her like this, but at the same time, she couldn't dare let him go too far. He had too much potential. She remembered thinking that he was one who could climb over her fortress walls.

He reached farther up her shirt, and his fingertips touched the lacy top of her bra. His hand slid to her cleavage and positioned a thumb and two fingers on the easy-release clasp, poised, ready to free her breasts. She suddenly wanted to push him back and scoot up on her stack of pillows.

Wait, she almost said when she felt his thumb and fingers work together to unbuckle the clasp, but before she could speak, he did.

"Is this okay?" he had asked gently.

"No," she said instinctively.

Gay stars, little stars, you are little eyes,
Eyes of baby angels playing in the skies.

Stars, 1914

Joyce Kilmer

CHAPTER 28

MOTHER'S PLACE

Ruth and Nicole were relaxing on the rocking chair porch at a little past ten o'clock when Owen's car snaked up the driveway. "Look, it's him," Nicole said with excitement, leaning forward in her rocking chair.

"Well, aren't you going down there to meet him?" Ruth nudged her.

Nicole stood, reluctant at first, but the nearer he came, the more she wanted to go to him. Shortly, she was halfway across the lobby and heading to the front door. As she went, she remembered Garland telling her to invest her interest only in someone who was also interested in her. She decided at that moment she wasn't going to let a little thing like being terrified of heartache keep her from giving herself to him. No more staying out of reach, she whispered. She skipped down the steps to meet him as he drove up and stood by his door as he switched off the car.

Ruth stood against the porch rail and watched. When Owen emerged from the car, Nicole put her arms around his neck and gave him a brief kiss and then a longer one, and he put his arms around her waist and pulled her close to rid the space between them. Ruth grinned and remembered the day she had spent with Michael up on the mountain when he had held her tight against him in the shadows of the tall trees where nature took its course, and they finally consummated their marriage on their wedding blanket.

The couple exchanged words Ruth could not hear but was not worried about it because she could see they were all said with warm smiles. Owen kept rubbing Nicole's arm, and she finally took his hand and led him up the front steps, into the lobby, where he dropped his bag, and then onto the porch to introduce him.

"Granna, this is Owen," Nicole said, smiling wide.

Owen leaned toward Ruth's rocking chair, reached out to clasp her outstretched hand with both of his, and then wouldn't let go. He held her gently and said, "I apologize for not arriving with Nicole."

"I'm so pleased to meet you," Ruth said. "I've heard so much about you."

"I hope some of it was favorable," Owen responded.

"Oh, a little, maybe," Ruth said with a grin.

"More than a little, Granna," Nicole admonished.

"Hush yourself, Nicole," Ruth scolded. "We don't want his head to swell."

"I deserve a little criticism," Owen conceded as he shuffled his feet. "Maybe a lot. I certainly have my share of flaws. Nicole is very forgiving of me."

"We're all flawed," Ruth said, "and doing the best we can in this struggle we call life. You show me a perfect man or woman, and I'll show you where the leprechauns hide their gold. Now let's go inside and get you settled in." She reached for the screen door, but before she could grab the handle, Owen was there and opened it for her. As she passed through, she nodded at Nicole with an approving smile and then asked Susan to have Owen's bag taken to his room down the hall. "A key will be waiting for you on the counter when we get back," she said to him.

Ruth led the trio into the innkeeper's suite. She went to the kitchen sink to rinse her mug, and Nicole grabbed Owen's arm and dragged him down the hall, where she kissed him again. "I'm so glad you finally made it," she said when they separated.

"I'm so sorry we fought," Owen apologized. "I hope we get a chance to be alone; there is so much I want to talk about."

"We'll have time alone; I'll make sure of it," she promised.

Ruth stepped into the living room and saw them leaning into each other in the shadows of the hallway. She grinned and turned away. "When you two are ready, I need some help getting our things out to the convertible. I'll give Owen a tour of the place when we return."

"She's taking us to the Joyce Kilmer forest," Nicole said, leading Owen back into the living room.

"As long as I'm in the company of you two lovely ladies, I don't care where we go," he said loud enough for Ruth to hear him.

"He's such a flirt," Nicole carped playfully.

"Oh, he's a flirt, all right," Ruth agreed. "And he's handsome, too. I just hope he's also strong because he's carrying the picnic basket."

The trio gathered their things and made their way to the car. With the top down on Big Red, they pulled away from the inn, Nicole driving and Owen sitting in the center of the back seat so he could lean forward to hear the conversation of his tour guides over the sound of the whipping wind. Ruth sat sideways on the passenger seat, her back pressed against the door so she could easily look at both of her young companions. During the short drive, she questioned Owen about his important case. He answered every question and then asked her to tell him about the forest. He listened intently and she appreciated his enthusiasm for her story, especially when she spoke of establishing the park. Nicole kept winking at her grandmother and watching Owen in the rearview mirror.

Spotting a directional marker that pointed to the park, Nicole slowed the car, turned onto a narrow road, and headed higher into the mountains. Owen leaned back and stared in awe into the trees that overshadowed them. Still watching him in the rearview mirror, Nicole reached over to pat Ruth's leg and pointed to the back seat. Ruth looked. "It's beautiful, isn't it?" she remarked.

"It's spectacular," Owen said.

"Just wait," Ruth teased him, "we aren't even there yet."

The roadside views became even more remarkable as the car climbed higher, gently rolling from side to side with each ascending curve. Cabins on the hillsides, rows of dried corn stalks, and fading pastures below. Not a billboard, communications tower, or skyscraper in sight. Nicole slowed to a near crawl when she came to a turn where a wide shoulder provided for pulling over and taking a look. "Look, there's the inn," she said, pointing toward Brysonville, "and there's the courthouse."

"I see a church steeple," Owen said.

"We'll go there tomorrow," Nicole said. "I want to show you the family plot. But let's not talk about that today. Today is Granna's day. It's all about her for now."

"This day belongs to all of us," Ruth said. "We can talk about anything we want to."

"We're here," Nicole said shortly. She steered into the parking lot at the park's entrance. It was just big enough to hold two dozen cars. She pulled the wide Cadillac into a suitable spot near the trailhead.

"Yes, we're here," Ruth echoed.

"How long is the trail?" Owen asked, getting out of the car.

"Not much more than a few miles," Ruth answered.

"Is it steep?" he asked.

"Not really," Ruth answered. "It's mostly gentle slopes and some stairs in a few places. Why, are you worried it might be too much for you?"

"I'm thinking about you," he said.

"I may be an old woman," Ruth quipped, "but I'm still a mountain girl. I've been walking these trails all of my life. A little exercise is still good for me."

"She'll be fine," Nicole assured. "She can probably hike farther than we can."

"Enough of this silly banter," Ruth said, opening her door. "We've got things to do and places to see." She effortlessly lifted herself out of the car. It was as if being in the woods had erased a few of her years.

Owen heard the gurgling sounds of a stream running over rocks and walked toward it. He found clear water running over small boulders, some speckled with moss and lichen and others naked and burnished smooth by the unrelenting water and passage of time. The opposite bank was covered in rhododendrons and azalea bushes, and tall trees cast dense shadows all around except for where sunlight managed to break through the thick foliage and shine like spotlights on decades of fallen leaves. He breathed deeply, savored the absence of traffic and telephone noises, and loved the way the cool air felt as it filled his lungs. Just up ahead, he saw a footbridge crossing the stream. There, the trail entered the forest.

Owen returned to the car and found the women waiting by the open trunk. He slipped on a backpack and picked up the picnic basket. Nicole tightened her shoelaces and slung her camera bag over her shoulder, then reached into the trunk and retrieved her grandmother's hiking staff. Ruth took it, tapped it several times on the ground, and then leaned on it to make sure it was still sturdy. Made from a sturdy branch of hardwood, it stood about four feet tall with leather strapping wrapped tightly around one end to provide a good grip just below an eagle head carved into the top of the staff.

"That's nice," Owen said. "It looks like it's been here a few times before."

"It does, doesn't it?" Ruth agreed. "An old friend carved it for me years ago."

"Bear?" Nicole asked.

"Yes, Bear," Ruth answered.

"Who is Bear?" Owen wanted to know.

"Come on, let's get started, I'll tell you as we walk," Ruth said, heading toward the bridge. Owen and Nicole followed. When they reached the bridge, Nicole stopped to have Owen take a photo of her hugging her grandmother. He snapped the picture, and as he lowered the camera, he saw Ruth rise up and kiss Nicole on the cheek. "Let's go," she called out, motioning for him to come along.

He stepped onto the bridge and looked over the handrail at the fast-moving stream below. The water foamed as it plunged over the rocks, loud and bold, and then slowed when it reached a wide basin where it lingered before continuing downstream, gentle and placid until it reached another steep slope where it picked up speed again and darted around and over more rocks. He looked up and saw the tall trees overhead. He guessed they were at least eight stories tall and much larger in diameter than he could reach around with both arms. He was reminded of the trees within Liberty Park.

"Have you never been in the woods before?" Ruth called back to him. She had already stepped off the other side of the bridge and was on the dirt path leading into the forest.

Owen laughed when he caught up with them. "Nowhere like this," he said. "It's just so beautiful."

Nicole waved for him to come alongside her. "She's taking us to a very special place," she whispered.

"Yes, I am," Ruth said, not missing a thing. "Then you will see what 'beautiful' really means."

They moved along the well-worn trail, occasionally meeting other hikers headed back to their cars. In some places, the trail was flat and wide, in others, it was narrow, uneven, and a tangle of exposed roots. In those places, Ruth held onto Nicole's hand and carefully made her way forward. The deeper into the woods they went, the taller the trees were and the more dense the shade became. Green moss was thick as a carpet in the places where the sun never dried the soil.

In single file, they climbed up a crude staircase made from logs sawn in half and wedged into the earth. Ruth, never short of breath it seemed, never stopped talking, sharing with Owen nearly everything about the forest she had already shared with Nicole.

They negotiated their way past rocks and exposed roots and reached a second bridge that let them cross a deep crevasse the water had cut into the soil. The bridge was made from fallen trees split in half just as the steps had been, and long branches had been lashed to supports to make handrails. The planks beneath their feet were rough-hewn, and Owen could see the water running below between the spaces where they were butted together.

"These were split by hand the old-fashioned way," Ruth said, tapping the planks with her staff as she walked across the bridge. "There isn't much done the old-fashioned way anymore." She scanned their whereabouts. "We're almost there," she said. "It's just around the bend ahead."

The hikers rounded a bend and approached a small clearing surrounded by towering trees. In the middle of the clearing was a large boulder, nearly as tall as Ruth's staff and perhaps eight feet in diameter where it protruded from the earth. Ruth led the way to the boulder and leaned against it to rest. "This is what we did together, Michael and me," she said, pointing. A large brass plaque bearing an inscription and relief sculpture of Joyce Kilmer's face was fastened to the stone.

Owen read the inscription. It told of Kilmer's service during the First World War and his poetry. "I remember learning 'Trees' in elementary school," he said.

Ruth elbowed Nicole. "He knows 'Trees.' I knew I liked him," she whispered.

"I like him, too," Nicole whispered back, but loud enough for Owen to hear her.

He looked at her and smiled. "What's this?" he asked.

"Just girl talk," Ruth said quickly. "Now come along," she said louder. "I have one more place to show you." She walked around the boulder and continued on the trail, going deeper into the forest. The path soon became steeper and more rugged. Owen gave Nicole the picnic basket and took her place, supporting Ruth as she carefully stepped along the trail. Her pace began to slow, and he saw that her forehead was wet with perspiration.

"Are you doing okay?" he asked.

"I'm fine, just gettin' a bit winded going uphill," Ruth said. "Let me keep a hold of your arm, and I'll be fine."

Owen looked over his shoulder at Nicole, and she nodded, assuring him it was okay to continue. They walked, more slowly now, another several hundred yards before Ruth stopped. "We take a detour here," she said, pointing into the trees with her staff.

"There's no trail," Nicole observed.

"I know. It's a special place, it's not meant for everyone. Now follow me," Ruth ordered. She stepped from the trail into the lush carpet of ivy that covered the ground. "We will be there when we get to the top of that ridge."

Nicole took the lead, moving fallen branches or holding back limbs so that Ruth could proceed without obstacles. "Thank you, darlings," she said as Nicole took one hand and Owen the other and helped her to step over a rotting tree that lay on the ground. Ruth needed to stop several times to catch her breath. "I sometimes forget I'm so old." Her voice was thin with fatigue, but determined, she pushed onward. Fifteen minutes later, they reached the top of the ridge.

"We'll stop here," she finally instructed, standing under a particularly tall poplar tree. "Help me clear a place to sit." Using the end of her staff, she began to push aside nature's debris. Nicole put down the picnic basket, Owen shrugged off the backpack, and they got down on their knees to brush twigs and small stones out of the way. "That's good," Ruth said after the ground was cleared of all but the leaves, a barrier of protection from the moist soil. "Owen, open that knapsack and take out the blanket, please," she asked.

He unzipped the backpack and pulled out a large folded blanket. It was made from horsehair and wool and showed the wear that comes with age and routine use. Unfolding it, he saw that it bore an American Indian design. "Is this real?" he asked, giving a corner to Nicole for her help spreading it out. They placed it on the ground.

"Sure it is, hand-woven by a Cherokee Indian woman," Ruth said. "I've had that blanket for years and years. Now take off your shoes and get comfortable." Holding onto her staff for support and with Nicole helping her, Ruth sat down, unlaced her shoes, and pulled them off. Owen and Nicole followed suit, and then Nicole set the picnic basket in the middle of the blanket.

"Is this the wedding blanket?" Nicole asked. Ruth nodded and confirmed that it was.

"Yum, lunch," Owen said as he reached for the food and set it out. "What blanket?" he asked.

Ruth blushed, and Nicole thought of how difficult it must have been for her grandmother and Michael to brave Nicolas's disapproval, have a secret wedding on the reservation, and then sneak into the mountains to consummate their marriage on this blanket at this very spot. Owen was only trying to love her, and she was making it difficult, she thought, starting and stopping as she did, and all the while laying down bricks high and wide to keep him from getting too close to her. She looked at him and he smiled, and she began to melt.

"I need some water, honey. Please pass me a bottle," Ruth asked Nicole, interrupting her thoughts.

Nicole pulled out three bottles of water. She also found a corkscrew, wine bottle, and plastic cups. "Wine, Granna?" she asked as she opened a bottle of water and handed it to her.

"Why not? It's my birthday, isn't it?" Ruth declared.

"It is indeed. Happy birthday, Granna." Nicole leaned forward and kissed the birthday girl.

"Yes, happy birthday," Owen added.

"I'm so glad both of you are here," Ruth said. "Your presence will make my birthday party so much more special."

"We're glad, too," Nicole said.

"Now let's eat," Ruth urged. "Owen, please open the wine for us."

Owen pulled the cork out and poured the wine. They ate thick sandwiches of chicken salad made with walnuts, along with sliced tomatoes and onions, a cold bean salad, and a sliced apple.

Owen studied the considerable oak, hemlock, chestnut, and poplar trees that reached for the sky all around them. The soft bark of a few of the trees was grooved where bucks had rubbed their antlers. He could not see the trail from where they sat, and except for their own presence, the forest was unspoiled, he observed. "I know I keep saying it, but I can't help myself. This place is so beautiful," he said. He took a sip of wine and wiped his lips with the back of his hand. "I like it here."

"So did Michael," Ruth said.

"Is this where you and Michael came?" Nicole asked.

"This was our place, dear; this is where we escaped to be alone."

Nicole smiled wide and reached for Owen's leg. She squeezed him when she asked her next question. "Just how special is it, Granna?"

"Oh, Nicole, you're embarrassing me," Ruth protested.

"I'm sorry, but I have to know for certain," Nicole said. "Tell me, Granna, please."

"Oh, if I must." Ruth looked first at Owen and then at Nicole. "Your mother was conceived on this very spot, right here under this tree."

"Wow," Owen said. "I wasn't expecting that."

"I love it," Nicole said. She leaned over again to Ruth and hugged her. "Thank you for bringing us here."

"I haven't been here in a long while," Ruth said. "I wanted to come."

"Look," Owen whispered, pointing into the trees. Ruth and Nicole followed his outstretched finger.

Not fifty feet away stood a whitetail deer, a big, powerful buck wearing a wide crown of antlers. Unafraid, the deer casually watched the hikers.

"There's no need to whisper," Ruth smiled. That's Ol' Buck. He's just curious about who I brought with me. For years, he's been greeting me whenever I come to this place."

"That same deer?" Owen asked, almost doubting Ruth.

"Sure, I recognize him. See that blaze on his forehead? That's very uncommon on a whitetail; that's Buck, alright," Ruth said.

The deer tossed his head as if to confirm who he was and then casually trotted a short distance into the shadows.

"Do you hike up here often?" Owen asked, watching the deer until it was out of sight.

"I did back when I had more gumption," Ruth said. "But now, I just come when I feel strong enough. I like to think I'm visiting Michael when I'm here. I like to think he comes to sit with me." She looked around with great admiration. "'The forest is filled with many spirits,' Bear used to say."

"That reminds me of a ballet, Giselle," Owen said out of the blue.

"Exactly, just like Giselle," Ruth said, impressed with Owen as she beamed at him.

"Who's Giselle?" Nicole asked, her head cocked to the side.

"I bet he reads more than you do, doesn't he?" Ruth teased.

Owen leaned back and laughed. "I'm not saying a word; I plead the fifth."

"Stop it," Nicole warned, punching him in the arm. "Now, who is Giselle?"

"She's the main character of a ballet," Ruth explained. "She lived in a village in the forest and was in love with a prince. She died young but her spirit lived on in the woods. Every night, the prince, who never stopped loving her, went into the woods searching for her, and when he found her, they danced until dawn."

"Michael is Giselle, and your grandmother is Albrecht, the prince," Owen added.

"He even knows the Prince's name," Ruth said, beaming now at Nicole. "I'm so delighted with this young man. Let's keep him."

"You think he's worth keeping, Granna?" Nicole asked.

"Oh, I know so," Ruth said, looking at Owen. "Young man, how do you know about Giselle?"

"A librarian I befriended years ago thought I needed a little culture. She dragged me to the only ballet I've seen in my life, and it happened to be Giselle. It made a lasting impression on me, watching how much my friend enjoyed what was happening on stage, that and the notion that two people could love each other so much that even death could not separate them."

"I believe that," Ruth said. "Death ends a life, but not the love that filled it."

"It's a beautiful sentiment," Nicole said. She lowered her head but lifted her eyes, looked across the blanket on which she knew love had bloomed, and a baby had been made, and stared at Owen. A wish surged up that her grandmother wasn't there with them so that she could ask him to make love to her right then and there under the trees. Why she had not given herself back to him yet, she was no longer certain or even sure there ever was a good reason to deny him in the first place.

She began to pick at a stubborn hangnail, and it, unwilling to let go, started to bleed as she tore the skin away from the nail.

"Stop." Owen reached out and covered her wounded finger. "You're going to hurt yourself."

She looked into his eyes and then down at their hands and saw that he massaged her palm with his thumb, rubbing gently in that soft place between the Life and Fate lines.

The private hope that she had secreted away impatiently demanded to be revealed, but words never came easy to her, as practiced as she was in the art of never being vulnerable. "I've been thinking so long about how not to get hurt," she confessed. "I've forgotten how to just let go," she managed to eke out.

"Let me remind you," Owen said. He stood and pulled her up with him, led her off the blanket and onto the leaves, where they stood close enough to kiss. He slid his right hand around her waist and, with his left, raised her right hand. "Put your left hand on my shoulder," he whispered, absorbing the willing expression on her face. "Now, just follow me." He began to waltz, slowly stepping forward and taking Nicole with him, then to the right, the back, to the left, and forward again, marking out a box in the leaves, one large enough for both of them.

Ruth smiled and sipped her wine and watched her granddaughter fall in love with the man who waltzed with her in the woods to the sweet music of birds and a gentle wind blowing through the trees. "This is going splendidly," she whispered to herself.

Nicole heard something shuffle through the leaves and looked over Owen's shoulder. "Look, the deer," she whispered. "It's walking right toward us."

"You don't have to whisper, Nicole. Ol' Buck is not afraid of us," Ruth said. "He's just curious and coming back to see what we're up to."

The buck stopped within ten feet of the blanket and lowered his head a dip, and then raised it up again as if he were nodding a hello. The muscles quivered across his back and shoulders, and he watched the couple as they returned to dancing in the fallen leaves.

Ruth started to push herself up on her staff, and Owen was quick to help her to her feet. "He wants to join us for lunch," she said. She extended her hand and offered the deer a few slices of apple. He boldly stepped closer and took it, and she slid her hand up his nose and rubbed him between the antlers while he chewed.

"I'm amazed that he isn't afraid of us," Owen said.

"He's not afraid at all," Ruth mused. "He always acts like we've known each other for a long time."

When Ruth finished feeding him the apple, the buck courteously bowed his great crown and then slowly turned away and disappeared into the trees.

I have seen all of the joy
Of the world on the innocent
Heart of a maiden.

Vision, 1914

Joyce Kilmer

CHAPTER 29

LETTING GO

Even though the hike back to the car was easier going downhill, Ruth was tired again by the time they reached the parking lot. She fell asleep almost as soon as she took her place in the front seat and let her head fall back against the headrest.

This time, Nicole sat in the middle of the front seat to hold Ruth snuggly in place and Owen slid in behind the wheel. He carefully maneuvered the hulking car out of the parking lot and headed back to Brysonville.

"You dance well," he spoke softly to Nicole and winked. He reached over the back of the seat and draped his arm around her. "Why they ever stopped making cars with bench seats, I can't understand," he said.

"You're so old-fashioned," Nicole laughed.

"And yet you picked me," Owen laughed back at her.

"I most certainly did," she confessed as she placed her hand on his leg and began drawing slow circles on his thigh with her fingertips.

"Have you enjoyed yourself the last few days?" he asked, enjoying her touch.

"I should've made this trip a long time ago," Nicole said. "I feel awful that I've not spent more time with her."

"She doesn't seem to be upset with you," Owen reassured her.

Nicole glanced over at Ruth, whose head rolled gently side to side each time the car dipped into a curve. Whatever she was dreaming about had put a smile on her face. "Her best trait is her ability to love people in spite of themselves," Nicole said.

"We should all be like that," Owen said.

"Are you ready for the hearing?" Nicole asked.

"I can't find the damn guy who wrote the Ordinance, the only real expert on the matter in town," Owen groaned. "It's going to be impossible to prove corruption if I can't question him. And, I've done everything else I can think of. I've read every rezoning case on record, reviewed tons of environmental data, and even tried to think of a new way to lay out the parking garage to impact fewer trees. But nothing feels right yet; I still don't have a hook."

"Have you talked with Quinn?" Nicole asked.

"Briefly," Owen answered.

"How'd that go?" Nicole pressed further.

"I was politely rude to her," Owen answered, bracing for more questions. He looked in the rearview mirror and could see Nicole watching him as he drove, her face aglow and full of color, her hair licking at his ear. She nestled into him and put her head on his shoulder, keeping one arm extended and holding onto her grandmother.

Owen looked into his own eyes in his reflection in the mirror. There's never a good time to spoil a perfect moment, he thought. "About Quinn," he began.

"Are you going to tell me you want to get back together with her?" Nicole interrupted.

"No, I'll never want that," Owen said.

"Then, unless you need to talk more about the case, I don't want to hear another word about her," Nicole said without malice. "Let's let the rest of the day be just about us." She stretched to kiss his neck. "You should forgive her. I think that'll make a big difference in you, letting go of the past. One thing I've learned these last couple of days is the past only has the power you choose to give it."

"You think so?" Owen asked as he glanced at her. "And what about you?"

"I'm working on it. I'm sure it'll make a big difference in both of us," she said. She closed her eyes and, within seconds, joined her grandmother in sweet slumber, leaving Owen alone to navigate their way back to Brysonville.

After arriving back at the inn, Nicole helped Ruth to the family suite and into her bedroom while Owen unloaded the car and put the convertible top back up. After parking the car in the garage, which took him three tries, he found Nicole waiting for him in the lobby.

"Let's go to your room so we can talk privately," she said. She held up the room key she had swiped from the front desk, took his hand, and led him across the lobby toward the guest rooms. Her eyes met Susan's as she and Owen walked past the front desk. Susan nodded with a furtive smile, and Nicole suddenly blushed.

"I'm sorry I disappointed you," Owen said as they strolled down the hall. "I should have tried to do more to delay the hearing."

"Let's just let it go, okay?" Nicole asked softly. "Everything has worked out just fine after all."

"Then may we kiss and make up?" Owen asked. He cracked a flirty smile.

"Only once," Nicole said before quickly kissing him on his cheek. She kept her arm wrapped around his waist until they reached the door of his room.

She opened the door and stepped inside, pulling Owen along with her. Before the door was completely shut, she wrapped her arms around his neck and began kissing him deeply. "I love you, Owen," she said when she came up for air. Her heart pounded in her chest.

"You've never said it quite like that before," Owen said, almost shocked. "You sound like you really mean it."

"Let's not spoil the moment with too much talk," Nicole said.

"I love you too," he said in return.

"Then make love to me," she whispered.

"You're serious, I hope," he said.

"Too much talk," she said. She kissed him again, pressed her hips into his, and moaned.

He pulled his shirt out of his pants and began to unbutton it. "I am sweaty," he said. "I should take a quick shower first."

"No. Not now," Nicole insisted.

Owen, aroused, grabbed her by the waist and guided her back toward the bed, kissing her along the way, not letting their mouths separate. Her soft, plump tongue and the sound of her impassioned breathing nearly sent him over the edge. Everything he had held back for weeks suddenly surged. He yanked her shirt out of her jeans and rushed his hand up her flank to her breast. His fingers slid under her bra, and she moaned with sounds of approval. He gave her a firm push, and she fell backward onto the bed.

He looked down at her and could hardly believe that what he thought he had lost and since seen only in his fitful dreams was now about to come back to him.

He ripped off his shirt and flung it across the room as he danced out of his shoes and pants. His boxers did nothing to hide what he had, and he climbed onto the bed and straddled her, waiting only long enough to make sure her eyes still said yes. He leaned down to kiss her again and unbuttoned her blouse. Her eagerness swelled, and she helped him to remove her clothes. The last button free, she spread her shirt open. He started in the divot in her neck just above where her collarbones joined and then slid his fingers down between her breasts. With a deft flick of the clasp, the bra sprung open.

"I wish my breasts," Nicole began.

"Shush, no talking, remember?" He put his fingers to her lips and then ran them down her neck and over her breasts and found her nipples. He kissed her body again and again, here, there, and everywhere. She tasted salty-sweet from a day of hiking and dancing, her skin was damp-hot against his cheek, and he loved it.

Nearly crazed by his suckling and falling deeper into his charms, wanting him to explore more of her, Nicole ran her fingers through his hair and then pushed him farther down her torso. Soon the only sounds in the room were those of two people purring enthusiastically, appreciatively, finally gladly giving in to what they had denied themselves and each other for too long.

"You have no idea how much I've wanted you again," Nicole said after a half-hour had passed.

Owen's eyes slowly surveyed the details of her naked body, all beautiful and flushed and glistening with sweat from their lovemaking, her chest rising and falling as she caught her breath. He looked into her eyes. "I wanted you more," he said.

She blushed again. "I've wanted you; I just didn't let it show," she said.

"I'm so glad you've come back to me," he said.

"Me too." She stroked his chest and her fingers came to rest on his scar. "Does it ever hurt?" she asked.

"Oddly, and thankfully, not anymore," he answered. "For the first time in a long time, it doesn't hurt at all."

"That's great," Nicole said.

"I'm sure you had something to do with it," Owen said.

"What do you mean," she asked.

"You've made all my worry and stress fade away," he answered.

They rested in silence for some time, their legs and arms woven together like kudzu, cooling down in the mountain air that bathed over them.

"You have never made love to me quite like that before," Owen said. "You are full of surprises today."

"What do you mean?" Nicole asked, turning her head toward him and looking into his eyes.

"You know, it was different," Owen said. "More intense and more intimate at the same time, if that makes any sense."

"Are you complaining?" she asked.

"Oh, hell no. I loved it," he said. "I think you gave more of yourself to me today, like you were more caught up in it than you have ever been before."

"I am finally giving all of myself to you, Owen," Nicole said softly, "completely and without reservation."

"So what's changed?" Owen asked carefully.

Nicole smiled at him. "All is well in my world for the first time in a long time. Everything finally feels just right," she said. "That, and I'm not afraid of you anymore, sir." She chuckled, slid her arms around his back, and pulled him to her for more.

*****

Owen lay propped up on his elbow and lightly traced his fingertips across Nicole's body while she slept. His hunger for her was not yet satisfied, his heart beating strong in his chest; he leaned down and kissed her lips to rouse her.

"I'm yours," she whispered as she stretched.

"Mine?" he asked.

"Yes, yours," she said.

"You've certainly never said that before," Owen said. "I'm both so happy and so surprised to hear those words coming from you."

"If only these walls could talk," Nicole said. "There is no telling what words have been spoken in these rooms during all the years."

"Confessions, proposals, and prayers, I imagine," Owen began to list.

"Arguments, breakups, and breakdowns as well, sadly," Nicole added.

"Don't forget the tears," Owen said.

"Countless, I'm sure," Nicole said. She opened her eyes and plumped the pillow under her head. "Things are going to be different from here forward, Owen," she said.

"What do you mean?" he asked.

"I mean, I realized that I had a lot of unfinished business with my mother. I didn't realize it until I walked up to her grave marker," Nicole explained, "but when I did, it was clear to me that I needed to forgive her, let go of my anger and resentment, and move on with my life."

"Forgive her for what?" Owen asked. "I have always thought you two were close, but in a quiet sort of way."

"Yes, we were close, at least most of the time," Nicole said. "I loved my mother, but it wasn't the typical affectionate mother-daughter relationship. We didn't demonstrate our feelings for one another very much. Our love went mostly unspoken. Eventually, there was anger between us, too, and for better or worse, it also went unspoken. But now it is dealt with, all that stuff is behind me, and I am ready to just let go and move on. I've learned it's better to have loved even if it ends in heartbreak than it is to protect your heart and never love or be loved at all." She turned to Owen. He smiled at her and waited. He had been waiting for a long time, she thought, probably longer than she should have made him. "I always heard my mother second-guessing me," she continued, "making me feel guilty for being even the slightest bit vulnerable. I've realized vulnerability isn't going to change who I am. Granna helped me to see that it's okay to stop being so guarded. She told me, 'Listen to your heart, not your head,'" Nicole said.

"And what does your heart tell you?" Owen asked.

"That it wants to belong to you if you'll have it," Nicole said.

"I'll take good care of it," Owen said.

"I know," she said.

"Maybe I should spend some time alone with your Grandmother," Owen said. "Maybe she can help me, too."

"Help you with what?" Nicole asked.

"You know," he said before he laid back and rested his head on her pillow. "The guard at the office started in on me about working on a Friday night. It got me thinking about my priorities. Nicole, becoming a successful lawyer doesn't mean more to me than you do. It never did." He looked into her eyes. "I should've come here with you on Friday, just like we planned. I could have done more to make that happen and do my work here."

"Don't worry about it another minute," she reassured him. "I'm glad things turned out like they did. Having some time alone with Granna gave me a chance to get close to her again and to discover a few things I've needed to know." She paused with a twinge of the all too familiar urge to change the subject, but she didn't. "I shouldn't have held back so much from you," she continued. "I've been intimacy-challenged most of my life, I guess. You've always been forgiving of me, even when I didn't deserve it," she said.

"Hey, I've fallen short of your expectations more than a few times," Owen said, moving closer to her. "If you forgive me and allow me, I'll make it up to you."

"You have always given more to this relationship than I have, Owen," she said. "You have nothing to make up for."

"I love you, Nicole," Owen said. He stroked her arm and then clasped her hand. "Being with you really is all that I want."

"You've been so patient with me," Nicole said appreciatively.

"Yeah, well, that part hasn't always been easy," Owen snickered.

Nicole quickly reached behind her head, grabbed her pillow, and swung it around, hitting him and nearly knocking him off the bed. She sprang up and pounced on top of him, sitting on his hips and pinning his shoulders against the mattress with her hands.

"I'm teasing, I'm only teasing," he pleaded, laughing happily.

"You'd better be, or I'm going to kick your ass!" she said.

"I am! I am!" he said, gasping through laughter. "Please, please, don't kick my ass."

She looked down at him, suddenly serious again. "It's true, isn't it?" she asked.

"What's true?" he asked.

"I challenged your patience; I know I did. I don't know why you put up with me." Her throat tightened, and her stomach lurched with the realization. "Anyone else would have left me, but you didn't."

"I won't leave you," he said, reaching up to hold her face in his hands. "But let me be honest, I don't want us to be the real-life version of Rachel and Ross," he said.

"I don't understand," Nicole said.

"You know," Owen said, "the couple on *Friends*. The couple who loved one another but never could get on the same romance page. Their love dance was more a tug of war than a waltz. We must waltz."

"That's a fair request," she admitted. "Ugh, my family drama was much more complicated than I thought it was. It's no wonder I am such a mess."

"You are not a mess," he said. "And, I have family drama as well. To tell you the truth, I think we both made it far more complicated than it needed to be."

"What do you mean," she asked.

"We both knew there was something more between us," Owen said. "Something deeper and more powerful than either of us were willing to acknowledge because fear held us back." He brushed his fingers gently through her hair as he spoke. "I don't know about you, but I feel like we've been dancing around this for long enough. I know I've been afraid, but I'm also tired of pretending that I am not deeply in love with you. That foolishness comes to an end right now."

"You really won't leave me, will you," she declared, looking deeply into his kind eyes, finally believing that he would not.

"No, I won't. I finally believe we can have the kind of relationship I want, one based on sincerity, authenticity, and genuinity," he said.

"Genuinity!" Nicole blurted out in laughter. "Is that even a word?"

"Don't be criticizing my rhymes," Owen retorted.

Nicole rolled over and dropped her weight onto his chest. He slid his hands around her back and pulled her tight against himself.

"I want you forever," Nicole whispered carefully.

"What do you mean?" Owen asked.

"You know," she said sheepishly.

"I want to hear you say it," he responded.

She drew a nervous breath, kissed him again, and then whispered in his ear. "You know," she said again, and without a second thought, "I want to be your wife."

Owen slowly rolled her off his chest and onto the bed. Their foreheads touching and eyes locked on one another, he smiled. "And I want to be your husband," he said.

It is stern work,
It is perilous work,
To thrust your hand in
The sun and pull out a
Spark of immortal fire
To warm the hearts of men.

The Proud Poet, 1917

Joyce Kilmer

CHAPTER 30

REVELATION

The happy couple remained sequestered for nearly another hour, continuing to be affectionate and playful with one another. They repeated over and over again how much they loved each other, both finding the words surprisingly easy to say now that they had finally been uttered aloud. They daydreamed about when and where they would marry and easily agreed that they would do so soon. There was no need to wait, seeing how much time they had already wasted. The wedding would be held at the inn.

Eventually, the pair showered together and got dressed for the evening's event, Ruth's birthday party. The starry-eyed couple returned to the lobby, walking hand in hand, and they found Ruth sitting on the same sofa where Nicole had found her on the night she had arrived. Ruth, too, had freshened up and was now wearing a dress. It is hard to believe that only a few days have gone by, Nicole thought. So much has happened, so much has changed, so much has finally been brought into the light of day, she mused.

Owen observed that Ruth still looked tired, but she reassured them she had had a restorative nap and was now feeling fine. "Let's go outside on the porch and have another glass of wine," she suggested. "We can watch the sun go down."

"I need to use the telephone first," Owen said, "and then I'll join you." He kissed Nicole tenderly before she walked with Ruth toward the porch. He watched them talking cheerfully as they crossed the room and pushed open the screen doors. Ruth suddenly erupted with smiles and laughter and hugged her granddaughter. Apparently, Nicole had shared the good news, Owen thought. He smiled and headed into the family suite.

Inside, he picked up the book of poems he had seen earlier on a side table and thumbed through it until he found what he was looking for. He pulled his phone out of his back pocket and a slip of paper from his wallet. He dialed a number while glancing at a page in the book.

"Hello," an ancient voice answered.

"Emma?" he said.

"Yes," she said.

"This is Owen, your attorney," he said.

"Owen, you don't have to remind me who you are," Emma chuckled. "I ain't that dim yet. Now, how are you?"

"I'm fine, just fine. And you?" Owen asked.

"The Lord blesses me every day," she replied. "Are you ready for Tuesday?"

"Actually, that's why I'm calling," he said. "I have to ask you something. Have you ever heard of the poem, 'Trees'?"

"'Trees'?" Emma asked, confused.

"It's a little poem by Joyce Kilmer," he explained. "It says that man cannot make anything as beautiful as what God can."

"Can you say some of it for me?" Emma asked.

"Sure," Owen said. "It goes, 'I think I shall never see a poem lovely as a tree.'"

"Oh, yes, yes. I learned it back in grade school," Emma recalled.

"Do you remember when you first heard it?" Owen asked.

"We recited it at the ceremony when we planted our trees around the school," Emma replied. "Mother practiced and practiced with me until I could say it just right."

"Can you still recite it?" Owen asked.

"Oh, Lord, no," Emma said. "We planted those trees more than seventy years ago. I've long since forgotten how to say all of that poem."

"Emma, this is very important. You've got to memorize it again," Owen urged.

"Again? At my age?" Emma asked.

"I know you can do it, Emma. Now please go and get some paper. I want you to write it down as I read it to you. And Emma," Owen added, "I'm also going to need you to do one more thing."

Owen read the poem a word or two at a time while Emma labored with her twisted fingers to hold a pen. When they were finished, she asked a few questions, and he gave her his last instructions. Their call ended after a minute of cordial southern chit-chat about this and that. Owen shoved his phone back into his pocket and made his way toward the porch. Before he got halfway across the lobby, something caught his attention.

On the mantle above the fireplace was a small figurine, a mother and child in repose. He was confident he recognized it but picked it up and turned it over to be sure. "Yes, it is a Hummel," he whispered. "Just like the one Mother owns, the one Father gave her the day Joel was born." He pictured it on her nightstand next to a photograph of Joel.

Suddenly, his heart softened a second time that day and his mind flooded with unexpected but affectionate memories. It was his mother who had taught him how to ride a bicycle so many years ago. It was his mother who had handsewn his hard-earned merit badges onto his Boy Scout sash. It was his mom who had held his hand wrapped in a blood-soaked dish towel above his heart while his father drove to the emergency room to have his nearly severed pinky finger stitched up. It was his mom's voice he heard whispering favorite childhood lullabies into his ear while he struggled to wake up from anesthesia after his heart surgery.

He looked out the screen doors and onto the rocking chair porch and saw that Nicole and Ruth, sharing a private joke or embarrassing tale, were lost in their laughter and probably wouldn't notice if he took a little longer to reappear. He pulled his phone out again and found a club chair in a quiet corner of the lobby. He plopped down, dialed a number, and waited, turning the Hummel repeatedly in his hand.

"Hi, Mom," he said with deferential kindness and an almost forgotten affection when she answered her phone.

"Hello, Owen," she replied.

"I spoke with Dad," Owen began, "and he told me about Joel."

"I know," she said. "He told me."

"Did you know?" Owen asked. "During all of this time, did you know?"

"Yes, I knew," she answered in a near whisper.

"Why didn't you tell me, Mom?" he asked.

"Joel asked me not to tell you, Owen," she said. "He was so afraid of what would happen to him. He didn't want anyone to know and then worry more than he did."

"Mom, don't you think I should have known?" he said.

"I do, Owen. I wanted to tell you," she said. "But Joel made me promise not to share his secret with anyone. You know how people react to this sort of news. He was so worried you would think less of him if you were to find out why he was sick."

"I could never think poorly of Joel," Owen said with a whimper. "He was more than my big brother; he was my best friend. He could never do anything wrong in my eyes."

"I'm so sorry, Owen," she said. "I was only trying to honor his wishes."

"I'm so sorry, Mom," Owen said quickly. "It's me who needs to apologize. I've been blaming you, and you never deserved that."

Blanche began to cry softly.

"I'm so sorry, Mom," Owen said again.

"I miss him so much," Blanche said as she wept.

"So do I," Owen said.

"I love you, Owen," she said. "I love you so very much."

"I love you, too, Mom," Owen said tearfully. "Please forgive me."

"That's already been done, son," she said.

"Mom, I want to see you when we get back to Atlanta," Owen said.

"Did you make it to North Carolina?" Blanche asked.

"Yes," Owen answered. "I've spent the day up here with Nicole and her grandmother."

"Owen, does Nicole make you happy?" Blanche asked. "I mean, really happy?"

"Yes, Mom. She does," Owen answered. "Very happy."

"All I've ever wanted was for my sons to be happy," Blanche said softly. "If Nicole does that for you, I will welcome her into our circle if you give me the chance."

The pleasantest sort of poet
Is the poet who's old and wise,
With an old white beard and wrinkles
About his kind old eyes.

Old Poets, 1914

Joyce Kilmer

CHAPTER 31

BIRTHDAY PARTY

That evening, the dining tables were set with pressed white linens, fresh-cut flowers, candles, and place cards, all carefully arranged to ensure the grand birthday was celebrated in style. The room smelled like a field of just-bloomed spring flowers, and the candle flames gave off a warm, romantic glow that caused the shadows of the guests to cover the walls with animated silhouettes. Owen and Nicole stood beside Ruth as her legion of friends and a few longtime regular guests of the inn filed past to greet her upon entering the room. Some of the guests remembered Nicole from years ago as a little girl following her grandmother around Brysonville. Garland gave her a big hug and then peppered Owen with polite but discerning questions.

Quickly a nearby table was piled high with cards and gifts, and wine was poured liberally while plates were being dished up back in the kitchen. Before the butter could melt into the flaky cheese biscuits, one of Nathaniel's nearly secret recipes, laughter, and celebratory chatter filled the dining room.

Eventually, the lights were dimmed, and the guests, finding their respective places, took their seats. An aromatic southern meal of all Ruth's favorite seasonal dishes was served. The preacher, a self-professed teetotaler, offered a polite but hasty prayer and toast, hoping nobody would notice before he could finish that his tongue was getting a little thick from secreted libations. Ruth snickered at him, and then urged everyone to eat well but reminded them to leave room for birthday cake.

After the sopped-up and scraped-clean plates were removed from the table and replaced with dessert dishes, a giant birthday cake was rolled out from the kitchen. All sang "Happy Birthday," and many came to

Ruth's table to hug and kiss her after she blew out the candles, eight big ones, and five small ones. After making sure that a slice of cake had been served to each guest and those who desired it received a cup of steaming coffee, Ruth stood and toasted Nicole and Owen, announcing their surprise engagement. As the applause rose, Nicole blushed, and Owen beamed when he raised a glass to his future bride.

After the gentlemen loosened their belts, most of the tables were pushed aside to make room for dancing. A string quartet entered the room, and Owen was the first to dance with Ruth. Soon, other couples joined in, and everyone swayed to the music and allure of the evening. The mood was infectious. Owen guided an effervescent Nicole across the floor, sometimes forgetting they weren't alone in the room.

Ruth danced slowly but confidently with Garland, Martin next, and then sat down to watch her granddaughter float in the arms of the man who loved her. She's happy, Ruth thought, finally getting what her life has been missing for so long. She approved of Owen. He had the patience and understanding that a woman required, she thought, and Nicole was finally able to give of herself in the way that holds a man's attention. "They remind me of Michael and me," Ruth whispered to Garland as she watched. "I only wish her mother could be here to see this."

"It would make her so happy," Garland said.

"I'm certain it would," Ruth agreed.

"You should open your gifts, Miss Ruth," Martin suggested. "It's getting late."

Everyone gathered around as Ruth unwrapped and admired each gift, taking care to graciously thank the guest who had brought it. There was nothing insincere about how honored she felt to receive all the attention.

After the last gift had been opened and all the cards had been read, the guests slowly began to take their leave. Wishing her well and promising to return for another party next year, everyone kissed Ruth again before departing for home. When only Ruth, Nicole, and Owen finally remained in the dining room, Nicole began to dab her eyes and turned away to hide her face.

"What is it, Lady Bug?" Ruth asked as she put her arm around Nicole. "Why the tears all of a sudden?"

"I'm just so happy," Nicole said. "Happier than I've ever been. I didn't know I could feel this way."

"Well then, cry all you want to, darlin'," Ruth said. "Happy tears are always welcomed. In fact, I'm happy, too, so I might just have to shed a tear with you."

Nicole threw her arms around her grandmother. "I love you, Granna. I love you so very much. Thank you for all you've done for me," she said.

"I'm just doing what grandmothers do, child, plain and simple," Ruth said. "And I love you too." She pulled away from Nicole's tight embrace. "Now, you lovebirds, follow me. I have something for you."

"For us? No, Granna," Nicole protested. "It's your birthday. You should be the center of attention."

"No questions or fussing, just follow me," Ruth insisted, pulling the couple out of the dining room. They passed the display of letters and photographs, and Nicole caught a glimpse of her great-grandfather in a photo pinned to the corkboard behind the glass case.

With a woman on each arm, Owen strutted proudly into the lobby. Some guests sat before the fireplace, reading from the collection of old magazines. More than a few, relaxed by the emerging sounds of the night and the slow cadence of the inn, dozed in the comfortable chairs scattered about the room. A mother drinking a cup of hot tea sat at the long table in the center of the room, playing a game of checkers with her two young sons.

"I sure do love this place," Ruth said as her eyes briefly rested on each of her comfortable and satisfied patrons.

"It's a wonderful place," Owen said. "I want to come back sometime when we can stay longer."

"I was hoping you'd feel that way," Ruth said, pushing open the door of the innkeeper's suite. "Now, have a seat on the sofa and wait a moment." She disappeared from the living room and then returned shortly with two wrapped packages cradled in her arms. She sat down next to Nicole, balancing the packages on her knees. "This is just a little something from me to each of you. Something for you to remember me by," Ruth said.

Nicole reached for her grandmother's hand. "I don't need anything to remind me of you," she said. "You're not going anywhere any time soon; you said so yourself. Besides, I could never forget you, Granna."

"I know you won't forget about me, Lady Bug, but take this anyway," Ruth said. "It'll give you something to tell your children about." She took the larger package from the bottom of the stack and handed it to Nicole. "Go ahead," she said. "Open it."

Nicole took the package, and from the feel of it in her hands, she immediately knew what the gift was. She peeled back a corner of the wrapping paper. "It's your blanket," she said with awe.

"No, it's your blanket now," Ruth said.

"I can't take this, Granna; it's too important to you," Nicole said.

"Yes, you can," Ruth insisted, "and you will. You like it, don't you?"

"I love it," Nicole said, reaching out to hug Ruth and thanked her with a kiss. "I can't believe you're willing to part with it."

"This blanket was special for Michael and me," Ruth whispered into her ear, "and I hope it will be special for you and Owen one day. I'd like for you to use it," Ruth said in a suggestive whisper, "if you know what I mean."

Nicole burst into laughter.

"What's so funny?" Owen asked.

"Now it's his turn," Ruth said quickly, pushing aside his question but not without blushing a little. She gave him the smaller package.

"You're too generous," Owen said as he accepted the gift. "You shouldn't have."

"It's important to me to give this to you. I hope you'll see why," Ruth said.

When Owen pulled the wrapping paper off, he was holding an old book. "It's your Joyce Kilmer book," he said. "I was just looking at it."

"Granna!" Nicole exclaimed. "You can't give that away."

"I certainly can, and I'm doing so right now," Ruth said, "so don't fuss with me. Besides, it's fitting for Owen to have it. Like I said, he is to you what Michael is to me." She leaned across Nicole's lap and reached out to grasp Owen's hand. "Now you save those nice peoples' trees, young man."

"Thank you," Owen said, looking at Nicole for direction. She nodded with approval.

"Thank you," Owen said. "If I do, it will be because of this book. You have no idea how much you helped me by taking me into the forest today."

Ruth, perplexed, waved him off. "I don't know how I could've helped, but I'm glad if I did," she said.

"You reminded me of 'Trees'," he said. "And believe it or not, Emma, my client, knows the poem, too."

"I'm not sure what all that means," Ruth said, "but I do know that everyone likes a good poem. Now sit still, I have one more gift to offer, and it is for the both of you."

"Granna," Nicole protested again, "you've already given us wonderful gifts. No more, please. It's your birthday, not ours. This day is supposed to be all about you."

"I want to give you the inn," Granna blurted out, ignoring Nicole. "I want you to have the inn after I'm gone." Nicole opened her mouth to speak, but Ruth cut her off with an authoritative wave of her hand. "I've thought about it for some time now, Nicole, and it's what I want to do, so don't argue with me. I've always meant for you to have this place, and now that I know Owen, well, let's just consider it an early wedding gift for both of you."

"It's an incredibly generous gesture, but," Owen began to say, but Ruth raised her brow over steely eyes and stopped him mid-sentence.

"Susan and the rest of the staff take good care of the place," Ruth said, "and I've already asked Martin to help keep an eye on everything for you. So you see, you can help me to keep the inn in the family and you won't have to lift a finger to run it. You don't even need to live here. You can stay in Atlanta and just visit the place once in a while. That's all I ask. Just come up to the place now and then, and don't forget to visit me at the church when you come."

"Granna," Nicole reached out to hold her hand. "We...."

"Just say 'thank you,' or nothing at all, honey," Ruth said.

"Thank you, Granna," Nicole managed. "I can't begin to thank you enough for all you've done."

"Good. I'm glad to see you know better than to refuse a gift," Ruth said as she stroked Nicole's hair. "No more tears, my little Lady Bug; this is supposed to be a happy occasion."

"I'm overwhelmed," Owen said. "I don't know what to say except thank you and promise you that we will come here as often as we can."

"I know you will," Ruth said, sitting back on the sofa and grinning wide, pleased with all that had unfolded.

"You know," Owen said, looking at Nicole. "We could even move here one day if you would like that."

"Owen, I would love that," Nicole said. "But how could that work? What about your law practice?"

"They don't call it the 'World Wide Web' for nothing," Owen teased in response. "It's everywhere. Eventually, the technology will reach Brysonville, making it possible for me to work from here. Mark my words, one day, clients will have no idea that their lawyers are sitting in their Bermuda shorts behind a desk and working from home." He turned his gaze to Ruth. "We will move here one day. We will raise our children here, run this inn in a manner that honors you in everything we do for our guests, and we will grow old together right here in this room," he said. He sat back in his chair and grinned. "If Nicole can be persuaded to agree," he said.

"Do you agree, Nicole?" Ruth asked.

"I reckon I do," Nicole said as tears rolled down her cheeks.

"Look at you," Ruth laughed, "You're finally speaking Mountain English!"

The trio stayed awake and talked for another hour, and to her own surprise, Ruth invited Owen to remain in the suite for the night. "For all intents and purposes, you're family now," she reasoned. Nicole read poems from the book, and Owen used her camera to photograph the two women, who giggled about bridal showers and honeymoons.

Eventually, eyelids grew heavy, and all agreed it was time to go to bed. Ruth hugged Nicole and Owen and sent them off to bed, and then walked through the suite to turn off the lights. She stood alone in the living room, waiting for her eyes to adjust to the sudden darkness. When she could see again, she looked around the room that was now dimly lit by the scant moonlight that managed to slip past the branches of the trees outside and make its way through the windows.

"I surely do love this place," she said quietly.

There is no place to hide
When Age comes seeking for his bride.

Age Comes A-wooing, 1911

Joyce Kilmer

CHAPTER 32

GRIEF

Nicole stirred under the bedcovers and woke to the warmth of Owen's all-night embrace. They had slept pressed together, he behind her with his arm wrapped around her and a hand wedged between her breasts. She smiled; sensations from the afternoon and night before remained with her, her body grateful to have been explored, indulged, and used so passionately in the way it had been. She was happy someone other than herself had given her the pleasure, that Owen had owned her in a loving combination of tenderness and hunger.

She blinked and reached to rub the sleepiness from her eyes. She was thirsty but didn't want to move from the bed, lingering to take in the sights and sounds of morning at the Poplar Inn. Shadows of the trees outside moved across the walls as the wind gently tossed branches about. A ray of sunshine hit the beveled mirror over the dresser and separated into the colors of a rainbow. Outside the open window, birds chirped, and children laughed while running along the path that passed below the rocking chair porch.

Suddenly, she jolted upright in bed, throwing the covers back and waking Owen. "Something's wrong," she said, the pitch of fright cracking her voice.

"What is it?" Owen asked as he reached to pull the covers back up over himself.

"I don't hear her," Nicole said, springing from the bed. She ran across the floor to the window.

"Hear what?" Owen asked, but Nicole didn't answer. Naked and uncaring, she leaned out the window and looked onto the porch. Her grandmother's rocking chair was empty. She gasped and ran into Ruth's room.

*****

"Ruth's heart stopped sometime during the night, probably in her sleep," the coroner said. "She felt no discomfort, I assure you; her death was most certainly sudden and painless. I'm so glad her last night in this world was a celebration of her." He dabbed a handkerchief to his eyes.

Nicole had found her grandmother under the bedcovers wearing her nightgown, her head high on a plump pillow. She clutched a faded photograph in her hand, held close to her heart. It was a picture taken long ago of a young girl wearing a sun bonnet and a young man dressed in a forestry uniform.

Nicole was nearly inconsolable, and Owen held her for a long time while she cried and talked to Ruth, stroking her hair and straightening her gown. They remained alone with her until a knock at the door disturbed them. Owen opened the door and found that a guest had heard crying through the walls and notified the front desk that something might be wrong. Owen explained to Susan what had happened and requested that someone call a funeral home.

It didn't take long for word of Miss Ruth's death to spread throughout the inn and all of Brysonville. People began arriving to confirm the sad news and find comfort in each other's company. Martin cried nearly as hard as Nicole did.

Before noon, the rocking chair porch and lobby were filled with those wishing to pay their respects, and more than a few requested to see Ruth one last time, to say goodbye to her while she was as yet untouched by the funeral home. Nicole consented, and a line quickly formed at the entrance to the family suite. With the help of Owen, Nicole arranged Ruth's body for viewing. She combed her hair and applied makeup to give color to her lips and cheeks.

Nicole sat in a chair at the bedside and shook the hands of the mourners who passed through the room until she was too drained to speak to another person. Owen politely informed those outside the door that Nicole wished for privacy, and everyone graciously complied and turned away.

Owen and Nicole spoke with the funeral director when he came to take the body. Nicole wanted to have her grandmother cremated and then buried in the family plot next to her father, mother, and daughter. The funeral service would take place in two days.

Nicole fell into Owen's enveloping arms as she watched the covered gurney roll out the back door into a waiting hearse. "I'm so glad you are here with me," she whimpered, "I couldn't handle this alone."

"I'm going to call Emma and the office," Owen said, "to let them know what has happened. Someone will have to make the court appearance for me. I'm sure the judge will reschedule, considering the circumstances."

"No," Nicole said without a blink of an eye, "you won't. Granna wouldn't hear of it. She told you to save Emma's tree, and that is just what you will do. Don't take any chances with the judge. You can't do that, Owen, you just can't. That woman, that neighborhood, is depending on you."

Owen tried to reason with her, but Nicole was steadfast. He tried to disregard her wishes when he thought she wasn't looking, but she admonished him when she caught him trying to make a phone call. No matter how much he tried to persuade her otherwise, Nicole remained determined he would argue the Liberty Park case the next morning. Reluctantly, he finally agreed to return to Atlanta for the hearing but insisted he would return in time to attend the memorial service. He privately prayed the case wouldn't spill into a second day.

By the end of the day, the inn was so full of endlessly arriving people that latecomers had to gather outside on the lawn beneath the shade of the trees. Everyone shared with each other and Nicole their favorite memories of Miss Ruth, showing how she had touched so many people during her long life. Nicole marveled at the outpouring of love and found comfort in learning so many others were as fond of Ruth as she was. By the time the last mourner left, Nicole's mood was calm and resolute, her tears all dried up.

"Are you sure you won't let me stay?" Owen asked again before he put his bag in his car.

"I'm sure," she said.

"Are you going to be okay?" he asked.

"As long as I have you, I'm fine," she said. "Losing Granna hurts like hell right now, but I will be okay." She looked into the darkening sky. The stars were beginning to sparkle. She whispered quietly as if she were speaking only to herself. "It's as if she waited until she knew I had you in my life."

Owen put his arms around her and pulled her close. "I'll do my best tomorrow and then get back here as fast as I can," he said.

"Owen, you save those trees," Nicole said. "Granna believed you could, and so do I. Now go do it."

He got into his car and began to pull away but stopped when Nicole waved at him. She leaned into the car window and kissed him goodbye once more. "I love you, Owen," she said, liking how the words felt rolling off her tongue.

She stood in the parking lot and watched his car disappear into the darkness as it turned the curve near the bottom of the driveway. When the taillights were out of sight, she returned to the suite to get her keys.

Thank God for the bitter and ceaseless strife,
And the sting of His chastening rod!
Thank God for the stress and pain of life,
And Oh, thank God for God!

Thanksgiving, 1917

Joyce Kilmer

CHAPTER 33

ENLIGHTENMENT

Owen almost hated himself for leaving Nicole alone but knew he needed to appear in court the next morning. It was a holiday weekend, and it would have been impossible to prepare someone to stand in for him on such short notice, much less find the judge and give him notice. And the last thing he wanted to do was give Quinn more time to prepare. To her, it was just an argument over a stand of trees, he was sure, but to him, it was so much more than that. It was now more than it had ever been.

He checked his watch and decided it wasn't too late to call Emma. She answered on the first ring. "Are you ready for tomorrow?" he asked.

"I'm as ready as I'm ever goin' to be," she said. "Are you?"

"I'll be ready, Emma," Owen answered. "I promised you I wouldn't let you down."

"You still at the office?" she asked.

"No, I'm driving back from North Carolina," he said. "I managed to break away and spend some time with Nicole after all."

"Good, I'm so glad you could," she said. "Did it make her happy?"

"Yes, it did, at least for a while," he said.

"Is everythin' all right?" Emma asked.

Owen looked out into the growing darkness, and a stand of trees flashed briefly in his headlights. He thought of Ruth as she climbed the path to the ridge where she had taken them to picnic. "Not exactly," he said. "Her grandmother died last night. Nicole is pretty upset right now, but she sent me away with her blessing."

"I'm so sorry; please tell her I'll be prayin' for her," Emma said.

"Thanks, I'll tell her," Owen said.

"Was it hard for you to leave her?" Emma asked.

"I tried to stay, but she wouldn't hear of it," he said. "She insisted I come back to help you; she said it was the right thing to do. Her grandmother loved trees, too. We spent her last day on earth together, walking through the forest."

"What is the last thing Nicole said to you before you left?" Emma asked.

"She said she loves me," Owen said.

"You see there?" Emma said.

"Excuse me?" Owen said, perplexed.

"Owen, you should always be thinkin' about why you are doin' whatever it is you are doin'" Emma explained. "Sometimes you might be doin' something for fun, or you might be doin' it for money. Then again, you might be doin' it for love. Well, you should be havin' fun every day, but that ain't no excuse for doin' the wrong thing. And money is the Devil's way of temptin' us, so that's no good either. But love, now that's the best that you can hope for, but it can slip right through your fingers if you ain't careful. If you're doin' somethin' for love, then it's always the right thing to do, Owen. That's why she sent you home; she loves you. She knows you need to do this even if it ain't what she wants right now."

Owen scratched his head and stared at the road ahead in silence. After a moment, he exhaled deeply. "Nicole understands me more than I have given her credit for," he said. "She knows that the only person I need to prove anything to would be Owen Montgomery. You are very wise, Emma," he said.

"Child, I've been blessed with a long life. I've learned a lot of lessons durin' my years," she said.

"Thank you, Emma. Thank you for enlightening me," he said.

"Don't thank me, just follow your heart," Emma said. "That's all I want you to do."

"I will, I promise," he said.

"Remind me, are you a promise-keeper or a promise-breaker, Owen?" Emma asked.

"I'm a promise-keeper," he said with a grin.

"I know you are," Emam said. "Now, what time are you pickin' me up in the mornin'?"

"Seven-thirty," he answered.

"I'll be ready. Goodnight, Owen." She hung up before he could say another word. He settled back and let his thoughts reach for Nicole. Now more than ever, he wanted to be the kind of man she needed. Now more than ever, he wanted to become the man he hoped to be. He thought back to one evening while helping Florence Darden reshelve discarded law books. It was then when he told her of his predicament, caught between his desire to help the poor in their pursuit of justice and his fellow law student girlfriend's plans, that they hone their reputation in the ranks of Atlanta corporate law before moving to New York where real money was to be made.

"I've met many a law student as I've moved around these tables collecting books," she said, "and I've learned to size them up rather quickly. You will be a good lawyer, Owen," she said. "And you could be a wealthy one at that if that was what you want. But I must warn you that work won't embrace you at night, or care for you when you are sick or after you grow old. I beg you not to let your ambitions cause you to lose sight of those most important to you."

He saw that the moon had climbed high above the treetops and now illuminated the night sky in a haunting blue-grey light. As the stars sparkled bright, the trees along the roadside swayed rhythmically as his car whisked by. He envisioned himself dancing with Nicole beneath the poplar trees on a carpet of leaves.

He reached for his phone and dialed.

"Hello," Nicole answered.

"Hey," he said.

"Are you almost home?" she asked.

"No, I just wanted to talk to you," he said. "I couldn't wait another hour to call. How are you doing?"

"I'm sort of blue but otherwise fine," she said. "I'm so grateful I had this weekend with her. It's hard to believe there will never be another one."

"I'm so glad I had the opportunity to meet her," he said.

"Owen, if I didn't have you, I'd be all alone now," Nicole said, beginning to sniffle.

"You're not alone, Nicole," Owen said. "From now on, I'll be by your side. I promise."

"And me with you," she said, gathering herself. "I went back to Mom's grave after you left."

"You did?" he asked.

"I wanted to tell her about Granna and not to worry about me because I have you now," she said.

"You do, Nicole, you do," he reassured her.

"We're really getting married, aren't we?" she asked.

"As soon as we can," he said. "I've been thinking; we really could move to Brysonville one day, and I could set up a small law practice. Then we could live at the inn and raise our family there. Would you like that?"

"We're going to have a family?" Nicole asked.

"I certainly hope so," he answered.

"I'd love to do that, have your children and everything else, but," she began to laugh, "I just can't see you as a small-town lawyer."

"I can," he said quickly. "Nicole?"

"Yes?" she answered.

"I always intended to be the man you've dreamed of, to win your heart, but I thought taking it slow was best," he said. "But the truth is I became selfish and distracted. I was worried more about things I now realize do not matter as much as you do."

"We've both been distracted," she said, "but not anymore."

"I need to tell you something," Owen said slowly.

"Yes," Nicole said.

"I spoke with my mom yesterday," he began, "and I talked with Dad a bit before that. Do you remember when I told you Joel killed himself because he was depressed that he would not get into medical school?"

"I do," Nicole answered cautiously.

"It turns out it wasn't about that at all. I have been wrong all along and unjustly cruel to my mother. I have held her responsible for what Joel did, but I know now he made the decision for his own reasons."

"Why did he do it, Owen," Nicole asked carefully.

"According to Dad, he had AIDS and just couldn't face the future that he knew was ahead of him. He chose to die quickly by his own hand rather than waste away slowly," Owen said. "And now it is him that I am mad at. He should have told me," he said as he white-knuckled the steering wheel. "And Mom should have told me too. I would never have been so mean to her had I known the truth."

"If there is one thing I've learned this weekend, Owen, it is that people handle the truth in very different ways," Nicole said. "Some of us get right to it, and others need a minute, or years, to digest it," she continued. "The same is true for secrets. Some have no problem dropping the charade when the time for the truth comes along, but others just can't even then. It seems the longer they've kept a secret, the more difficult it is for them to unwind it."

"And where did you acquire this wisdom?" Owen asked as tears streamed down his face.

"From Granna," Nicole said. "She taught me a lot this weekend." She could hear Owen crying softly. "Are you alright?" she asked.

"Yes," he said and exhaled. "I'm so embarrassed about how I've treated Mom and you. I'm embarrassed I wasn't the one who proposed," he muttered painfully.

"You can always ask me now if you want to," she said.

Owen looked into the trees again and wished he were making love to her in the woods, with only the moonlight and crickets to witness. He cleared his throat and drew a deep breath. "Nicole, I want to spend the rest of my life with you. Will you marry me?" he asked.

"I'll have to think about it," she answered playfully.

"What!" he burst out.

"So, you want children?" Nicole asked, teasing him.

"Two or three," Owen said nonchalantly, wiping his face dry.

"Slow down, let's take this one baby at a time," she laughed.

He paused again and then spoke softly. "Nicole?"

"Of course I will marry you, silly," she said, yawning. "I'm so sleepy. Call me tomorrow. I'm going to dream about you tonight."

"And I'll dream of you, too," he said.

"Goodnight, my future husband," she said, blowing a kiss into the phone before hanging up.

Poems are made by fools like me,
But only God can make a tree.

Trees, 1915

Joyce Kilmer

CHAPTER 34

TREES

The following morning, Owen looked at his watch. It was nearly seven-fifteen. He looked in the mirror, tightened his necktie, returned a stray hair to its place, and then made his way through the house and into his car. It was time to pick up Emma.

He parked in front of her house and found her sitting on her porch talking with neighbors who had risen early and come by to wish her good luck. He walked up onto the porch, and everyone greeted him warmly. The men shook his hand, and Ruby kissed him on the cheek. "It's time, Emma," he said after a few minutes of small talk. She rose slowly and took his hand, and together, they crossed her front yard and got into the car.

As he pulled away from the curb, he looked over at Emma. She was wearing a navy blue church dress with white flowers and a white straw hat encircled with a blue ribbon. She carried a small purse in her lap. "You look very nice," he told her.

"Thank you. So do you," she repaid the compliment.

"I like your fragrance, too," he said.

"Thank you," she said. "It's lavender."

He smiled knowingly. "Do you have it?" he asked, letting the car roll slowly down the block.

"It's right here," Emma said, patting her purse.

"Good," he said. Momentarily, he stopped the car alongside the curb in front of the park. "Well, let's do it."

"Yes, let's," Emma said.

He grabbed a small bag from the back seat and exited the car. He helped Emma climb onto the curb, up the stone steps, and onto the old school grounds. They walked through the dew-dampened grass and moved to her tree. Emma stood leaning against it while Owen walked back a few paces. He stopped, opened the bag, and pulled out an old Polaroid camera he hadn't been able to throw away. He focused, took a picture, and then waited for it to develop. After a few minutes, he walked back to Emma and showed her the photograph.

"Will it do?" she asked.

"It's perfect," he assured her. "Come, it's almost time."

Moments later, Owen and Emma entered the courtroom, and other Liberty Park residents who were already seated waved to greet them. Owen pulled out the chair for Emma and helped her sit down. He then seated himself and looked over at the defendant's table. He saw Quinn and the developer whispering to one another. He thought he heard a chuckle within their murmur and noted that the skirt she wore today was even shorter than the last one. He stood and moved to her side.

"A word, please," he asked, standing over her shoulder.

Quinn's eyes glanced momentarily at her client, then the empty judge's chair, and back to Owen. "Sure," she finally agreed. They exited the courtroom and stood in the hall. Removed from curious ears, they faced each other. Quinn had her arms crossed rigidly and one foot extended, and Owen had his hands comfortably stuffed deep in his pockets.

"Yes?" she queried impatiently.

Owen cleared his throat. "I've done a lot of soul searching in the last few days, and I've confronted a few things about myself that I've...."

Quinn's arms went lax, and she withdrew her foot.

"...well, the truth is," Owen went on, "I just want to apologize to you. You were right not to marry me; I wasn't ready."

Quinn's eyes softened, her jaw relaxed, and her lips parted in surprise.

"I just want you to know I'm not angry with you anymore," he continued. "I shouldn't have been in the first place, and I hope you'll forgive me for how I've acted."

Before Quinn could react, the same burly bailiff called out his marching orders, and they returned to the courtroom just as Judge Hardwick approached his bench. The lawyers quickly returned to their respective places, but not before Owen wished Quinn good luck, and then the proceedings began.

Owen presented his opening statement first, a summary of the Tree Protection Ordinance and his view of why it justified his petition. Quinn followed, politely asserting that the zoning variance was legally obtained and there were no grounds to reverse that decision. Owen then cited legal precedents for overturning the zoning approval, presented statistics and charts that detailed the loss of green space in Atlanta during the last twenty-five years and produced copies of Environmental Protection Agency reports warning city officials about Atlanta's growing smog problem. He summarized research from the University of Georgia that asserted the cleaning effect of poplar trees on air pollution and told of the Georgia Tech findings that Atlanta's tree canopy declined by nearly a half-acre every day during the last five years. He told of the city's arborist getting fired and how, mysteriously, none of the law firm's contacts at City Hall knew where to reach him.

Judge Hardwick nodded occasionally while Owen spoke, and Quinn, disarmed, never raised an objection.

When not on the stand herself describing the efforts of the Liberty Park Neighborhood Association, Emma sat attentively at the plaintiff's table, constantly smiling and nodding her approval of Owen's performance. An occasional "Amen" arose from her neighbors, who were equally confident in their attorney. Emma threw a disapproving glare at Quinn now and then, even though Owen had urged her not to. "I just couldn't help myself," she whispered to him.

In her turn, Quinn rose, and to Owen's surprise and perhaps the dismay of Hardwick, she stood in place behind her chair. She described how her client had lawfully obtained the rezoning approval, and she presented expert opinions projecting an overall increase in property values because of the new condominiums. She claimed that new businesses would move into the neighborhood to serve the new residents, and the city itself would benefit from improved tax revenues. With the help of the bailiff, she presented an artistic rendering of what the park and condominiums would look like after the construction of the parking garage was completed. The rendering depicted mature trees, not the saplings that Owen knew would be planted. When she finished, she sat down and referred to her notes with little more than vague interest. Her client huffed with obvious dismay. "What was that," he hissed harshly.

"Do you wish to reply, Mr. Montgomery?"

"Yes, Your Honor, I do." Owen moved to stand before the bench and began with what he had saved for last.

"The first Arbor Day was established on April 10, 1872, by a man named Sterling Morton. His objective was simple: to plant trees in a desert known as the Nebraska Territory to give the pioneers something to remind them of home. Ten years later, our nation's schools adopted Arbor Day and began the tradition of young children planting trees to improve their surroundings. Seventy-two years ago, my client, Mrs. Emma Troutman, planted this tree at her school." He reached into the breast pocket of his jacket and pulled out a photograph. "May I present this to you, Your Honor?"

"I'll see it," Judge Hardwick responded, reaching out to take the photograph. He sat back in his chair and studied it. It was old, faded, and tattered around the edges, but what it depicted was clear. It was a young girl wearing a long dress and ankle boots standing next to a small seedling tree. The girl and the tree were nearly the same height. She stood with an extended arm, her hand grasping the trunk as she proudly displayed her young tree to the camera.

Owen reached to pull another photograph from his jacket pocket. "And this, Your Honor," he said, "is that little girl and that same tree today."

"Objection," Quinn stated automatically.

"Overruled," Judge Hardwick said. "You opened the door when you failed to object to the first photograph."

"Your Honor," she started to protest, rising from her chair.

"I said, 'Overruled,' Counsel. Be seated," Hardwick said, pointing to her chair with his gavel.

Quinn sat down and folded her arms on the table.

"Hand it to me," Hardwick instructed. He took the second photograph and compared it to the first. It was the picture of Emma leaning against her tree that Owen had taken that morning. The tree towered above her head, its total height not captured in the photograph, but Hardwick could tell from its girth that it was indeed a large tree. And despite the offending red X that had been spray-painted on it, he could see from Emma's smile that she was still proud of her tree. He looked back at

Owen. "Do you have any other surprises for us, Mr. Montgomery?" he asked as he handed the photographs back to Owen.

"If I may, Your Honor," Owen answered. "I would like to call my client, Mrs. Emma Troutman, back to the stand. I have a few additional questions to ask of her."

"And the nature of these questions?" the Judge asked.

"I wish to ask her to explain the first photograph, Your Honor," Owen said.

"You may," Hardwick consented.

Owen escorted Emma once more to the stand and supported her as she climbed the few steps to the witness chair. After she was comfortably seated, she looked up and waved quickly at her neighbors. Owen stood before her and smiled, waiting for her to let him know when she was ready. She nodded, and he began.

"Mrs. Troutman, please tell us about this photograph," he asked, placing the old photograph before her.

"That's me when I was just eight years old," Emma said. "It was taken the day I planted my tree during an Arbor Day ceremony on the playground where I attended grade school. That's my tree there next to me."

"And who took this picture?" Owen asked.

"A man from the newspaper," Emma said. "He took one of each of us children. I was in the paper that Sunday."

"Mrs. Troutman, on the day that you planted your tree," Owen proceeded, "did you have anything to say to those who were there watching the celebration?"

"Yes, I did," Emma said.

"Can you tell us now what it was that you said?" Owen asked.

"We children recited a poem," she answered.

"Do you still remember that poem?" he asked.

"Yes, I do," she said.

"Then please tell it to us," Owen encouraged her.

"All right then." Emma cleared her throat, sat forward in the chair, and placed her hand on the rail of the witness stand to hold herself steady. She began speaking. Her voice shook a little at first, but soon, her nerves settled, and then she sounded clear and strong. "I think I shall never see, a poem lovely as a tree. A tree whose hungry mouth is prest, against the earth's sweet flowing breast. A tree that looks at God all day, and lifts her leafy arms to pray. A tree that may in summer wear, a nest of robins in her hair."

And then she suddenly forgot the next line of the poem. Her chin began to quiver, and she looked at Owen with fear drawn across her face.

Owen stood nervously, praying that her memory would return to her and that she would finish the poem. It startled him when he heard Judge Hardwick speak.

"Upon whose bosom snow has lain," he said, kindly prompting Emma.

Emma turned to him, nodded, and smiled. "Yes, that's it, thank you." She looked back at Owen and continued. "Upon whose bosom snow has lain, who intimately lives with rain. Poems are made by fools like me, but only God can make a tree."

Love has bent down in his old kindly fashion,
And breathed upon her his immortal breath.

In Memoriam, 1911

CHAPTER 35

ROCKING CHAIR

It was just after sunrise on Tuesday, Nicole's fourth morning waking up at the inn. She had switched off the alarm clock the night before, wanting to sleep as late as she could, anything to avoid the painful tasks that awaited her today.

A noise interrupted her slumber and prodded her awake. At first, she fought it and tried to force herself back to sleep. She was simply not ready to deal with the realities she had to face. She rolled over and pulled the pillow over her head, covering her ears in an attempt to drown out the noise.

"What is that noise?" she asked herself.

She suddenly realized she knew that sound. It was, in fact, very familiar. It was the rhythmic sound of rockers creaking on the old front porch floorboards, the sound of her grandmother's rocking chair.

Bolting up, wide awake and her chest rising desperately hopeful, praying that her mind had played a cruel trick on her, that Granna was alive and well and waiting outside on the porch, she flung the covers off. In one swift motion, she grabbed a flannel shirt and slipped it on. She didn't bother to button it but wrapped it around her torso like a robe. She darted to the window, her mind racing, praying, pleading, and bargaining with God as she went. Who will I find sitting in the rocking chair? She thought as she reached the window. Her hand was shaking, her eyes blinking nervously, and she pulled back the curtain and peered outside.

There was no one, the porch was empty. The chair was only rocking gently in the wind.

She looked into the trees. The leaves and branches were still, and the curtain was stagnant in her hand.

There was no wind, she realized.

I must be dreaming, she thought. She quickly buttoned her shirt and stepped into a pair of jeans before exiting the suite in her bare feet. She headed for the porch.

Distraught, she passed quickly through the lobby where a few employees and a handful of early-rising guests were engaged in small talk that ceased when they saw her. Everyone nodded, expressed their sympathies and grief with their eyes, and wondered among themselves who should go comfort her.

Nicole pushed the screen door open and stepped out onto the porch. Her knees shook, and her steps felt heavy with despair.

The rocking chair was empty. Her heart sank as a stone dropped into a bottomless well. She would have traded anything at that moment to have found her grandmother alive and waiting for her with the old coffee mug in hand. Tears came to her eyes.

Nicole stood in the still morning and, with unbelieving eyes, stared at the chair. It still rocked. Afraid but compelled, she drew near it. The creaking sound of rockers faded with her each step forward and then stopped altogether when she was near enough to sit down.

The chair sat still. Nicole could only stare at it longingly.

Finally, she drew a slow, hollow sigh and, full of hesitation, took the last step. She put her hands on the corner knobs of the rocker's tall back and let her fingers trace the edges of the weathered wood. Her jaw trembled as she pictured her grandmother sitting in the chair. My grandmother, the grand matron of the mountains, my dear friend, the last member of my family, she thought mournfully. Thank God for Owen, she whispered out loud.

She gently pushed the chair to make it rock, to hear its music once again.

After a moment, she moved to take a seat in it, to feel closer to her grandmother, to be where the woman who helped her to find herself held court. She turned and pressed her calves into the rungs, but before she could sit down, something caught her attention. Something moved across the lawn below the porch. She stepped to the rail and looked toward the woods.

It was a whitetail deer. A graceful, beautiful doe walked slowly across the yard, leaving a trail of dainty, ballerina-like footsteps in the morning dew-dampened grass.

Nicole leaned across the porch rail to let her gaze follow the doe, and when she did, she sucked in a hurried breath of startled surprise. Another deer, much larger than the first and carrying a proud crown of antlers, stepped from the shadows of the trees at the edge of the lawn. He sauntered assuredly toward the doe.

Nicole's pulse raced, and her heart pounded in her chest. The second deer had a bold blaze on his forehead.

It was Buck, she realized.

The animals approached one another nervously at first, but that gave way to warm, expressive recognition, Nicole thought. Stepping closer, their noses came together. Buck's shoulders quivered, and they pressed into each other.

It is as if they had been waiting for each other, Nicole thought. At that moment, the deer turned away from the inn and stepped into the shadows, disappearing into the trees.

Nicole stood and watched for nearly an hour but saw nothing more of the deer. She did not ask herself again if she had imagined everything, for she knew she had not. She knew what she had witnessed. And then she remembered something her grandmother had told her. "Love is an echo that will remain long after we are gone, Nicole," Ruth said. "It is a melody that could be heard if only you stop to listen for it. It is in the rustling of the leaves, in the chirping of the birds, and in the laughter of children. Love is an echo that will last as long as you want to hear it."

Nicole stepped away from the porch rail and gently sat down in the rocking chair. She leaned back, pushed her feet against the porch boards, and rocked in a strong, steady rhythm. She smiled and then laughed, softly at first and then with release. Her grief drained away, and her heart filled with joy as she imagined how the deer would spend their time together on this day that had come to pass.

Eventually, mourners began to appear at the inn. The innocent questions and laughter of their young children exploring the grounds were pleasant and welcome in contrast to the grey silence punctuated only by the occasional whisper that fills rooms before and after funerals.

Nicole, still on the porch and waiting for the right moment to return to the family suite to prepare for the day, tuned her ears to the songs of children and birds and the rustle of leaves in the nearby trees.

A gentle breeze stirred, and something fluttered on a small table that stood within arm's reach of the rocker. Where did this come from? Nicole thought. Reaching toward it, she fingered a small envelope. Her name was written across it in a man's handwriting.

Opening it, she found a single sheet of paper, a brief note from Garland.

Nicole, I cannot imagine how much you must be hurting right now. I am heartbroken myself. I'm going to miss that wonderful, grumpy old woman, nearly as much as I'm sure you will. I want to reassure you that you made her last days very happy ones. She told me so and said how much she liked Owen. I'm so glad you are taking a chance on love, Nicole. As your grandmother used to say, 'Can't never could.' You will be happy with Owen; I know you will.

We think there is never a good time to admit we've made mistakes, but that isn't true. We should confess our wrongdoings and make amends right way. Nicole, I lied to you. I beg you to forgive me. I meant only to honor your mother's wishes, but now I see she was wrong. Your father's name is Thomas Brown. When he left Brysonville, he moved to Falls Church, Virginia. I would begin looking for him there.

With much love, and may God have mercy on all of us, Garland.

The air is like a butterfly
With frail blue wings.
The happy Earth looks at
The sky and sings.

Easter, 1916

Joyce Kilmer

CHAPTER 36

ONE YEAR LATER

"A tree that may in summer wear, a nest of robins in her hair. Upon whose bosom snow has lain; who intimately lives with rain," Nicole recited, lying on her back on her Indian blanket and looking up into the tree branches overhead.

"That's it," Emma said. "You're gettin' it." Nicole grinned, and they finished the poem together. "Poems are made by fools like me, but only God can make a tree," they sang.

"Ain't it a coincidence, that bein' your granny's favorite poem?" Emma remarked. "And the judge's too," she added.

"Yes, it is," Nicole agreed. "Granna would be so happy with how everything has turned out."

"I still can't hardly believe Owen saved my tree," Emma said. "And he didn't charge me a penny!"

"He certainly did save it," Nicole said, smiling proudly. "He saved all of them." She reached across the blanket and placed her hand on his knee, giving it a squeeze. They smiled at each other, their gaze locked as a gentle breeze stirred the leaves overhead. It was late November, the last throws of a change of seasons. Leaves were the colors of gold, red, and cinnamon and tumbled about in the wind.

"They sound like crushed ice in an empty tea glass," Owen said. "You should come up to visit us sometime, Emma," he added. "At least come for the wedding. We'll arrange for a driver to take you."

"I'm too old for travelin', Owen," Emma said, "but I'll be there in spirit. You're always welcome to stop by and see me, though, when you're in Atlanta."

"I'm afraid that won't be often, at least not for a while. Starting a new law practice takes a lot of time, especially when you're new to a community," he said.

"We'll see you when we come down to visit his parents," Nicole insisted politely.

"Have you found your daddy yet?" Emma asked carefully.

"Not yet. He's moved, I suppose. But I will, even if I have to write to every medical board in the country looking for him," Nicole answered.

"Are you sure you want to find him?" Emma asked. "It may not go the way you hope."

"I'm going to give him a chance," Nicole said. "I want to give him the opportunity to surprise me."

Emma nodded with all the earnest approval she could muster. "Forgiveness is a beautiful thing," she said and then turned to Owen. "You're a good lawyer, Owen, and I think Brysonville is going to treat you just fine."

"We won't forget about you, Emma," Owen said.

"I know 'cause you promised me you wouldn't." She grinned wide, and her eyes sparkled.

"Who's hungry?" Nicole asked. "I'm famished." She started to stand.

"Eatin' for two does that for you," Emma laughed.

Owen helped his friend rise from the old bamboo folding chair. Then he and Nicole folded the Indian blanket, Emma doing her best to brush off the leaves that would not let go of it. Once cleaned and folded, Nicole tucked the bundle under her arm and took Emma's hand. Owen grabbed the chair, and they began to walk across the park toward the car.

"Now, when's the baby comin'?" Emma asked again.

"We've got three-and-a-half long months to go," Nicole said, holding her belly.

"Have you thought of any names yet?" Emma asked.

A broad smile erupted on Nicole's face, and she turned to Owen. He winked and nodded.

"If it's a girl," Nicole said, turning back to Emma, "we'll name her Elizabeth Ruth, but call her Ruthie. If it's a boy, Michael Fischer Montgomery will be his name."

All characters in this novel are entirely fictitious, and any resemblance to actual persons, living or dead, is purely coincidental.

The Joyce Kilmer Memorial Forest is located in the western part of the Nantahala National Forest, about 15 miles from Robbinsville, North Carolina.

Brysonville is a fictional city loosely based on a composite of Bryson City, NC, and Lawrenceville, GA.

The Poplar Inn was inspired by the Fryemont Inn in Bryson City, NC.

Author's Note

Even though I have written more than forty books since my first publication in 2002, many people do not regard me as a serious author because I have not yet published a work of fiction. In 2007, I, an alumnus of the university, was invited to attend a luncheon hosted by Mercer University Press. There, I met Terry Kay, the novelist best known for his book, To Dance with the White Dog, who was at the event autographing his newest work, The Book of Marie.

To Dance with the White Dog was one of my mother's favorite books and I shared this with Mr. Kay, to which he replied, "She has good taste." He saw that I was wearing an Author's name badge and asked me about what I had written. I told him of my gift book series as well as shared how I had learned I would not be judged a "real" author until I could point to a book of fiction bearing my name. He laughed and asked me if I thought I might one day attempt a novel. I confessed I had started one a few years earlier but struggled to finish it, and no matter how many times I attempted to, I could not bring the story to a satisfying conclusion. He scratched his fingers through his beard and said to me, "Just keep writing. One day, the story will finish itself."

I worked on that manuscript for five more years and finally finished it, but it was still not to my liking. It wasn't anywhere close to standing in the shadows of To Dance with the White Dog, Bridges of Madison County, or The Notebook, so disillusioned, I lost my drive to become a novelist and abandoned the project in 2012.

In January 2023, sick and tired of the worldwide viral pandemic and its adverse impact on nearly every aspect of life during the previous three years, I sat down in my library, my little happy place, surrounded by books, art, and family photographs. Sitting on the sofa, I glanced over my shoulder, and my eyes landed on a worn and yellowed paperback copy of To Dance with the White Dog. Remembering my conversation with Terry Kay, I opened it and began to read. Three days later, I sat it down and smiled. Surprisingly, I found myself inspired to return to my dormant manuscript and give it another go.

I hope you like the end result of the rewrite of my book, To Echo and Remain, a book twenty-two years in the making that might not have seen the light of day had I not reread To Dance with the White Dog and remembered Mr. Kay's words, "Just keep writing. One day, the story will finish itself." I wish I could tell him, "Thank you." Maybe Ol' Buck will deliver that message for me.

Acknowledgment

I owe a great deal of thanks to many who have helped me bring this simple love story to life. So many people have read a version of this book that I've lost track of who said what and when to help me improve the story and shape the characters. Nevertheless, I would be unjustifiably remiss if I didn't give credit where it is so obviously due – thank you to Arthur Goldberg, Heather Schoenrock, and Deanne Beesley, who plodded through the early drafts and made many valuable suggestions, to Kim Harris, Amy Brueck, Patty Beelen, Becky Stottlemyer, Cayce Buchanan, DeeAnn Geeslin, Amy Lykins, and Donna Graham, who contributed significantly to the final editing and polishing of the book, and to my wife who not only walked the Joyce Kilmer forest with me again and again until I could do it justice with my representation but also made sure I kept the story believable and relatable. Without you, Jill, I would know nothing of love at all.

www.ingramcontent.com/pod-product-compliance
Lightning Source LLC
Chambersburg PA
CBHW070748280626
47162CB00018B/2775